Methods of Interrogation

A fist thudded against the side of McKay's head. It was a very large fist, powered by a very large arm.

McKay barely felt it. His brain seemed to be packed in those little plastic intestine things they used to ship stereo parts in.

Colonel Ivan Vesensky, former operative of the KGB and current traitor, shook his neat narrow head. "Such technique. You'll jar any information they have out of their minds before you get it out of their mouths, that way."

Major Llewellyn stood massaging one hamhock fist, smearing blood over the knuckle he'd cut on the edge of McKay's tooth. "You were part of this little setup, Russki. Why don't *you* tell us the details?"

The trim head shook again. McKay fuzzily regretted not being able to break it open. . . .

THE ![flag] GUARDIANS
PLAGUE YEARS

RICHARD AUSTIN

JOVE BOOKS, NEW YORK

THE GUARDIANS: PLAGUE YEARS

A Jove Book / published by arrangement with
the author

PRINTING HISTORY
Jove edition / December 1988

ISBN: 0-515-09841-8

Jove Books are published by The Berkley Publishing Group,
200 Madison Avenue, New York, New York 10016.
The name ''JOVE'' and the ''J'' logo
are trademarks belonging to Jove Publications, Inc.

PRINTED IN THE UNITED STATES OF AMERICA

10 9 8 7 6 5 4 3 2 1

For Eliza Shallcross:
M.T., as promised

PROLOGUE

Rubble crunched underfoot. The bearded man's arms pin-wheeled as a head-sized chunk of cement twisted underfoot. He went to one knee, and for the first time he forgot the idiot repetition of the song in his head as his ankle groaned agony.

His voice echoed it, but softly. He had to keep quiet, if only for the discipline. The wolves would be on his trail soon. He had to be tough. Even two years after the Third World War, the one they called the One-Day War, he hadn't had much experience at that.

He lurched the rest of the way across the mound of debris that had been a street, fell into a doorway, and paused for a moment, panting beneath a tattered maroon awning. His heart pounded like a hammer in his ears. Trying to be quiet seemed futile; surely anyone could hear his pulse a block away.

He brushed a straggly strand of hair from his eyes. They had always ragged him about the length of his hair, back in the compound. They said it made him look like one of the Street People. It irritated M.A.; he said it looked unsoldierlike, as if a scientist had to worry about shit like that. Or even a technician. Cromartie had stood up for him, though. That was one thing you could say for the grimy rat-faced little bastard.

The thought of Street People made him flick his eyes up and down the street, suddenly wary. Not even M.A. could do anything to keep the streets of Chicago safe. In that respect maybe things hadn't changed that much since the war.

He pushed out of the doorway's shelter. His right leg buckled beneath him. He dropped to the sidewalk with a despairing cry, just catching himself with one hand, sobbing as broken glass lacerated his palm. *Got to find a crutch of some sort,* he thought.

Rummaging in the debris that had slumped from the building's cratered red-brick face, he tore through shreds of weather-faded fabric that disintegrated to the rough fumbling of his fingers, designer dresses from a yuppie boutique, dropped by looters caught in the sudden firestorm of ambush. The Loop district had suffered greatly from the SS-17 warhead that had detonated over the lake, but this block had received most of its damage later, during the riots or the fighting with the Effsee expeditionary force.

His fingertips found cool hardness that rasped ever so slightly. They came up with an aluminum rod, still shiny, that had been used to crank the awning up and down. Not great, but it would do.

He drove the pole down through rubble to cement and climbed painfully upright. Grasping his crutch with both hands, he hobbled on, keeping his eyes on the ground to prevent a second misstep that might cripple him for good and leave him helpless to wait for the Street People or the inevitable pursuit from the Citadel. *Wouldn't that be a hell of a choice?* he said to himself. The thought raised a twisted half-smile.

The song came again, the damned stupid hackneyed song: *Chicago, Chicago, that toddlin' town.* He'd lived here almost his entire life, and he'd always hated that song with a passion. Now as he was running—well, gimping—for his life, it came back to haunt him.

State *Street, that* great *street, ta-tum, ta-tum, ta-tum.* What was worse was he couldn't remember all the damned *words.* But fuck it. It gave him something of an idea. It wasn't such a great street anymore, on its way down even before the economic hard times and federally mandated closings before the war, but there were a few underground parking garages where not even Street People liked to go. He could duck in one of them for the night—not even the overriding need to avoid detection was going to make him chance one of the bridges by night, and it was unlikely he could get across one with his ankle fucked up like this.

A wind from the lake raised swirls of dust around his ankles as he limped toward State. Funny, back in the bad old days before the war he used to dream of what life would be like after the Holocaust. He was a scientist—well, a qualified lab technician, anyway. He reckoned that should make him king (one of his buddies, Rosenberg, always said that was fine unless the people decided to blame science for their plight and grease all the scientists. Rosenberg always was an asshole. He was glad an I-beam had fallen on him).

He'd set himself up and lord it over a populace whose very survival depended on the technological nuggets he doled out sparingly. They'd fill his every need, his every desire, and be grateful for the opportunity. . . .

And he'd gotten that last part. No doubt about it; Cromartie

demanded the best for his people, give him that, and M.A. obliged.
He'd done it with more women than he'd ever thought about, in
ways he hadn't imagined even as an adolescent—they were eager
to suggest tricks you hadn't heard of, once they saw what happened
to their less cooperative sisters. There was always a need for
experimental subjects in the lab—

But he hadn't been king. He'd been a flunky, in fact, with a
jerkoff for a supervisor and that nutbag Cromartie in charge, and
all of them subordinate to M.A. and his goons. That wasn't all
that bad, he admitted—trying to fight off that fucking song again—
when you thought about the fringe benefits, to say nothing of the
alternatives.

But then they'd come up with their plan. M.A. and Cromartie,
the fuckers. And it had been too much for him. He never thought
he was squeamish; he thought most people were lumps, sheep,
and that he was just naturally better than they were. But he'd
discovered to his own surprise that his sense of superiority had
limits.

He patted a pocket of his windbreaker. It was all there, on an
oppy disk he'd copied before cutting out. Somewhere somebody
would have a laser-disk drive capable of extracting the information,
and the odds were good those people would have the means of
rewarding him. Handsomely. They damned well would, too, and
be glad to, once they realized what he'd saved them from.

Ahead was a stretch of State turned into a pedestrian mall in
an attempt to bail out the merchants and property owners in the
moribund inner city. Where he was going was a problem. He
didn't want to stray too close to the Marina City Towers to the
northwest, and he *really* wanted to stay clear of the crazies who
nested in the skeleton of the Sears Tower, which the Lake Michigan
blast had toppled into the Chicago River. The thought of what
they'd do to him made his flesh creep. Due north along State,
maybe, even though M.A.'s people would be watching that. But
there was plenty of cover, after all. He'd show Llewellyn that you
didn't have to be some kind of Green Beret asshole to use cover.
He'd show them all, and then maybe he really would be a king,
deliverer of a grateful populace.

In fact, come to think of it, he'd been small-time in his fantasies.
Why settle for some crummy clump of *Mad Max* chump survivors?
The whole fucking *country* would be in his debt. . . .

The debris began to mount around him, riding a rising blast of
wind from the lake at his back. Damn, it was cold, and the sun

filtering weakly through a scum of clouds did little to warm him.
He'd have to find some way to make a fire tonight, without letting
the light be seen. . . .

The trash rose higher and higher, papers swirling around him
like moths ganging a light, and then he felt a distinct *downblast*,
through his hair right down the collar of his jacket.

He turned around and saw a helicopter.

For a moment he just stood and gaped, the aluminum rod slipping
from fingers numbed by blood that suddenly ran at the temperature
of liquid nitrogen. It hung tauntingly before the blank face of a
looming Bauhaus box that had somehow survived the SS-17, not
fifteen meters above and behind him. A predatory, insectile shape,
a dark silhouette against the brightness of the sky, its muffled
rotors sweeping a ghostly circle above. The chain gun in its chin
could kill an APC, would splash him across half the block with
a single short burst. But it was pointed straight ahead, not at him.

He wasn't getting off that easy.

Forgetting the pain in his ankle, he turned and ran blindly toward
State Street. He floundered, feet sinking to the ankles at every
agonizing step. The song drummed in his temples to the pounding
of his pulse: Chi*cago,* Chi*cago,* that *toddl*in' *town.*

The helicopter was a Stealth gunship, whisper-quiet. He felt
more than heard it as it swept past him and then pirouetted neatly
around its rotor shaft to face him with sun-dazzle whiting out the
curved windscreen. It hung there, taunting him with a blank Cy-
clops glare.

Gotta get undercover! He turned and darted toward a bank
building, the shatterproof glass of whose floor-to-ceiling windows
had long since failed to live up to warranty. The damned thing
couldn't follow him in there. He'd be safe for a moment, able to
collect his thoughts.

State Street, that *Great* Street . . . There was a snarl, and
sparks danced and crackled off the sidewalk and cement facing
as explosive shells raked the bank scant meters ahead of him. He
shied, squealing like a frightened horse, tried to run in the opposite
direction.

The chopper jock let him get close to the building opposite,
then laid another burst right across his path, herding him away
from shelter.

He was limping now with comic exaggeration, hanging on to
his thigh with both hands, hauling his protesting leg by main force.
The chopper swooped at him, once, twice, eerie-quiet, a nightmare

made of plastic and glittering steel.

His lungs were bursting as he lurched onto the herringbone bricks of the State Street mall. The chopper darted at him like a sheepdog, driving him out into the middle, far from any possible refuge. He started running north, a strange crippledy flailing gait, the last ecstasy of desperation before collapse.

Something bounced off the bricks before him with a metallic clang.

He turned, trying to hold the breath he'd ripped halfway out of his lungs. But it was too late. He couldn't see it, couldn't smell or taste it, but he could feel it, or imagined he could, infiltrating his nose and streaming eyes.

He tried to run in the other direction. His nose was running now, his eyes blurred by tears brought on by more than the horror of what was happening to him. His hand rooted frantically in the pocket of his jacket as he felt a band of iron close around his chest. Maybe if he gave the damning disk back, they'd take him back, save him, not let this happen to him. He was one of them, a natural lord over the sheep, they couldn't do this, it wasn't right. Wasn't fair—

His lungs seemed to be turning solid within him. The tears streamed freely as he fought futilely for breath. His hand found the optical disk and his fingers clenched on it in his last willed action. Then the spasms overtook him. He flailed his arms, kicked, writhed in the debris the helicopter's rotors washed over him like surf. And then he died.

CHAPTER
ONE ————————————————————

Billy McKay came awake with a hand over his mouth.

Fuck me, he thought frantically. He'd always known this would happen: the Guardians would start imagining themselves to be safe here among their allies in San Antonio, capital of the Republic of Texas—as if anywhere in the crazy quilt the One-Day War had left of America could possibly be safe for the elite unit charged with putting it all back together.

But there was no time for regret, no time to speculate where the killers had come from—Randall James Hedison, governor of Texas in exile in Oklahoma City; *Cristeros* up from Mexico and pissed off about the Guardians making off with their beautiful teenaged prophet, Sister Light; a hit squad courtesy of their old buddy Yevgeny Maximov, reaching out across the Atlantic from his European domain to Touch Someone. Whoever had invaded the bedroom of the house the Republic was letting the Guardians use, the intruder had only given McKay time to *act*.

With any luck at all, that would turn out to be a fatal sort of mistake.

With one hand McKay grabbed the wrist attached to the hand on his mouth. With the other he grabbed for the combat-modified .45 in the Milt Sparks holster tucked between mattress and box-springs. Then he threw his hundred-plus kilogram weight off the bed, dragging his attacker across the bed and onto the floor.

He fell on top of the intruder. Breath exploded from the bedroom invader in a *whoof*. McKay noticed that his assailant had recently brushed his teeth; mighty considerate assassins they had in these parts. In fact, the midnight visitor smelled clean, even faintly perfumed.

Then he noticed that the body beneath his wasn't struggling, and that it was *soft*. Not mushy-soft, but the soft of padding over firm muscles. He reared up feeling with the hand that wasn't waving his Colt in the air.

It closed over an unmistakably feminine and unmistakably bare breast. The nipple poked into his palm like a fingertip.

"Jesus fucking *Christ*," he muttered. "Eklund, if you're playing games—"

But he already knew it wasn't Marla Eklund, lieutenant colonel
in the armed forces of the Republic of Texas and comrade in arms
to the Guardians. He'd rolled around with her often enough to
know that this wasn't her six-foot weight lifter's body pinned
beneath his. To know that what he was smelling wasn't the smell
of her. A few splinters of starlight fell in through the venetian
blinds, but not enough to make out details.

The intruder drew a deep breath. "Jesus, *vato,* if you're going
to try to ²quash me—" A hand slipped behind his neck and pulled
his head down. The mouth that met his was warm, moist, and
waiting.

He was already rock-rigid inside his skivvies. *What the fuck,
over?* he thought. He probed with his tongue. The intruder met it
with hers, which writhed like a snake with a broken back. She
writhed, too, grinding against him. He felt and heard the rustling
rasp of pubic hair on his crotch.

Growling low in his throat he raised himself. He felt fingers
tugging his prick out of the fly of his shorts, planting the head
firmly against the wet lips of a cunt. He might not have been the
brightest dude in the world, but he didn't need any more clues.
The intruder cried out as he thrust into her.

They went furiously at it, ignoring the chill hardness of the
bare wood floor beneath. Whoever she was, she was pretty incred-
ible; she had a long, lean build, not too many inches shorter than
Eklund after all, breasts large for a willowy frame. Though she
lacked Eklund's well-molded muscle mass, she was also pretty
damn strong: as her passion started to mount she began arching
her back, lifting him into the air even though he had to outweigh
her by a hundred pounds.

After a frantic interval of the *slap-slap* of skin on skin and bare
buttocks on wood, McKay felt her clench about him. He roared
like a bull and let go himself.

He collapsed on top of her. She lay with her head to the side
and her hands limp as dead things on his T-shirted back, panting
as if she'd just run a mile in two minutes. McKay let his forehead
slump past her shoulder, feeling the hardwood floor through a
lush mat of long hair. He enjoyed the cool. He was feeling pretty
wrung-out himself.

After a time she began to nibble at his ear again. He felt his
cock, still half inside her, begin to respond. But this was getting

to be too much even for him. He always thought of himself as a stud, but there were limits.

He hoisted himself onto his elbows. "Pardon me, but I don't believe we've met."

The lights came on. McKay froze. That was all he needed, for one of his teammates to be checking to see if he was all right, drawn by the commotion McKay and the mysterious stranger had created. Even Tom Rogers, who had liquid nitrogen where most people had blood, would never be able to resist ribbing him about this till the sun went out.

Then he realized he was gazing down into the cat-green eyes of Claudia LaRousse, virgin daughter of the president of the Republic of Texas. On second thought he struck the *virgin*. Not recently, anyway.

He opened his mouth. "Fuck—" he began.

"Billy McKay, you two-timing blue-belly son of a bitch," came the familiar parade-deck roar of former drill sergeant Marla Eklund her own demure self. *"Just what the hell do you think you're doing?"*

"—*me*." he concluded.

Claudia smiled. It made her look even more like a cat . . . one that had finally found the latch on the parakeet cage.

"I thought I just did," she purred.

An empty vase the former residents of the house had left on the dresser shattered against the wall, showering clumps of black dirt and terra-cotta shrapnel down on McKay's close-cropped head.

"Billy," the voice of former fighter-jock and current Guardian Casey Wilson asked from the doorway, "are you all right, man?"

Lights and music spilled into the street from both sides. Down by the Alamo was a honky-tonk sort of district, where music and laughter alike were too loud, even in the middle of the night. It suited McKay's mood.

He stopped outside a place with ROSE OF CIMARRON engraved and painted on a wooden sign above the door, lit by a pair of kerosene lamps. For a moment he pondered, hands stuck deep in the pockets of a tan windbreaker. His breath came in wisps of fog. The music coming out of here was mariachi, which always sounded to McKay as if it should be being cranked out of one of those old-time barrel organs you used to see in Marx Brothers movies. He didn't especially care for mariachi music, or salsa, or any of that stuff. But it did tend to leaven the country music, which he could hack even less.

The fact was, cowboy music just naturally lent itself to going on a good old-fashioned red-eyed low-life binge of the sort McKay felt badly in need of right about now, and so did this Mexican stuff. McKay rubbed the raw red spot high on the cheek where Eklund had caught him with a right hook, and went in.

''—outbreak of a mysterious disease in a sizable community of survivors of the One-Day War in Cleveland, Ohio,'' the television was saying over a dwindling song. The doors swung to behind McKay as he paused to look around—double-hung doors, of course; sometimes Texas seemed almost frantic to live up to its movie image.

It was a pretty standard post-Holocaust bar, with a few variations. City power was expensive enough only to be tapped to power the refrigerator compressors and the TV flickering above the bar, tuned to one of the two local channels. For illumination the Rose depended on kerosene and pressurized-methane lamps hung above the obligatory pool tables and nailed to the square posts that pretended to hold up the ceiling. The dim light they gave off only added to the proper bar ambience, especially when filtered through bands of tobacco and marijuana smoke.

The jukebox cranked up another one. From his recent trip to Mexico McKay recognized *"El Camino de Guanajuato,"* "The Guanajuato Road," which their guide, Judy Betzinez, had gleefully called to their attention because it contained the classic line, *"La vida vale nada en Guanajuato."* Which meant, "Life is worth nothing in Guanajuato." The Guardians' expedition hadn't taken them to that city, famed primarily for its deceased citizens, mummified in the local soil and displayed in a variety of amusing and entertaining poses in the catacombs. But if life *was* worth anything there, it would sure have stood out from the rest of the country.

Maybe the rest of the world, these days.

"Reports on the apparent epidemic remain sketchy, but our Action News team has pieced together . . ." The music drowned the latest evening blues, and McKay bellied up to the bar.

Specialty of the house was something called a Poco Loco, which was a sort of post-Holocaust boilermaker, a shot glass filled with fuel-grade ethanol cut with whatever was handy, chased by a mug of Bexar beer, a local brew. The shot was cascading like napalm down his throat and he was vigorously chugging the chaser when he was suddenly jostled from behind.

Beer slopped down the front of his jacket and the T-shirt he still wore beneath. He turned around, sputtering and scowling, but secretly pleased. This was just the kind of therapy his wounded spirit needed.

"Who the fuck you think you're pushing?" he demanded.

"You, you Yankee meatball. Wanna make something of it?"

McKay did, but to his disappointment his would-be antagonist was a sawed-off bandy-legged specimen not more than five five in his pointy-toe boots, with a Levi's jacket and a white straw c'boy hat with a feather in the band and a face that was primarily nose.

"Shit, you ain't a keeper. I better throw you back, Shorty."

"Yeah? How about *him?*" The miniature shitkicker jerked a dirty-nailed thumb back over one shoulder at the junior-grade mountain standing there glowering at McKay from under the brim of his own hat. This one had a mashed-in Aggie tackle's nose and pig eyes and a beard that looked as if it had been drawn in makeup pencil by a careless artist, the kind that was enjoying another spell of popularity among the younger rednecked set.

"This dude botherin' you, Jesse?" he drawled, cracking scarred and swollen knuckles. He had biceps like most people have thighs.

"Thinks his size gives him the right to pick on me, Buford," Jesse said, spraying spittle onto the sleeve of McKay's jacket.

McKay was about to quick-punch ol' Buford in the beer belly when he saw a flicker of motion in the smoked-glass mirror, right next to an old *Playboy* photo of sex star Merith Tobias, doing her best golden-nude Monroe on a waterbed with her yellow hair all flowing out over a burgundy silk coverlet. He spun, snapping his right arm up in a quick *ol-gool* block.

A pool cue snapped off clean against his ulna. He barely felt it. That was the way a well-executed tae kwon do block worked—if it wasn't well executed, you busted your arm instead. McKay got a quick impression of an Adam's apple like an elbow and mouth hanging in a slack gape of surprise, and then he drove his fist into the middle of the cue wielder's bony face.

Bone and cartilage crunched. Blood splattered satisfactorily. The skinny shitkicker went flying into the crowd as if he'd been kicked by a mule.

"T-bone!" the little cowboy shouted in alarm.

Moving with a speed that would be the last thing you'd associate with his bulk, McKay whirled back, grabbing a handful of Jesse's shirt and hauling the little bastard bodily into the air—right into the path of the haymaker his good buddy Buford was launching at McKay's ear. The meaty forearm clipped him on the side of the head. He sagged in McKay's fist.

McKay smiled.

Then he heard, *real close,* the sort of sliding clack that means only one thing in all the world. He froze. His eyes tracked right, very slowly; when you heard that sound you didn't want to move *anything* fast.

The bartender was pointing a beautifully preserved Winchester Model 97 slide-action twelve gauge at McKay's ear. It wasn't personal; the barkeep was clearly ready to point the shotgun anywhere the incipient bar fight showed signs of breaking out again. Which, of course, was nowhere.

"The establishment thanks you for taking your differences out of doors, gentlemen," the bartender said.

About this time a Plains Indian who dwarfed even young Buford loomed up, grinning from a face like a jack-o'-lantern framed by long black braids, grabbed McKay and the semicomatose Jesse by the scruffs, and bum's rushed them out the door. A moment later the jack-o'-lantern's cousin pitched Buford into the gutter next to the front bumper of a Nissan pickup like a sack of feed, skimming his hat after him like a Frisbee.

McKay picked himself up and brushed at his knees. A weight landed abruptly on his back, long arms and legs wrapped around him, and a voice screeched, "I got him, boys! Fix his ass good!"

The third member of the trio had obviously opted to use the momentum imparted by a giant Kiowa jackboot to renew his attack. Without having to think about it McKay reached back and grabbed a short hank of hair. Then he jackknifed forward, sending T-bone flying over his head and into the open window of a powder-blue 1967 Ford Fairlane parked right in front of the Rose of Cimarron. His boots flailed uselessly at the air. The soles were separating, down by the toes.

As McKay was congratulating himself his arms were yanked behind him and two enormous hands closed on the back of his neck in a full nelson. He'd forgotten about Buford.

Even at this hour of the morning the sidewalks were thronged. The passersby just sort of navigated around the disturbance, except for a few who stopped to watch. Obviously people were accustomed to letting adults settle their own differences, hereabouts.

Jesse picked himself up, crammed his somewhat crumpled hat back on his head. "You just hang onto him real good, Buford. Real good."

He stooped, picked up a beer bottle, busted it on the curb. McKay tried to wrench free, but Buford held him tight, grunting rhythmically into his ear in a way that indicated he was either laughing or horny.

McKay's .45 was nestled out of sight in its combat rig beneath his jacket. He hadn't even thought of using it; that wasn't the point of the exercise. Now he wished he had, but it was too late; the piece was trapped between two sweaty, straining bodies, and he couldn't get his arms loose, and in general he was fucked.

Then a black Thunderbird roared off from the head of the block, only to lock its brakes almost at once, right in front of the Rose. A heavily accented voice hollered, "*La Araña* sends his greetings," and the short mean muzzles of a pair of Skorpion machine pistols poked out of the passenger-side windows.

By unspoken accord Buford and McKay both just dropped like rag dolls. Jesse took a moment to gawk, then sucked pavement just as orange fire started billowing from the little Czech guns—trademarks of the Mexican Federal Security Directorate, whose boss the Guardians had caused to lose his job, to say nothing of his bid to run the country. Glass and cement dust exploded from the bar's facade.

McKay clawed for his gun as the sharp little bullets cracked overhead. "Fuck," he grunted, "this just ain't my day."

Alertly, the locals were taking cover—on the *other* side of the street. And McKay's side lit up like an exploding scoreboard.

The Republic of Texas had not been founded on the principle that a disarmed citizenry was a safe citizenry. The machine pistols had scarcely opened up when there were guns *everywhere*.

To his open-mouthed astonishment McKay watched the most amazing assortment of sidearms appear out of holsters, pockets, and even purses. Cowboy guns as long as his forearm, big automatics, belly guns, everything. A young Hispanic woman who'd been sashaying past with a wiggle of hips in a velveteen miniskirt that McKay would have found quite interesting if he hadn't been fixing to get the shit beat out of him whipped an army-style Beretta out of her purse, propped it professionally on the Nissan pickup's hood, and cut loose. Jesse was firing a tiny chromed Jetfire .25 past the rear bumper of the Fairlane.

Shotgun flame vomited from the blown-out windows of the bar.

One of the Jolly Green Kiowas appeared in the doorway, blasting away with an Ital-Alpine paratrooper assault rifle from the hip, and the recoil of the big 7.62 millimeter rounds seemed to make him no never-mind at all.

The Mexican hit men were surprised.

As bullet holes appeared in the side of the car like spots of ink shaken from a fountain pen, the Skorpions fell silent pretty quickly. With commendable presence of mind the driver tried to put the T-Bird in gear and peel away, but there was this stout black man in a gray three-piece suit and bolo tie with a silver-and-turquoise longhorn clasp kneeling a little ways along the sidewalk pumping slugs from a snubbed .41 magnum into the engine block, and all four tires already looked as if they'd been driven across one of those pop-up dragon's-tooth barriers they have to keep people from sneaking into drive-in movies without paying. He didn't make much headway.

Steam poured out from under the buckled hood. The car *thump-whumped* about eleven feet and stopped with a loud sigh. The pedestrians all began to run out of ammo more or less at once. As the shooting died, so did the car, collapsing on its shattered suspension with a crash.

The ensuing silence was louder than thunder.

"Fuck," Billy McKay said. He was holding his own Colt unfired in both hands. He only heard his own voice because it reverberated inside his head.

A skinny kid approached the Thunderbird holding a Ruger single-action ready and peered gingerly in. He went green beneath his freckles.

"Shoot," he said. "Looks like the debutante ball after Jason went home."

Buford was already on his feet, tucking a Llama .38 auto into his belt. He held a huge hand down to McKay. McKay eyed it a moment. *What the fuck, over?* He put the Colt away and took the hand.

Jesse came swaggering up as Buford hoisted McKay aloft. "Let's go back inside," he said. "Buy you boys a beer."

The Fairlane's door opened and T-bone got out stuffing cartridges into a snubnosed revolver. The four of them staggered back into the Rose of Cimarron.

The Kiowa bouncer held the door for him. He still had his BM-59 by the pistol grip with its hot barrel in the air. He looked at the ruins of the T-bird and shook his head

"Stupid motherfuckers," he said. "Didn't they know this was Texas?"

Dawn was slopping like curdled milk over the stony hills to the east when McKay staggered up the front walk to the house where the Guardians were billeted. One arm was draped around the bearlike neck of Buford, the other rested on Jesse's skinny shoulders. He was leading his new friends in a stirring rendition of a song that had been popular back in Beirut:

> *"Jingle fucking bells, jingle fucking bells,*
> *Jingle all the fucking way.*
> *What fucking fun it is to fucking ride*
> *In a one-horse-fucking open sleigh."*

"That's dumb," T-bone slobbered. He brought up the rear, gimping slightly. He'd fucked up his knee some when McKay had thrown him into the car. "Christmas ain't for eight, nine months yet."

"Shit," Jesse said with disdain, "you just ain't got the holiday spirit, you dumb peckerwood."

The door opened. Sam Sloan stood there, already dressed in gray Guardians uniform coveralls. "Where the heck have you been?" he asked.

McKay waggled his hands from his buddies' shoulders. "Winning hearts and minds. Hearts and minds."

Sloan looked him up and down, his long rectangular Jim Garner face carefully deadpan. "Well, you better brace yourself for a man-sized jolt of Tommy's best hangover cure."

McKay scowled. "Wha'fuck for? Party's just begun."

"No. The party's over, McKay. We're supposed to turn up at the presidential offices pronto. The fertilizer has hit the fan."

He was already starting to get sober. Duty did that to him. "Whuh—what happened?"

The former navy officer shook his head. "You wouldn't believe me if I told you. *Trust* me."

CHAPTER
TWO ————————————

"We caught him sneaking into town a little after 0300," the young officers was saying as they swung down the fluorescent-lit corridor of San Antonio's city hall, now serving as seat of government to the Texican Republic.

Striding alongside him, McKay tried to keep his eyeballs under control. They kept wanting to flick back over his shoulder at the bulk of the president, coming right behind. *Shit, I wonder if he knows I shagged his daughter?*

There was no way LaRousse could've found out. Not this soon. Unless, of course, his loyal officer Eklund informed him, out of a sense of duty, of course. Or Claudia . . . could *she*—?

A trooper with a slung M16 was holding a door open for them just down the hall. From inside a voice was saying wearily but determinedly, "I beg your pardon, but I was not *sneaking*. I was arriving quite openly."

McKay's head was a buzz of fatigue and booze and adrenaline. People were talking, but it wasn't registering. If the crusty old bastard knew, he was thinking, it would be just his style to call him out: *High Noon* for true, six guns on main street. Or maybe he'd just break McKay's neck. He was seventy if he was a day, but the way he was built he could still make a pretty good go of it.

McKay's bootheel stopped on the runner across the bottom of the door as if it had suddenly been magnetized. All of a sudden he *knew that voice*. It was impossible, but he knew it.

Then he looked at the man sitting in the orange plastic auditorium chair with his manacled hands resting in his lap. Sea-green eyes met his. Thin lips smiled.

"Gentlemen," McKay said, "you better believe him. If Colonel Ivan Vesensky *was* tryin' to sneak in, not even you boys would've caught him."

He heard a double intake of breath from Casey and Sloan, trailing after President LaRousse. He walked into the briefing room and leaned back against the wall. He folded his oak-limb

15

forearms across his chest. The buzzing fog had cleared abruptly from his brain.

Vesensky inclined his head courteously. "Good morning, Lieutenant," he said in his anchorman's baritone. His English was impeccable; the only accent was the barest hint of British inflection, and that fit seamlessly with the covers he tended to affect: playboy, skier, photojournalist.

McKay stared down at him. "Colonel," he said roughly. "You're a little better dressed than last time I saw you."

The Russian laughed. The last time McKay had seen him, he'd been wearing nothing more than a pair of briefs and a coating of Gulf Coast seawater. On that occasion he'd interrupted a romantic interlude between McKay and Marla Eklund during the *Cristero* siege of the Bernardo de Galves Seawater Desalinization Facility, another piece of the Blueprint puzzle.

This morning he had on a navy-blue turtleneck with a CPO jacket buttoned over it, black jeans, black athletic shoes.

The Texicans were all staring at McKay as if he'd sprouted horns. "You know this man?" demanded a long, narrow, uniformed man with a waxed brown mustache and a brushstroke of gray at either temple.

"That's right," McKay said. "At least, I do."

"We're familiar with his reputation," Sam Sloan said, halfway beneath his breath.

He and the other two Guardians had filed in and were staring at Vesensky with open interest. Only McKay had encountered their long-standing antagonist at close range before. Casey had seen him, too—at a kilometer's distance, through the scope of his high-tech sniper's rifle in the rubble of Washington, D.C. And even then the Russian's face had been largely obscured by the heavy-metal makeup he'd applied for his role as the Witch King of the Ruins.

"Well, anytime you're ready to quit playing games and give us some solid information, I'm ready," the mustache said.

McKay tracked his eyes to him under lowered brows. "His name's Vesensky, like I said. He used to be with the KGB. Now he's *numero uno* hit man for old man Maximov."

A fresh-faced Texican lieutenant gasped. "You mean the chairman of the Federated States of Europe?"

McKay took a Cuban cigar—booty from Mexico—from the pocket of his silver-gray coveralls and unwrapped it with elaborate casualness. "No. I mean Leo Maximov, used to run a deli on Boggs, back in Pittsburgh. What the hell do you think, Junior?"

The mustache put what he must have thought was a penetrating gray gaze right to McKay. "Suppose you tell us why he should turn up here at weird o'clock in the morning, asking for you boys?" His tone hinted treason.

"How the fuck should I know?" he said, lighting the cigar. "Why don't you ask him, Captain?"

He puffed a cloud of smoke. The mention of delis made it remind him of the bagel-flavored steam near vendor's carts on cold Pittsburgh days. The officer turned the color of boiled beets. McKay had not failed to notice the oak leaves on his shoulders. But what the hey; the Republican armed forces knew how to fight, but they handed out promotions like a newly minted Third World dictatorship.

"Mr. President, are you going to let him say that in your presence?" the major demanded when he got the power of speech back.

Lamar Louis Napoleon LaRousse chuckled, a sound like rocks being shaken in an oil drum. "Say what, son? It sounded like the man made a perfectly good suggestion to me. Say, you have a spare one of those evil ropes, Billy?"

McKay pulled out another cigar and handed it over. He caught a glimpse of Sloan's face, which was a sort of mesquite green. The navy man wasn't too fond of cigar smoke at the best of times.

"Well, you gonna stand there looking like a stepped-on toad frog," the President asked, unwrapping the cigar, "or would you like to ask the question while you're still a major?" He flicked a match alive with his thumbnail.

The major gave McKay a final hate look, reluctantly let it slide to the Russian, who was doing a passable job concealing his amusement. "Well?" the Texican barked. "Spit it out, spy."

Vesensky looked at LaRousse. "I'd like to thank Your Excellency for giving me the chance to say what I came here to say."

LaRousse waved the cigar negligently. "Think nothing of it, son. And don't call me Excellency. Call me Mr. President, or Lamar, or hey you. Just don't call me late for supper."

Vesnesky gave McKay a sidelong look. McKay rolled his eyes slightly. President LaRousse could take some getting used to, whether you were the boss Guardian or the former blue-ribbon assassin for Department V-for-Victor, the "wet affairs" bureau of the Department of State Security.

"I've come to ask for the Guardians' help," he said. "And offer my own."

The major inhaled about an inch more height. "What the fuck are you talking about?" McKay demanded.

"I'm talking about a danger that threatens not only the Federated States of Europe—and the not-so United States of America—but quite conceivably the entire world." ·

"If you're talking about the Pan-Turanians, Colonel, save your breath," Sam Sloan said. "You don't seriously expect us to think they're a threat to America, when you've started to throw them out of your European empire?"

Vesensky shook his sleek blond head. "Not at all—Commander Sloan, is it? I'm talking about a weapon against which there is no known defense. Biological warfare, Commander."

McKay frowned and took the cigar out of his mouth. "Slow down a minute, here, Colonel. Did you come all this way to threaten us?"

Vesensky shook his head. "No, no. I told you, this threat hangs over all of us." The exasperation in his voice was the first crack his composure had shown. "Europe and America alike could be depopulated, unless action is taken, and quickly."

From the dossiers Major Crenna's Blueprint intelligence boys had been able to assemble on Vesensky, the former Soviet agent was in his middle to late thirties, though he could pass for mid-twenties. Now for a brief instant his face was that of an old man: worn parchment. Even Billy McKay, not normally a sensitive kind of guy, could recognize naked fear. The kind of fear that was hard to fake.

Of course, Colonel Ivan Vesensky was one hell of an actor.

"He's talking Cleveland, Billy," Tom Rogers said quietly.

McKay opened his mouth and shut it again. His whole head seemed to be ringing like a brass bell.

Vesensky nodded.

President LaRousse pulled a chair around and sat with his arms crossed over the back. "Suppose you tell us about it, son," he said. "I'll try to keep my smoke away from you, since it looks like it bothers you."

The Russian nodded amused acceptance. The amusement didn't last. "First of all, I don't want to give away any secrets my colleagues the Guardians prefer to keep," he said.

"The Texicans were with us at the Galves plant," McKay said, drawing on his own cigar. "May have slipped your mind. They're hip to the Blueprint. And why your man Maximov's so hot to get his hooks on it."

Vesensky gave a have-it-your-way shrug. "Very well. Then I assume President LaRousse is aware that during the fraternal occupation of America by FSE forces sent to restore the rightful president, William Lowell, to power—"

McKay growled low in his throat. "Maybe you should give the propaganda a miss, Colonel," Sam suggested.

Vesensky grinned. "At any rate, sir, for a time the Expeditionary Force military command as well as Lowell's government were situated in a giant subterranean complex in Iowa called Heartland. Before the arrival of the FSE contingent Heartland was headquarters for Project Blueprint, of which the Guardians are a part, as well as seat of power for the usurper President MacGregor.

"Heartland was destroyed by terrorist action—and before my esteemed associate Lieutenant McKay leaps for my throat, let me assure him and you that that's purely the official FSE description of the course of events, and I'm here, after all, as a representative of my government—"

"Why does the phrase 'like a thief in the night' come to mind?" Sloan murmured.

Vesensky drew a deep breath. "In any event, before the destruction of Heartland by the Guardians, a good deal of its database on the Blueprint for Renewal was liberated by FSE technicians. As I assume the Guardians have told you, the master key to the Blueprint was lost with President Lowell's National Emergency Aerial Command Post. Unfortunately, we didn't recover it when we bought the president back from the Quebecois separatists—to skip the euphemisms in the interests of harmony. The Guardians and the Blueprint technicians backing them had been able to piece together a good deal of the master plan, but they put a lock on the files so that even now our own analysts haven't been able to extract all the information in them. In addition, we have assembled a fair amount of data on our own since the loss of Heartland.

"As I also presume you know, both the FSE and the Guardians have been in a race to identify and secure major Blueprint facilities since the One-Day War. Each side correlates extant data with information garnered from various other sources."

He paused. "Six weeks ago our analysts determined, to an eighty-five percent probability, that a Blueprint facility devoted to recombinant-DNA research existed in the Midwest. Analysis of intelligence gathered during the occupation of Chicago indicates a high order of probability that the lab is located somewhere in or near that city. Finally, a recent reassessment of the data points very strongly to the lab's being biowar capable."

McKay shared a look with his comrades. The Guardians' comm units, calculator-sized and capable of picking up subvocalized speech and transmitting it through bone-conduction phones behind the Guardians' ears, insured secure—and secret—communication even in a crowded room. But there was no need for speech, even subvocalized. Each of them was thinking the same thing: that for the FSE to share this information with them was like the Israelis offering the Syrians the Bomb at a discount.

"This is the most ridiculous load of horseshit I've ever heard," the mustache said. "Mr. President, I strongly suggest— "

"Who the fuck asked you, Jocko?" McKay said. "You Texicans are always making such a big stink about being a sovereign nation and all that shit. How 'bout butting out and letting the U.S. and the FSE handle their own affairs?"

"Mr. President—" the major began.

It wasn't his morning to get to complete a sentence. "Lieutenant McKay," LaRousse said, "I got a definite hunch this matter concerns the welfare of the great and sovereign Republic of Texas every bit as much as the U.S. of A. and the Effsees. Maybe Major Compton would like to wait outside."

"Mr. President, I really must protest—"

LaRousse frowned. It made him look like an extra head on Rushmore, in a pissed-off mood to boot. "*Vamoose,* Bob. Hit the highway."

The major coughed and sputtered and left. When the door to the corridor was shut, the president cocked a white-thatched crag of brow at Vesensky.

"All right, son, I ain't saying I believe you and I ain't saying I don't. But even if what you're saying's true, why did you take the risk of coming here to tell us about it?"

Vesensky met his gaze levelly. "The Cleveland outbreak, sir. Cleveland is five hundred kilometers from Chicago. Not terrifically far by American standards. One of the closest reasonably large collections of survivors of the war, in fact."

Sam Sloan frowned and rubbed his chin. "Still, it's not exactly next door. Bit far for an accidental release."

"But, yes, Commander. Quite so. Not too far, not too near: ideal for an experiment. And a warning."

Casey turned pale under a surfboard tan that not even the long winter had made much of a dent in. "You mean it was, like, a deliberate release?"

Vesensky nodded. "Koblenz theorizes that the Blueprint DNA research facility has fallen into what your entertainment media might quaintly have termed 'the wrong hands.' I concur in that assessment.

"Gentlemen, unless we pool our resources immediately and effectively, someone is going to be holding a sword at the throat of the entire human race."

CHAPTER
THREE

"So, Billy, like what do you think?" Casey Wilson asked. Worry lengthened his boyish face.

" 'So, Billy, like what do you think?' " McKay mimicked savagely. "Jesus, Casey, do you always have to talk like such a freak? Life ain't just one long song by the Eagles."

Casey's face crumpled as if McKay had driven a pile-driver fist into it. He took off his yellow Zeiss shooting glasses, which he tended to wear at any hour of the day or night, and began polishing them, gazing down into the pool of fluorescent light jittering on the Formica top of the commissary table. The youngest Guardian wasn't your average swaggering, hard-drinking, don't-mess-with-me-weenie fighter jock. On the other hand he was the top-scoring American ace since Korea, with the only five-kill mission any American had racked up in the jet age.

Sam Sloan stared at McKay across his steaming cup of tea, for once too shocked even to voice disapproval of his leader's crudeness.

"Billy," Tom Rogers said, in that gentle, Southern-inflected voice of his. He always used that tone of voice, whether making love or passing sentence of death.

McKay said nothing, just sat with his bulky body leaning forward and his bare forearms resting on the cool Formica, staring at a cork bulletin board with notices for roommates and day care and a staff square dance tacked to it.

"Billy," Tom said the same way. "Don't you think that was a little rough?"

"Fuck," McKay said in disgust. "Don't be such an old woman. I just can't hack this California mellow bullshit sometimes."

Casey polished his glasses some more. Tom just stared at McKay. His expression remained mild. His eyes were the gray of armor plate, shark's eyes.

McKay shifted his bulk in the plastic chair. The little rubber boots on its tubular sheet-metal legs squeaked on the linoleum floor. He was already aware he was an asshole. But Tom was

22

reminding him in his own downbeat way, all the same.

It wasn't treatment he'd take from just anybody. Tom was the unit morale officer and medic. Sometimes that meant playing babysitter to the Guardians' temperamental leader. But that wasn't the only reason McKay let Rogers lecture him—as he was doing now, unspeaking or not, in a way Zen enough to satisfy even Casey's flaky streak of mysticism.

Though he was built along the general lines of your standard cinderblock, Rogers was a good sixty pounds lighter than McKay and seven inches shorter. As a rule, McKay feared no evil, because he was the meanest sonofabitch in the valley. But there was one shining exception. On the basis of four years' close association, and a nodding acquaintance with his reputation in the shadow-world of dirty warfare before that, McKay reckoned Tom Rogers to be the deadliest specimen of humanity he'd ever encountered.

He made blades of his big scarred hands and drummed a slow beat with them on the tabletop. "All right, all right. I'm sorry, Case. I had no excuse to fly off the handle like that. So I'm a shitbird, okay? Fuck."

"So answer the question," Sloan said.

McKay blinked. "Huh?"

"Answer his question. What do you think? Is our old friend Ivan on the level?"

"No. No way. It's a scam."

After dropping his bombshell, Vesensky had permitted himself to be led away to confinement under guard in the truncated San Antone City Hall while the Guardians, their superiors, and their allies tried to figure out what the hell was going on. Commo officer Sloan had bounced accounts of the interrogation off a satellite to President MacGregor on one coast and Dr. Jacob Morgenstern, head of Project Blueprint, on the other. Experts in DC and California were combing through their own Blueprint data, which they'd mostly stolen back from the Effsees after the juvenile hackers of Vista Systems penetrated FSE computer security using codes the Guardians had liberated during the breakout from Heartland.

For the moment the Guardians were to sit tight and wait for orders. Even at the best of times that wasn't an easy task for any of them. Different as they were in temperament, each of them was action-oriented, comfortable only when he had a mission in mind, a goal before his eyes.

Sloan sloshed his tea in a slow circle in a white ceramic mug with WORLD'S GREATEST SECRETARY printed on it. It was an herbal blend imported from New Eden in California—another Blueprint facility, and one of the most fought-over. Just the smell of it turned McKay's guts over. *Why would the Texicans trade for that junk, anyway?* he wondered. *If they wanna drink stuff that smells like that, there's plenty of cowflops to boil.*

"You sure?" Sloan asked.

"Huh?" McKay said again. He'd wandered off in his mind, thinking about drying, shredding, and packaging Organic Prairie Frisbees for sale to the natural food set. He could own California in six weeks, no question. "Am I sure about what?"

"I'm tempted to say 'anything,' but I'll be dutiful and refrain."

"Hey. That's big of you."

"What I mean is, are you sure this is a trick? This whole crazy biowar business."

"Hell, yes. Our old buddy Ivan Vesensky is one tricky sonofabitch. The only one trickier is his main man Maximov. If they knew where a Blueprint facility was—especially as high-power a one as this is supposed to be—why would they tell us about it? No way."

"Unless they were on the level, man." Casey stuck his shooting glasses back on. "If they were, like, real scared."

McKay started to say something, shut his throat tight, let his breath out in a moment as a sigh. "Casey, this ain't your department, okay? I mean, you're good at what you do, you're the best, but when it comes to covert crap you're out of your depth. I'm sorry I came down on you earlier, but that's just the way it is. Right, Tom?"

Tom's jaw was set more firmly than usual. He was looking nowhere in particular. "I ain't sure, Billy."

"Say *what?*"

"I'm not sure this is a trick. I can't see their angle on it."

McKay bounced his hand-heel off his forehead. "This is not my day. This is a trap, all right? How do you like that? Chairman Max wants us taken out for good and all, and he's dangling little Ivan for bait."

"But Vesensky's his heavy-hitter," Sam objected. "He's pretty big bait."

"So we're, like, chopped liver? Come *on.* They've been making plays for us for two years. Maximov sent his hand-picked goon squad after our butts three months ago. We're the Guardians, remember? We're worth a few risks to put us out of the picture."

"What about the outbreak in Cleveland, Billy?" Casey asked.

"Coincidence. Or maybe it gave them the idea to pull this stunt. Can't you see the setup?"

"You're certaintly talking yourself into it, McKay," Sloan said.

"Hey, I just got it all worked out, that's all," McKay said with his best shit-eating smirk. He *was* talking himself into it.

Sloan ran a hand through his shock of dark brown hair, which he wore quite a bit longer than McKay's parade-deck cut—which wasn't saying much.

"Would they give away the existence of this lab, just for a trap? This could be as big a find as Starshine, and they sent a whole army after it."

"They might reckon we'd figure it out on our own anyway," Tom said, "or lift the information off them. Neither one of us's every really stole a march on the other yet."

"Yeah." McKay took out the stub of a cigar and chewed on it. "Besides, how do we know there really *is* a Blueprint designer-gene thing in Chicago, or anywhere? They might be jiving us about that, too."

But Tommy was staring at the wall. "With what we stole outta their database, they got to know their info's not much better than ours. They know we have that data. We can check if the whole thing's out in left field."

Sloan cocked his head at McKay. McKay frowned and lit the cigar. Mostly to gig Sloan, but also to help concentrate his thoughts, which were starting to break apart like a fogbank in the sun again. For a guy supposedly on inter-mission downtime he was leading a hell of a life.

"Also," Tom went on, thinking aloud, which he seldom did, "I ain't quite happy with the idea of Chairman Maximov using up Vesensky just to take us down. The colonel's his biggest asset in this hemisphere, in a lot of ways. Maximov burned a bunch of assets with that Liberator thing, and Iskander Bey's still got a big foothold in Europe. Chairman don't strike me the type to ride a losing streak till he's busted."

McKay rolled up one hand into a fist and put his chin on it. "What are you telling me, Tommy? What do *you* think's going down?"

"I don't know."

McKay sat and stared at him, smoke trickling up around his nose and into his eyes from the cigar jutting from his fist. Tommy was his rock; secretly he harbored the conviction that Tommy knew *everything*. And here he was showing doubt, the same evil nut-cutting thing McKay felt so often as leader and never let himself show.

It wasn't like Rogers to let him down like this.

He let his arm pivot forward, slamming the cigar to death in a hideous pink adobe ashtray. "Right. I'm outta here."

"Where to, Billy?" Casey asked.

"I'm gonna work out." They had a gym there in the building, which hadn't been blown off by the warhead that took out Randolph AFB and, incidentally, the top half of City Hall.

Sloan smirked. "Ah. The solution to every dilemma: go pump iron."

McKay showed him a nasty smile. "Naw. My solution to dilemmas is go look for bozos to punch out. But I did that last night. Don't want to fall into no rut."

He pumped like Arnold on speedballs for an hour and a half, until his arms weighed like lead and felt like wet paper and his abs quivered like the thighs of a fat girl getting eaten out. His strength went quickly, for him. Lifting on no sleep, and the multiple aftershocks of booze and adrenaline did that.

Unfortunately, his brain didn't quit working. If he wasn't thinking of Eklund it was Vesensky, or Claudia, or Claudia's dad, or all of the above intercut like a thriller on its final run to payoff. His usual cure for that sort of wheel-spinning was to get shit-faced, but circumstances had changed drastically in the last few hours, and unfitting yourself for action in a situation like this was something they used to stand you against a wall for.

So there was nothing for it but to pull on a borrowed pair of gray sweat pants and do a little road work. McKay *hated* road work.

But one thing was certain: he'd go nuts if he did any more *thinking*.

CHAPTER
FOUR

Nobody looked twice at a six-three former marine drill instructor jog-trotting through the lobby of the administrative center of a self-proclaimed sovereign nation in a white T-shirt and sweats and combat boots and a web belt with a communicator clipped like a Walkman on one side and an old government .45 in a Sparks combat rig on the other. It was an unbreakable rule that no Guardian should ever go- anywhere unarmed, even off to take a dump. Fortunately, the Texicans didn't shy away from guns.

Outside was bright in a watery sort of way, with a definite taste of chill that said winter wasn't dying easy in the Plains to the north. McKay wasn't too fuzzed to leer at a pair of incredibly cute Hispanic girls clicking up the cement steps in blue jeans and high-heeled boots. He was too fuzzed to realize who they were until he was almost on top of them.

"Good morning," said Claudia LaRousse. Her jade-colored eyes were utterly innocent, but her voice came out of her like smoke, hot and smooth.

The girl beside her grinned and said something in Spanish. McKay looked hard at her. He'd met one woman in his life who managed to make unplucked eyebrows look foxy, and that was . . .

"Luz says good morning, too. She hopes you won't be cold, dressed so scantily."

"Luz?"

Claudia tilted her head toward her companion, who was hiding her mouth behind her hand. "Hermana Luz. She's dropped the *Hermana* part."

It was hard to believe that the smartly dressed teenager with most of her hair ratted up and back in a dark kinky cloud and a narrow Kiowa braid hanging beside either cheek in prewar high style had until a couple of weeks before been the adored prophetess of a million bloodthirsty fanatics.

McKay dropped his eyes from the Mexican girl's. "Uh, I didn't know Luz was her real name." He wasn't usually the bashful type, but even he felt a little funky looking into the eyes

27

of a pretty teenybopper he'd once been sent to kill.

"It's not. The Virgin told her she could keep that part of her name after she quit being Sister Light. Mexicans aren't too hung up on the names they were baptized with. It's pretty common for them to go by a name they adopt after a religious experience or as a religious duty. Kind of a survival of Indian naming customs. Also useful in a country where almost everyone's real first name is José or María."

She grinned. "Like me and my sisters. Our mamas insisted. None of them's real traditional, except about that."

McKay blinked. "Your first name's José?" He was fuzzing out again. Fortunately, she laughed. "You seem to know a lot about this stuff. You an anthropologist or something?"

"No. Daddy always encouraged us to study all kinds of things. I'm really an architect—I was studying to be, anyway, before the war."

"In high school?"

"U of T, San Antone. Just finished my freshman year when the balloon went up."

He raised his eyebrows. It was hitting him eerie that not many hours before this selfsame cool, self-contained young woman had snuck into his bedroom for the express purpose of playing fireman on his cock, on what was even by his standards mighty short acquaintance.

At least she wasn't as young as he'd thought. "Oh, so you're—"

"I started university when I was fifteen, Mr. McKay. They said I was a gifted student. I'll be eighteen in July." She said something in Spanish to Luz. "Well, we don't want to keep you from getting your exercise, Lieutenant. We don't want you getting out of shape, do we?"

Luz snickered, and they ran on into the building.

Seventeen, he was thinking, watching the two tight, well-muscled little fannies, pumping around inside their denim casings. *Fuck me.*

Oh well. He thanked God he hadn't run across Ms. Claudia—María Claudia?—a year earlier. In his mind there was this big difference between putting it to a seventeen-year-old and a girl who was only sixteen. But it'd probably make a difference to her old man, too: since she was all of seventeen, he'd probably shoot McKay before he skinned him, if he ever found out.

Somehow, that wasn't much comfort.

He was running down by the Alamo. None of the Texicans

made much of a big deal about it, which surprised him, especially
since Randy Jim Hedison has assured him the Republicans were
obsessed with it, back before he had "in exile" added to his title
of governor. In fact, they seemed kind of embarrassed by the
whole thing.

"Your Texicans aren't real enamored of lost causes," the Guardians' old buddy Dreadlock Callahan had explained. The former
biker chieftain was currently a mercenary major with the Republic's
armed forces. "And the whole Alamo trip was a fuckup from the
git-go. Besides, a lot of them had ancestors on both sides. Tough
to know who to root for."

He was passing an open-air market a block or two beyond the
mission when he stopped at an intersection to let traffic pass. As
an old El Camino with the front end sawed off just in front of the
seats rolled past with a clopping of hooves, on blacktop, he tracked
his gaze left and found himself looking straight into a pair of blue
eyes as big and hot as signal lamps.

One time he'd been creepy-crawling through a roll of German
knife wire looped around a fighter base outside Tripoli. He and
two of his buddies from SOG-SWAC were infiltrating, planning
to make a few unauthorized modifications to some of the MiG-29
Fulcrums and late-model Mirages stashed away in their revetments.
Something that would culminate in a bang, and a big colorful
nylon canopy floating down out of the Libyan sky—or maybe not.
They weren't cutting their way in; the idea was to leave no signs
of entry or egress, no evidence at all of their presence expect a
multimillion-dollar hole in the desert or the Med. It was a bitch,
doing razor tape that way; it called for an ultimate degree of
training and mental discipline, plus nerves cooled by liquid helium.

So there he'd been in the middle of this tangle of razor blades,
and suddenly a searchlight in a cement guard tower had come on
and swept *right across him*. His skin had just simply shriveled all
over his body; there was nowhere to run. Even if he hauled around
the silenced submachine gun strapped across his back he was
basically going to die.

He didn't die. The light tracked on, blind as a sailor on the
third day of a binge. Probably the boys in the tower had come
out of their *bhang* fog momentarily and decided to do something
to make themselves look busy. He never found out.

His skin shriveled just like that now, with Marla Eklund staring
at him from behind the wheel of a cammie-painted Toyota four-
wheeler. Maybe waiting for the bullets was a little easier.

The field-expedient wagon rolled by. It had a complete flush toilet sitting in the back. Marla gunned the engine, popped the clutch, and squealed off down the street.

"Wait!" McKay yelled, without having any intention of doing so. Heads that had been bent down to look at fading boxes of scavenged detergent and hand tools and Go-bots raised and turned to look at the big crazy *gringo* as he peeled off down the street in pursuit of the Toy.

He was no Sam Sloan—the former naval officer was the runner in the group, though his specialty was the marathon, not sprinting. McKay's powerfully muscled legs could give him a hell of a burst of speed at need, though. He was flying down the street behind the Toyota, *gaining on it,* before he even got around to wondering what the hell he thought he was doing.

It was like some kind of sadistic music video. After her initial burst of speed Eklund had eased off the gas a hair. So she flicked a glance up into the rearview, and there's Billy McKay looming up right behind waving his arms. Their eyes met, and held, and she put the pedal to the metal.

"Marla! *Wait,* goddammit—" He hurled himself forward in a full-length desperate lunge for the vehicle. He left about a quarter millimeter off his fingerprints on the rear bumper and went face first into a pothole.

Now, shit, what did you want to go and do that for? he was asking himself. His self pled the Fifth. He pulled himself up onto hands and knees.

A couple of sets of strong hands aided him the rest of the way to his feet. A Hispanic with gray-dusted hair and an impressive mustache brushed at the grit caked on his arms. "She was in a hurry. Your wife?"

"Just somebody owes me money."

He sacked out about 2100, which was early for him, but he was exhausted.

When the door of his room whispered open unknown hours later he wasn't exactly surprised, even snapping into wakefulness from deepwater sleep. Still, lying on his belly with his cheek buried in a pillow, he slipped his left hand surreptitiously over the edge of the bed and down to the Pachmayr grips of his Colt.

The grumbling SAPD evidence techs had had to take *la Araña's* elite hit squad out of their car with tongs and a sponge last night, so there hadn't been much interrogation done. On the other hand, if the FSD killers had any other little friends north of the Rio Grande looking for vengeance against the Guardians, McKay didn't want to roll over and face them with nothing but his stiff dick in hand.

But as he'd anticipated it was the latter that was probably going to be useful. "You don't really need that," Claudia LaRousse said, gesturing at the big angular sidearm. Her voice came lower and rougher than this morning. "Or did I really rape you last night?"

McKay made a face and tucked the pistol back in its holster. He rolled onto his back and snapped on the bedside lamp. He didn't say anything.

She was standing there in a man's trenchcoat with her hair done up in a bun, a contrast to the cowpunk dos she and Luz had sported earlier. "Would you like me to go away?" she asked.

He still said nothing. She slipped off the trenchcoat and hung it on a plastic hook on the door. He was half-disappointed to see she had clothes on underneath. A maroon turtleneck and a very conservative length denim skirt, black stockings and high heels beneath. But he wasn't disappointed long. She set about removing her clothing right away.

She managed to be matter-of-fact and teasing at one and the same time. "Where the hell did a little girl like you learn about garter belts?" he asked.

She only smiled, came to the bed, and slowly slid the covers down. She had unbound her long black hair. It hung down over one olive shoulder, beside a full breast. She held the hair back from her face with one hand and bent forward.

She knew a lot of unusual things for a little girl.

Later they lay side by side, clutching each other and breathing hard, skin drawn up into goosebumps despite the down comforter pulled high to prevent them both freezing to death as the sweat slowly left their skins. Gradually they relaxed away from each other, until they lay side by side on their backs.

McKay turned his face to hers. "You trying to kill me, or what?"

She laughed and ran a finger along his chin. It was a slender finger. The nail was clipped short.

"You're not so old."

"Huh. I'm old enough to be your dad."

"If you'd started real early. Come to that, *my* dad could be your *granddad*, if he'd started early instead of late."

McKay frowned up at the ceiling. "That's what I mean about

trying to kill me, Claudia. Your dad. What's he gonna do if he finds out about us?"

She hoisted herself to an elbow. A breast slid free of the covers and hung there, swaying slightly, like a ripe fruit. "Afraid of a shotgun marriage?"

He winced. *Marriage* wasn't a word he liked to hear. Especially not in circumstances like these.

"I'm afraid of death."

She laughed again. "I doubt that."

"Then that just proves you're still a kid, even though you're real grown-up in a lot of ways."

She frowned, and though she bore no physical resemblance to President LaRousse that McKay could make out, all at once she was very much her father's daughter. Then her forehead smoothed.

"Maybe I asked for that—and maybe you're trying to put me off. But Daddy's an old dear. He wouldn't mind if he knew. Really. He talks a lot about our not disgracing the family"— McKay went taut—"but what he means is he doesn't want us going to bed with anyone unworthy of us."

She ran a hand down his chest. "Somehow I don't think he'd think you're unworthy."

"Thanks." He laughed, with little humor. He looked her in the eyes. "You're really Daddy's spoiled little darling, aren't you? Just barging in here two nights in a row."

He expected her to blow off at him. Maybe he wanted her to, somehow. But, damn her, she laughed *again*.

"You're pushing awfully hard, aren't you, Lieutenant? Somehow I didn't think you were the kind to feel guilty. But my father's always taught me—taught us—to go for what we want. Life's too short for hesitation.

"As for being spoiled—I guess I am. But I've been able to support myself since I was fourteen. I'm a fully trained architectural drafsman, I can train horses, I'm a decent mechanic. And I've even waited a few tables."

McKay held up his hands. "Okay, okay. I surrender."

"I know what it is. You're guilty because of what happened with Colonel Eklund. I'm very sorry about that; I had no idea she'd come to visit you that late. Maybe I'm a little impetuous sometimes."

"So what the hell about you? You feel guilty?"

"I'm here. I'm sorry the colonel caught us, because she didn't deserve to have her nose rubbed in it. And no, I'm not ego-tripping because I was able to cut in on her; men aren't built to be faithful.''

McKay shut his eyes and shook his head. He'd had to get used to going to bed with self-assured women since the war, since he'd been running into so damn many of them. But Claudia LaRousse was almost too much.

—As she demonstrated by taking his cock between thumb and forefinger and beginning to work it over lightly again.

"Jesus!" he exclaimed. "Give me a break. I ain't one of your nineteen-year-old studs.''

Her eyes seemed to glow like jade. "I know.''

On the nightstand his communicator buzzed for attention.

They were all clustered in the communication center in City Hall, a sterile white room with walls encrusted in gray metal panels and blinky lights. Vesensky, Major Compton and his mustache, President LaRousse wearing a maroon robe thrown over dark blue pajamas. McKay ran a hand through the hair he almost didn't have and marveled at the way his eyeballs felt like somebody'd popped them out and rolled them around in sand for a while before pushing them back in place.

"Play it again, Sam,'' he said.

"You won't like it any better a second time,'' Sloan responded. His hair was awry, which made him look like Jim Garner gotten out of bed in the middle of the night. Which was what had happened to him.

The tape squealed as Sloan ran it backward. He gave it a minute, then came off REWIND and punched PLAY.

"This dude's name is Morrigan?'' asked Casey.

Sloan nodded. "First name William. Washington's running a make on him.''

"—must call upon all citizens of the former United States of America to submit themselves to my authority in the interests of restoring national unity and national greatness,'' a voice was saying. It was a rich voice but not an entirely smooth one, like a well-made machine that hadn't been lubricated recently. "The Cleveland epidemic was a warning, and that warning should be clear. We have the virus. We are prepared to release it again.

"You have but one choice: submit or die. There is no third course.''

CHAPTER
FIVE

"Company, Billy," Casey said from the driver's seat of Mobile One, the Guardians' battlewagon, command post, and mobile home rolled into one ten-tonne package.

Sitting in a fold-down seat in the rear of the Cadillac V-450 armored car, McKay looked up and met Ivan Vesensky's eyes past the aft edge of the turret root. Vesensky cocked an eyebrow as slim and sculpted as he was.

Faggot, McKay thought as he got up. *Commie faggot.* He moved forward. He heard the little irritable whining of the servos in the one-man turret, complaining as they tracked Tom Rogers and the two heavy automatic weapons he was manning forward.

Metal decking shuddered beneath his feet. Mobile One's bulk tended to damp road vibration, but this stretch of Oklahoma highway had gone through two years of sun and rain with little by way of upkeep—and maybe a few years before that. It was making its presence known.

"Tracking anything?" he asked Sam Sloan, who was holding down the electronic systems operator's seat next to Case.

Sam shrugged. The armorplate skin stretched over Mobile One's foamed titanium-alloy flesh was impregnated with sophisticated sensors, little marvels of hot-superconductor technology, layered with enough redundancy that the various holes and scrapes in its hide hadn't impaired any of their functions yet. They had been monitoring radio traffic since they'd left Wichita Falls just south of the Texas-Oklahoma border. It had been couched in biblical voice code they couldn't make out, but since the transmission sources had been traveling right along with them—Mobile One's RDF gear could pick up a radio set that wasn't even transmitting, just on, if it was close enough—it wasn't hard to figure what was happening. The miniradar had even picked up a light plane apparently keeping sporadic watch on them.

But while the freaks had stayed busy, ever since they had swung east to avoid the mess that was left of Forts Sill and Lawton—to the accompaniment of the occasional low-level squeak from the rad-meters, as they passed through remnants of the roostertail of fallout laid down by the warhead that had groundburst on the stratotanker base at Altus — they'd been picking up fewer and fewer radio frequency emission sources in their immediate vicinity.

Sloan shook his head. "Nobody broadcasting within ten klicks of us. You think that means they've lost interest?"

McKay glanced up through the glass-plastic laminate armor vision block in front of Sloan, and by way of response grunted and jerked his head. Sloan looked up.

"*Whoo*," he whistled. Overhead Rogers charged the .50-cal and the forty mike-mike auto grenade launcher with a hefty double clack.

A flotilla of chopped cycles and outrageously modified cars, trucks, and vans was materializing out of the ground haze a kilometer ahead, where the highway passed between low mounded hills. Spread out across the whole six-lane right-of-way, it rolled forward like a black surf bearing brightly colored flotsam at its crest.

"Friends of yours, Vesensky?" McKay said. The former Soviet agent was already beside him, bent down to look out through the block. Half subconsciously McKay sidled away from him.

"Road gypsies," the Russian said. He shook his head. "Not friends of mine, McKay. It was my late associate Trajan who dealt with this lot." When he wasn't consciously affecting an American persona, he tended to have a Midlantic accent sprinkled with Britishisms.

"I've seen them before, of course," he added. "Your media always used to recount their excesses in loving detail. Between your press making a constant spectacle of your decadence and your military trumpeting our invincibility, we really had no need for our expensive and bloated propaganda *apparat*."

McKay had pulled his Maremont lightweight M60E3 from the clips that held it against the hull and was checking the receiver. "Hey, I really want to thank you for sharing that thought with us, Ivan." He let the bolt slam home on a belt of 7.62 linked coiled in a plastic half-moon ammo box, a gimmick borrowed from the Australian SAS.

"What do you need that for, McKay?" Sloan asked over his shoulder. "These're friends of ours."

"Friends of *yours*, maybe, navy boy," McKay snarled around the cold butt of his cigar. "No friends of mine, as long as the pilot lights are still on in Hell."

Sloan *tsked* sarcastically and shook his head. He wasn't a lot happier with this arrangement than his fearless leader.

The automotive mob broke around them like a wave, swirling past to either side with a snarling of engines and a flutter of bright-dyed Mohawks. The gypsies raised spiked and leathered arms, waving weapons ranging from Japanese *katanas* to plastic AUG assault rifles from Austria. The audio pickups studded in the hall picked up shrill coyote yips.

Under normal circumstances—well, under normal circumstances Tom Rogers would have started to rock 'n' roll the instant the first Harley came into view. To have the gypsies on all sides at Molotov range like this would have normally been an indication it was time for the Guardians to kiss their asses good-bye. As it was the ride had just become a white-knuckle flight for everybody but Vesensky, who looked coolly amused by his companions' discomfort.

Fuck him, McKay thought. Where the road gypsies were concerned it wasn't water that was over the dam; it was blood.

The gypsy wave eddied behind Mobile One, reversing flow and forming into a wake. A single vehicle awaited them in the middle of the northbound road. It was bizarre even by nomad standards: from the giant cleated tires and small operator's cage tucked to one side it appeared to have started life as a piece of heavy equipment. Whatever it was, it was now as spiky with metal protrusions as some kind of undersea crustacean, with platforms—some equipped with pintle-mount machineguns—sticking out here and there. At the top was a larger dais, mounted with a tubular-metal throne with a massive roll bar arched above it.

The people manning the platforms were far less colorful than the road gypsies. Every last one was dressed entirely in black, and instead of having outlandish dyed plumes of hair their heads were shaven—even at least one woman McKay could see. But that didn't mean they were less dangerous than the gypsies—far from it. Compared to the Brothers of Mercy, fanatical elite of the Church of the New Dispensation, the gypsies were no more than rowdy puppies.

A tall man with skin the color of paper and a spearhead nose rose from the throne and held up a hand. "In the name of the Chief Prophet Nathan Bedford Forrest Smith, I bid you welcome in the abode of the Lord." His voice sounded like dried fingerbones being rattled in a pan.

McKay and Sloan were staring at him with boiled-egg eyes.

McKay's hands gripped the machinegun so hard his knuckles popped, and glancing sideways Casey was astonished to see plain murder on Sloan's face.

"Billy—Sam—what's the matter, man?"

McKay weighed the machinegun in his hands, then all but threw it down on the deck. "Stop this thing," he snarled to Casey, who was already slowing down as they approached the flamboyantly customized carryall. Then he went aft of the turret root, popped the hatch in the overhead deck, and climbed out into the cold breeze.

"Brother Mace!" he called out, standing up and stepping around the low one-man turret. Overhead the wide blue sky was streaked with bold brushstrokes of cloud. The rolling land around was covered in thick dun grass, showing only scant hints of spring green. The nomad horde was halted behind him, engines growling like a million sullen beasts. "It's been a while."

"I am now Associate Prophet Mace, Captain General and Eldest Brother of the Brothers of Mercy," the tall man said. His eyes burned from impossibly deep sockets. "I see that you remeber me, Guardian McKay."

"Fuckin'-A straight," McKay said, lighting his cigar. "You do your own torturing still, or do you got assistants for that now?"

The pintle guns stayed with their barrels pointed skyward, but their crews stiffened, faces twisting with hate. "Let us strike him down, Eldest!" the bald woman cried.

Mace smiled. "Forbearance, Sister Martha. Guardian McKay, I pray with love in my heart that the Lord in His mercy shall someday permit you to learn the answer to that question. But now it is my duty to escort you in safety to the Living Prophet. Many are your crimes; the temptation to seek retribution, usurping our Lord's prerogative, might overcome some of the more susceptible among our flocks."

For once McKay couldn't think of anything to say. Or rather, he could think of a whole lot more to say than he could actually get said in less than a week. He threw the cigar down in disgust.

"Litterbug," Sister Martha said.

"You're acquainted with that picturesque individual, I take it?" Vesensky asked as McKay let himself back down into the stuffy warmth of Mobile One.

"No shit," McKay said. "He was in charge of interrogating Sam and me when your buddies grabbed us in the Denver Federal Center, right after the war."

Vesensky smiled thinly and glanced out the forward vision
block. "No buddies of mine. Thank God. I've had to work with
some pretty motley types, as I'm sure you're aware." They were;
Vesensky had sent everything from former California Lt. Gov.
Geoff van Damm's crazy-quilt revolutionaries to Washington kid
gangs to Casey's new girlfriend's *Cristeros* after the Guardians'
hides. But the FSE puppetmaster who'd pulled the New Dispensation's strings had been a homegrown American traitor, one William
Soames Summerill.

The carryall lumbered around a semicircle like a huge strange
beast seeking a place to lie down and headed north. Casey followed,
trailing the road gypsy horde like a tattered cloak.

Vesensky slid open the armor shutter over a vision block set
aft beside the engine. "Odd, very odd," he said, shaking his
head. "It baffles me, how your most violently fundamentalist
Christians can be allied with road gangs devoted to drugs, violent
sex, and loud music."

"Holocausts make strange bedfellows," Sam told him.

They took the long way, swinging through largely depopulated
suburbs west of the city. Condescending to use the radio, Eldest
Brother Mace explained that a more direct route would expose
them to the righteous wrath of the faithful he'd mentioned before.

Vesensky laughed. "I wonder what it is they don't want us to
see."

McKay glanced at him. He was a pretty shrewd Commie faggot
sonofabitch, there was no doubting that. Otherwise he wouldn't
have come so close to making the Guardians dead meat on so
many occasions.

On the other hand he hadn't succeeded yet—which made the
Guardians some pretty shrewd American straight sonsofbitches.
And McKay was shrewd enough to wonder just what Vesensky
meant when he said *us*.

The heart-meat of the Church of the New Dispensation was the
campus of Nathan Bedford Forrest Smith University, in the north-
western suburb called the Village. The aluminum-sided neighbor-
hoods were well tended but showed few signs of life as Mace led
them past the former Lake Hefner, now known as Lake Coffin in
honor of the First Prophet of the New Dispensation, then down
an avenue that ran alongside a spacious, immaculately groomed
park with a pond in the middle of it.

"Look at that," McKay marveled. "Swans." He pointed at

several birds sculling placidly around the pond.

"What did you expect, McKay?" Sloan asked. "Dragons? Though maybe it's a little early in the season—"

"I believe what surprised the lieutenant was the fact that so many potential meals should be swimming around unmolested in the middle of a well-settled area," Vesensky said. "Perhaps this— what did he call him?—Living Prophet provides them a better standard of living than one might have anticipated."

Sloan glanced back over his shoulder. "You really think so?"

"No. I think he has the inhabitants scared green of what would happen to them if they molested any of his swans."

The Guardians laughed. Even McKay unbent to the extent of a chuckle—as far as he'd warmed to their not altogether welcome ally since leaving San Antonio yesterday.

Still, he said, "You folks're the ones who still support Reverend Forrie."

"Ah, and are you consulted in making your country's policy?"

"Huh?"

"Do you get to make the policies you're called upon to carry out and uphold? We occupy similar positions with our respective countries, you gentlemen and I. But if you have a sizable say in your nation's policies, than we differ in that respect."

McKay exchanged uneasy looks with Case and Sloan. They *used* to have some say in what they were sent to do, in fact, back when they were combination White House staff and bodyguards to President MacGregor. Back when he was as much their comrade-in-arms as their commander in chief.

Nowadays . . . nowadays it seemed they were glorified errand boys. The president might just as well be on another planet. And his chief administrative aide, Blueprint participant Dr. Marguerite St. Claire Connolly, would have preferred if they *were* on another planet.

"Uh, I see what you mean," McKay said.

"Look at this," Sloan said, gesturing out the viewport to his right.

McKay turned in his fold-down seat and slid open an armorplate shutter. They were driving along a humongous wall, maybe twenty feet high, with a red glazed brick face that sloped inward away from them. It gave off an impression of immense thickness, some-how.

"Jesus. Looks like this place was *built* for the Holocaust."

"It was, McKay," Sloan said. "Forrie was always a big believ in end-of-the-world prophecies. When he started laying out the fortune he'd raked in as a boy-wonder televangelist to build this place, he had in mind surviving nuclear war—or flood, or plague, or famine, or swarms of locusts. All the walls on-campus are slanted like that to resist the dynamic overpressure of a thermonuclear blast. The tower back there''—he pointed to a round, squat, twenty-story building visible above the barbed-wire tangles that topped the wall—''could withstand an earthquake. And even if it couldn't, most of the important stuff is underground, bunkered like Cheyenne Mountain.''

''Yeah, and Cheyenne Mountain's a gigantic fucking hole in the ground, remember? That buzzard-headed cocksucker up there stuck us in it to cook in the rads, for God's sake.''

The gate was black ornamental iron; there looked to be solid panels that could slide out of recesses in the walls in emergency, and the green-glassed guardtowers to either side were flanked by sandbagged emplacements atop the wall from which the barrels of recoilless rifles protruded. Armed men in black watched them with hot eyes as they rolled on in.

The grounds were broad and already starting to green up. There were trees and bushes and fountains, and on the whole the place looked like anything but the stronghold of the most serious rival to the power of Washington, D.C., in the formerly United States. The slope-sided buildings just looked like outsized tank traps, or the kind of urban-blight public art President LaRousse was trying to purge from San Antone.

The carryall crawled ahead of them at a stately pace, to the base of the looming red-brick tower, down a wide concrete ramp. Steel and cement doors groaned open in front of it. It disappeared into blackness.

Casey halted at the lip of the ramp. ''Are we about to make a mistake?'' Sloan asked, voicing the hesitance his buddy obviously felt as Mace's voice clattered through the speakers, demanding to know what the delay was.

''Probab-fucking-ly,'' McKay said. ''Drive on.''

CHAPTER
SIX ——————————————————

Beneath an acoustic ceiling of bullet-colored cloud, the breeze off the lake rolled slowly, thickened by the stink of burned gasoline and smoked human meat. William Morrigan shook back his thinning brush of hair, rested hands cased in thick leather gauntlets on narrow hips, and breathed deep of oily air. He savored the music of the Street People's camp burning.

The last popping pistol shots of the mopping-up had died away. The shabby, scabby rubble-crawlers had never had a chance. The first they'd known things were wrong was when the Whispering Death gunship swooped in above the wreckage of a block of low-rent apartments and lower-rent offices north of the Loop, so low its rotor-wash scattered their early-morning cookfires in smoky embers. The snarling of its chin-gun had been the signal for Llewellyn and his hand-picked team to rise up from the positions they'd infiltrated to during the night.

The fight was over before it began.

"Well," he said. "We win again."

"You got that right, M.A.," a trooper said, grinning through the streaks of blackout paint slanted across his face. "We surely do."

A vee appeared between Morrigan's fine eyebrows as he squinted to catch the man's name. HOSPERS, the stencil read. He'd remember it. He was always alert to reward such signs of initiative, especially among the lower ranks. It was how you maintained *esprit*.

"Colonel!" a voice called.

He turned. A trooper emerged from a decapitated brownstone dragging a grimy, mat-haired child of four or five by one arm. Its only garment was an incredibly filthy white T-shirt with the ghost of a teddy-bear appliqué barely visible. Only the way the shirt rode up showed the child was female. A burn glowed red on one stick arm.

"I found this hidin' in there, Colonel," the trooper said. He held an Uzi with folding stock extended, butt on hip, barrel high.

Morrigan's nostrils pinched. "Very well, Delgado. Now kill it."

The man paled beneath his war paint. "What?"

"You heard me. Obey."

"Colonel—you don't mean—" He stopped, looked down at the child, which clung to his hand and regarded Morrigan with dry smoke-reddened eyes. He swallowed hard. "Colonel, please, I *can't*—"

A large figure loomed up behind him. Despite its size it made no sound crossing the several meters of cinder-coated pavement. Delgado sensed it, started to turn. A huge forearm furred with thick red-gold hair wrapped itself around his neck. A hand enfolded his chin.

His gun ejaculated futilely into the sky as the big man broke his neck with one quick heave.

The arm let go. Delgado slumped to the sidewalk as if all his bones had melted at once. The little girl clung a moment longer to the lifeless hand, staring down with enormous hazel eyes. Then she ran.

Morrigan glanced to his right. "Hospers," he said softly.

The trooper dropped his own Uzi instantly to midpoint and triggered a short burst. The little girl pirouetted raggedly three times with arms outflung and fell. Her blood soaked into a mound of brick and stone dust that the elements had already started to turn into soil, staining a small twisted shoot of weed.

The tall man stepped across Delgado without a downward flicker of eyes behind red blue-blocker lenses and came to stand beside Morrigan. The black paint looked unearthly above his full red-blond beard.

"Well done, Hospers," Morrigan said. "Or perhaps I should say, *Lieutenant* Hospers."

The soldier looked blank. "I'm just a private, sir."

Morrigan blinked three times rapidly, then decided to overlook the contradiction. One couldn't expect too much of a man. "You're a lieutenant now, do you understand?"

"Oh, yes. Uh, yes, *sir.*"

"Listen up, everybody," Morrigan said, lofting his voice and turning around as if to scatter his words by centrifugal force. "Let this be a lesson to you all. I worship toughness. Only by toughness do we show that we deserve to survive. If we're not tough we're no better than the animals we exterminated today."

"Sure enough, M.A.," called a paint-faced trooper.

"That Delgado always was a pussy, anyway," another said.

Morrigan turned to the burly man. "A good day's hunting, Llewellyn."

The captain of his bodyguard nodded. A golden tail of long hair bobbed at the back of his head. It was an eccentricity Morrigan tolerated. Every man was entitled to his mark, if he earned it.

Morrigan looked around with satisfaction. Flame vomited from glassless windows, and a second-story floor gave way with a cracking and groaning of structural members and an inverted shower of sparks. The tribes of outlaws north of the river got insolent if you didn't teach them a sharp lesson from time to time.

But that wasn't his only reason for ordering the raid, of course, nor for personally taking the gunship's stick in his gauntleted hands. It was the tension. The great plan was underway, and the waiting game had begun. Diversions such as this morning's were vitally necessary to keep the stress bearable.

"The responsibilities of command," Morrigan said with a sigh, looking down at the body of the trooper Delgado. Llewellyn grunted.

Morrigan slapped him on the arm. "Let's get a move on." He turned and walked toward where his helicopter awaited him in the midst of an intersection half a block away, its rotors still swooping in slowing circles like drugged seagulls.

They were on an elevator bound endlessly down. Standing next to McKay with the other two Guardians and Ivan Vesensky strategically placed between them and Mace, Sam Sloan kept thinking of the Elevator to Hell scene at the end of *Angel Heart,* where Mickey Rourke finally goes where he belongs.

Looking at the domed crag of Mace's skull gleaming like bone in the fluorescent light, he couldn't be sure they *weren't* going to hell. For anything that looked like that, it would have to be a homecoming.

"Yeah, we just might be," McKay's voice said in his ear. He started. It was one of the hazards of wearing the special mikes—if you didn't watch out, thinking aloud became exactly that, at least for anyone tied into your commo net.

The elevator stopped just when they were looking at each other and wondering if it ever would—even Vesensky, who was a pretty cool customer himself. The door opened.

A man stood awaiting them. He was TV photogenic: just past six feet, raquetball kind of build, strong, sharply defined features, longish hair that was very yellow on top. He was dressed all in

white—three-piece, tie, shoes, the works. A whole mob of people
hung discreetly behind him.

"I am Na·" Bedford Forrest Smith," he said in a voice that
left no doubt ne was telling the truth. It was a voice the Guardians
had heard on a more or less daily basis for the better part of two
years, assuring the world—and them—that they in person were
bound for deep shit in this life and the next. "I wish I could say
I am pleased to see you. Nonetheless, I bid you welcome in the
name of the Lord."

Sam snuck a sidewise look at Mace. The Eldest Brother was
gazing at Smith with adoration glittering in the obsidian disks of
his eyes. Smith's eyes never so much as flickered in his direction.

But it was time to be diplomatic; that was a big part of his job
description as a Guardian, after all. "We appreciate the welcome,
Mr. Smith," he said. He let out a little more farm Missouri than
usual, reckoning Forrie would go for the folksy down-home touch.

"You may address the Prophet as 'Prophet,' " said a chipmunk
with a dark blond three-piece suit and matching sideburns, who
stood a little ahead of the throng of hangers-on, behind the left
shoulder of the great man.

"Certainly, Prophet Smith. I didn't mean any offense."

McKay's eyes flicked him like a quirt. The ex-marine wasn't
happy with the truckling tone he was using on a man who was a
bitterer enemy than Maximov. On the other hand that bullet-shaped
head wasn't bone clear through, and they were about half a klick
down in the depths of Forrie Smith's personal fortress, so he didn't
say anything.

The elevator doors were twitching open and half-closed like a
spastic colon. "No need for you to stand there. Come." Smith
held out a hand so perfectly scrubbed and manicured it might have
been laminated in plastic. The onlookers parted like the Red Sea.

McKay and Sloan fell in alongside Smith at the head of the
procession traipsing along corridors lit with fluorescents bright
enough to make Sloan's teeth itch, and floored in canary-yellow
carpets that seemed to swallow their boots like a bog. Next came
Tom and Casey, one calm, the other laid-back bebopping along,
and then Vesensky, hands in the pockets of his blue jeans and his
thin lips bent in a sardonic smile, and Mace like Doorman of the
Dead, and then the whole assortment of flunkies of two or three
sexes.

"I'm Samuel Sloan, Prophet," Sam offered.

"I know," Smith said. "I apologize I wasn't able to greet you earlier, but the Lord's business leaves me little time."

Sloan rolled his eyes to McKay, who stuck out his lower jaw and pouted out his underlip in reply. Smith had developed his on-camera personality long enough that he almost sounded sincere.

"Especially with this current crisis," the Prophet went on, scooping handfuls of air. His hands were surprisingly large and capable-looking for someone in his line of work. Maybe making fists at the Devil and his servants—pornographers, dope dealers, Guardians, the makers of *I Love Lucy,* people like that—was a good workout. Isometric.

"I believe it is to be the judgment of the Lord," Smith said. "He punished us with the Fire, and we were not chastened. Now the Plague hangs above us like a scourge prepared for our backs."

He glanced at the two Guardians in their silvery-gray dress jumpsuits, slate-gray berets stuck jauntily through shoulder straps. "If you were to embrace the Lord, say no to sin, it would be more than a symbolic step in the right direction—"

"No way, Mr. Prophet," McKay rasped.

Disneyland on Parade gave a many-throated gasp of surprise behind them. Mace made a sound like trying to shift gears when the clutch isn't all the way in. But Smith only flipped an almost Gallic shrug.

"I expected no more. You are steeped in the Devil's sin. Still, you serve the Lord now, in your own way."

"Parden me, Your Excellency—"

"Not *Excellency*," the chipmunk interjected from the rear.

"No, no, Dodds, that's quite all right." He showed Sloan a smile fit to sell toothpaste. "Go ahead, Commander. Please overlook the rude interruption."

"Uh, well, I was wondering, if Morrigan's virus is a judgment from Heaven, why have you agreed to help us try and stop him?"

His three buddies cleared their throats all at once. It was inaudible to the world in general. To Sloan it sound like a Kansas thunderstorm.

"Why don't you wait to talk him out of it until we get our asses out of here, all right?" McKay subvocalized in disgust. *"Hearts and minds. Jesus."*

Sloan paled. But Smith just smiled in two dimensions and nodded.

"I understand your confusion. But I see this as a test, of our will, of our worthiness to survive as a nation. If we find within us the character to triumph, we shall rise again in the radiance of

God's love like a green shoot thrusting up through frozen soil into
the sunlight of spring. If we do not"—another shrug—"we join
Sodom, Gomorrah, and Atlantis in the ash-pit of history."

"*Atlantis?*" McKay subvocalized.

Smith stopped in front of a beige-painted metal door. The
flunkies halted like a drill team. "In this room," he said, waving
one of those incongruous glossy meathooks, "awaits someone
who has come a long way to meet with you."

"Yeah," McKay said. "Dr. Nguyen. The Effsee biochemist.
We was to collect him here."

He'd been royally pissed-off at being saddled with a scientist
from the FSE—as if Vesensky wasn't bad enough—but even Doc
Morgenstern admitted the good guys didn't have any specialists
heavy enough for this assignment. But the only place the Effsees
would agree to hand their virus doctor over was right here in Forrie
Smith's fantasyland. *That* was all but too much.

Smith smiled. This time it actually looked real. "Dr. Nguyen
is here, of course," he said. "But that's not whom I've brought
you here to meet."

He gestured. The door slid open as of its own free will.

Inside was a long table. A man sat in a swivel chair with his
broad back to them. At the sound of the door opening he turned
around.

"Gentlemen, what a pleasure it is to meet you at last," said
Yevgeny Maximov, rising to his feet.

CHAPTER
SEVEN

So somewhere in the middle of *The Empire Strikes Back,* Han Solo, and the hot-pants princess, and the big hairy dude, and my man Lando are all smoking and joking down the corridors of this city floating in the sky, and they turn a corner and who should they find knocking back a few with the Stormtroopers but Darth Vader his own bad self.

Billy McKay felt just like Han Solo. As a matter of fact, Billy McKay felt like Han Solo a lot, but now more than usual.

Unlike most times McKay felt like Han Solo, this was not a high point in his life.

McKay's hand went up to the butt of the .45, of which he had mysteriously not been relieved—and froze there, ahead of Tom Rogers's cautionary hiss in his mastoid process. Yevgeny Maximov wasn't all that much smaller than David Prowse, but not even he was going to stop two hundred thirty grain ball ammo with one hand the way Vader stopped Solo's laser bolts. On the other hand, where His Royal Badness the Dark Lord had to put up with a lot of dickhead Stormtroopers who wore the Styrofoam spacers from stereo boxes on their bodies and couldn't hit Oprah Winfrey in the ass at five paces, Maximov had Ivan Vesensky standing about eight feet from Billy McKay. Vesensky didn't miss much, and didn't miss often, and if McKay made the one proverbial false move the Russian was going to blow his spine in two, no question.

Sam Sloan stepped in front of McKay. McKay had an indignant moment to wonder just who the hell he was protecting from whom, and then Sloan said, "Your Excellency, this is quite an unexpected honor."

Maximov tilted his head back and laughed. It was a big laugh. It was a big head. It was a big all of him, for that matter.

"By your tact, I gather you are Commander Sloan." He had a voice that boomed like a bass drum. His English was blurred with accent but quite fluent.

Maximov came around the table holding out a ham-sized hand.

He wore a midnight blue suit with muted pinstriping. His graying black hair and beard were perfectly ordered, but his eyebrows were dense and unruly as Amazon undergrowth. He carried a lordly gut the way most men carried a wallet. He was one of the reasons Russia was associated with bears; it might be trite as hell, but that was what he looked like, to McKay at least.

McKay was all geared up to show his disdain for the commie bastard—or whatever he was; his politics has always been slippery, except for the clear and overriding belief that he really ought to own the world—by refusing to shake hands. But Maximov grabbed his hand and worked it heartily, as if McKay's arm was a pump handle. Tom Rogers would have his ass if he even thought about playing the knuckle-crushing game with a head of state, even an enemy state, but the strength of Maximov's grip was such that he was glad for an excuse not to try it.

"You may not believe this, my boy," he boomed, slapping McKay on the biceps, "but it's a true pleasure to meet you after all this time. You do not disappoint my expectations."

But McKay did believe him as he stood rubbing his arm and Maximov lumbered on to shake hands with the others. He knew damn well that Maximov was the sort you'd likely believe even if—maybe especially if—he was telling a lie. But he believed his protestations of pleasure anyway. Maximov was obviously a man who relished everything about his life, even his opponents. Especially the able ones.

Maybe he wasn't that different from Billy McKay.

Maximov gave Vesensky the full treatment, throwing his treetrunk arms around him, pressing his beard to one cheek and the other, emitting gruff cheerful Russian greetings. Smith he nodded expansively to, then turned and said, "Shall we sit? We have much to discuss."

Smith frowned slightly, nonplussed at being given orders in his own stronghold. But he didn't protest. Maximov was as easy to say no to as a volcanic eruption.

"I hope I didn't give you too much of a turn," he said, settling his bulk back in the swivel chair. "I am—how would you say?— incurably theatrical. You got the reference, I trust?"

Sam looked blank. Despite himself, McKay chuckled. *The Empire Strikes Back.*

Maximov beamed. "Of course. Such a curious culture you Americans have, so childish and yet so vital. The Soviets called it decadent, of course, but they had no sense of humor."

Vesensky said something in Russian. It wasn't part of the smat-
tering McKay had absorbed. Maximov laughed. "My very dear
friend Ivan Vissarionovich disapproves of the flip way I refer to
his former masters. Neither of us is Russian, by the way. He is
Georgian, I am Ukrainian. Subject peoples, you understand."

He steepled his broad, blunt fingers. "But to business. You are
doubtless wondering why I flew all the way here to meet with
you, at great risk to myself, not to mention inconvenience."

"You might say that," Sam said dryly.

"Since you put it that way, uh, Mr. Chairman," McKay said,
"I thought you had a war on, back in Europe."

The huge head nodded. "I do. But I am a financier, an adminis-
trator; my field of expertise is not military endeavors. Overall
strategic direction of the war against those fanatical Pan-Turanians
is mine, of course, but at this stage the best service I can render
my generals is to leave them alone."

He smiled. His lips were full, slightly purple. "Besides, we
are winning.

"As to why I am here before you, it is simply because I wish
to impress you with the gravity of the situation, as well as the
depth of my commitment to setting aside our differences for the
duration of this emergency and working together."

"Yeah, right," McKay said under his breath.

Sam looked at him as if he'd just cut one. He hadn't meant to
say it at all. The words just forced themselves out.

"Your skepticism is understandable, Lieutenant." Maximov
leaned forward, endangering the buttons on his vest. "But you
and I, we both live on the same planet. And the madman Morrigan
claims he has the capability to destroy all human life upon this
planet. I will not pretend that this crisis has changed my goals,
nor do I delude myself yours will alter; barring unforseen circumstances we are enemies, and so we shall remain, though I
regret that men such as we should find ourselves at odds. But may
not the lion lie down with the lamb, should both be caught in the
same mortar barrage?"

"Maybe," McKay admitted grudgingly. "But I still feel funny
about all this. I mean, with respect and all like that, does President
MacGregor know anything about you're being here? We ain't
authorized to negotiate with a foreign power."

Forrie Smith leaned forward over the table. "I believe we can
set your mind at rest over that, Guardian McKay." He seemed
pleased at being able to shove an oar into the conversation.

Maximov half-turned in his chair. Suddenly the wall behind him lit up with the faces of President Jeffrey MacGregor and Dr. Jacob Morgenstern, many times larger than life.

"Lieutenant McKay," MacGregor's face said. McKay jumped and almost said *holy shit,* which probably wouldn't have been the thing to do. "Commander Sloan, Lieutenant Rogers, Lieutenant Wilson. It's good to see you."

Morgenstern just nodded sharply, his manner showing clearly that he had no time for nonsense. It was sinking finally through McKay's crewcut that there were two meter-and-a-half color LCD screens set in the wall two meters apart, showing images from both coasts.

"Good to see you, Mr. President—Doctor," McKay said. "Kind of surprising."

"Satellite feeds," Sam said.

"A little miracle of technology," Smith said smugly. "Not to be compared to the divine kind, of course. But in God's service, just the same."

"We were as startled by the chairman's visit as you are," Morgenstern said. "It does make sense, given the circumstances."

"Shall we review what we know, gentlemen?" Maximov asked. Obviously, he'd spoken to the other two men immediately before the Guardians' arrival.

"Perhaps we should," MacGregor said. He grinned, showing a touch of the boyishness that made him such a good running mate for the craggy Lowell. It mainly had the effect of reminding McKay just how much the president had aged in the last two years. "Our guests are looking pretty befuddled."

A thought struck him. *"Sam—Case. What chance is there this could be a computer-generated scam?"*

"It'd have to be pretty sophisticated, man," Casey subvocalized back.

"Possible," Sloan replied the same way. *"But Casey's right. That kind of gimmickry would be pretty heavy duty even by prewar standards."* He gave his head the tiniest of shakes.

McKay had a suspicious nature, and not a lot of subtlety. "Mr. President, Doctor, no disrespect or anything—but how do we know it's *you?*"

"Why, Lieutenant, who else might we be?" the president asked.

"Real-time computer-generated overlays masked onto live actors, Mr. President," Sloan said. "Difficult but not impossible, given the level of technology that makes this meeting possible even if things are as they seem.''

MacGregor frowned, puzzled and slightly irritated. Morgenstern looked amused in a dour way.

The doctor glanced out of the field of view, appeared to listen briefly, then nodded. A window appeared in the lower left quadrant of his screen. A round, female Amerind-Hispanic face looked out at them, chubby cheeks and bright black eyes framed by black pigtails and a lightweight headset.

''Jesus *Christ*,'' McKay exploded. ''Bonnie Sanchez! What are you doing alive?''

The other Guardians were staring; even Tom Rogers widened his eyes. ''I wasn't at Vista when Chairman Max's goons hit the place. I wish I could tell him what I think of him for what he did to my friends, but I promised I'd be good.''

''Good to see you, Bon,'' Casey said. The others echoed him. The stocky tech, a strapping, scrappy, compulsive tinkerer, had been one of the Guardians' big favorites among the computer whiz kids of Vista Systems in California, and one mourned most keenly after the Liberators massacred them for helping the Guardians penetrate FSE security.

''Thanks, Case, Tommy, Sam. Big kiss to you, Billy. I won't take more time, but you got to agree it's not very likely the Effsees'd know enough about me to fake me up.'' She blinked out.

The Guardians looked at each other. *''I'm not sure that follows,* Sam subvocalized, *''but if they* do *know that much—''*

''—we're screwed,'' McKay finished. *''Seems to me we're down here in the belly of the Death Star by Jeff's orders anyway, we got no choice but to take a lot on faith.''*

Smith was leaning over the table, looking like a kicked puppy. ''Mr. Chairman,'' he said, ''why didn't you explain to that young woman about the political—and moral, yes—necessities behind the purging of that California viper's den?''

''Because I had no wish to insult her obvious intelligence.''

MacGregor was sitting looking thoughtful. ''Perhaps it would help if I told Lieutenant Rogers that, ah, Mama Lion sends her regards.''

McKay looked at Rogers, but of course the former Green Beanie's face told him nothing. *Mama Lion* was a private nickname that Uhuru Assad, formerly a Black Liberation Army terrorist, now government liaison with the DC rubble gangs and Tom's girlfriend, applied to herself.

''That's enough,'' he said. ''Looks like everything's on the level.'' *And if it ain't—*. Mentally he shrugged.

MacGregor allowed himself to look relieved. Morgenstern was showing little emotion, just sitting there impassive like an undernourished Buddha. He was a man without a millisecond's patience for bullshit; evidently he approved of McKay's caution.

"Very well," Morgernstern said. "To begin, we shall review what we know of the man we're dealing with.''

The previously blank expanse of wall between Morgenstern and MacGregor lit up with the image of a man, full frontal and profile. He appeared to have been at the low end of middle age when the pictures were taken—they were dated five years ago. He had a head that sprouted from a skinny neck and widened as it went up, little triangle chin, straight nose, thinning hair. He was pretty nondescript, not at all the way McKay would picture an evil mastermind who was prepared to scrag all the poor sonsofbitches who were just congratulating themselves on having survived not just the One-Day War but seven hundred-odd Days After. Except the eyes. They were wide and brown, at once vulnerable and commanding.

A wimp, McKay thought. But a deadly wimp.

"Morrigan, William Arundel,'' Morgenstern recited. "Forty-five years old, height 188 centimeters, last known weight seventy-two kilograms. Small star-shaped scar in the middle of his left eyebrow—the details have been transmitted to the Citadel, and Prophet Smith has agreed to furnish you with hardcopies. Subject was born in Mascoutah, Illinois. Appointed to West Point, distinguished himself academically, was forced to resign in his third year; further references are unavailable.

"Served in Vietnam 1970 to 1973. U.S. Army Long Range Reconnaissance Platoon, and there's a reference to service with the Phoenix and SOG under OPLAN thirty-four.''

McKay blinked. The Phoenix was a special project designed to break up the Vietcong infrastructure—a polite, or at least governmental, way of saying a hit team. Acing commanders, cadre, and tax collectors wasn't the nice, clean, law-abiding war of napalm and heavy artillery and innocent bystanders dying in droves, so the liberals made them cut it out. "SOG" was Studies and Observations Group, a meaningless title somebody thought up to cover the real activity of the unit, which was to prosecute a dirty covert war against North Vietnam; the big picture was called Operational Plan 34.

Studies and Observations Group had been resurrected in the late eighties to operate against various of America's enemies in Southwest Asia Command, the Med, both communist and fundamentalist Muslim. Billy McKay had been part of it for a while.

So Morrigan wasn't a wimp. At least not physically. Mentally . . . there'd been wimps of *that* kind in SOG-SWAC, for sure. Dudes with too damn much to prove. Most of the atrocity stories the press got to toss around had their origins with that sort of operative.

"Received his MBA from Princeton in 1978," Morgenstern was saying. "Minored in chemistry, and got a degree in chemical engineering in 1985. By that time he'd been employed for several years by Tyrone Pharmaceuticals, a firm with ties to a number of Third World nations—and a wholly owned, not to mention wholly extra-budgetary, subsidiary of the Central Intelligence Agency. It's all in the hardcopies, if you care."

He punched the keyboard of a desktop computer, the edge of which showed onscreen. "Undertook assignments for the CIA in Latin America and Africa during the eighties and early nineties. Details unavailable. Belonged—"

Morgenstern hesitated for a moment, looked up, eyes heavy-lidded and unreadable.

"Belonged to the so-called 'Roman' faction of the Central Intelligence Agency, a group which apparently drew its name both from its aspiration to propel America to an overtly imperial role worldwide and from the futurist Club of Rome, with which some of its members were associated. Morrigan supposedly was known to the Romans by the code-name Marcus Aurelius.

Now he looked directly at Maximov. So did the Guardians. "Several of the Romans, most notably the late W. Soames Summerill, code-name Trajan, are known to have been suborned by your organization, Chairman Maximov."

" 'Suborned' is rather a strong word to use," Maximov murmured. "Mr. Summerill shared many of the high ideals of the Internationalist Council, of which I was chairman until it was superseded by the ruling council of the Federated States of Europe. He saw himself serving the greater interests of both his country and humanity."

"He had a damned strange way of serving the interests of his country," MacGregor said, with more vehemence than he usually showed. "Considering that he spent several months ruling the country as viceroy for a foreign power—you, Mr. Chairman.''

"Soames Summerill was a great American," Smith said.
"He—"

"The man in question is dead, and likewise beyond praise and
reproach," Maximov said, his deep voice rolling across Smith's
like a human wave assault. "We need trouble ourselves with him
no more. Now, in answer to the question you're hoping so desperately not to have to ask, Mr. Morrigan was at one time on our
payroll."

"Not too long ago, either, Mr. Chairman," Tom Rogers said.
Everybody blinked at him. He spoke only a little more often than
the heads of Mount Rushmore. "We fought him when we were
fighting your expeditionary force in Chicago, back before we took
Heartland. He was in command of your indigenous elements. We
called him the Butcher." He spoke without heat, matter-of-factly,
as if he were discussing which brand of deodorant the man used.

"Had we had a man of your ability in charge of our indigenous
elements in Chicago, we'd still be there, Lieutenant," Maximov
said.

"Well, then, what the fuck, over?" McKay burst out. Smith
gasped. "It's *your boy* who's got this bug-bomb, Mr. Chairman?
What kind of little game are you playing here?"

"Lieutenant," MacGregor said, appalled.

"Guardian McKay," Maximov said, "I know subtlety is not
your forte. However, you are no fool, and that question is unworthy
of you. If I exercised any manner of control whatever over this
man Morrigan, do you think I should be here?"

"Marcus Aurelius appears to have embarked on a purely private-
enterprise endeavor," Vesensky said.

"Our current conjecture," Morgenstern said, "is that Morrigan
somehow discovered a Blueprint facility in Chicago, under the
direction of Dr. Wendell Carter."

The views of Morrigan were replaced by two of a handsome,
worried-looking black man with gray in his Brillo-pad hair. "Dr.
Carter had no known connection with biowarfare research. On the
other hand, his subordinate, Dr. Magnus Cromartie—"

Carter was replaced by a white man with a snub nose and watery
eyes that seemed to lurk behind thick glasses, whose round head
seemed to spring from his slumped shoulders without benefit of
a neck. It wasn't that he was muscular at all; he just didn't seem
to have a neck.

"—was employed at the Rocky Mountain Arsenal and the Provo, Utah, facility before joining Dr. Carter's team. He is known to have been employed in research into and development of biological weapons."

"So you think Morrigan and this geek Cromartie've teamed up?" McKay asked.

"You have a fine grasp of the obvious, McKay."

"What are we supposed to do, Doctor?" Sloan asked.

"We've spent a good deal of time discussing the priorities, gentlemen," MacGregor said. "At this time it appears our most pressing need is to determine just what it is we're being threatened with."

"So you want us to go to Cleveland before we go grease Morrigan," McKay stated.

MacGregor swallowed. "That is, ah, correct, Lieutenant." He was clearly uncomfortable ordering a death, even by implication.

"This is a bit out of our line, Mr. President," Sam Sloan said. "None of us is a biochemist."

"Perhaps this might be an opportune juncture to introduce Dr. Nguyen," Morgenstern said.

Maximov nodded. No other gesture was made, and nothing was said, at least audibly, but a side door of the briefing chamber slid open. Maybe the Guardians weren't the only ones to use larynx mikes capable of picking up subvocalized speech.

A woman walked in. She was tiny, probably less than five feet tall. Midnight hair hung to a fine jawline to either side of her triangular face, and was roached up in the front, emphasizing a high forehead and pronounced cheekbones. She had very large, very dark eyes, with epicanthic folds; she was evidently Oriental. She wore a sweater of gray and blue sort of brindled together, and black parachute pants bloused into low black boots.

McKay nodded to himself, approving. She was a pretty little piece, though it surprised him Reverend Forrie—never a fervent integrationist—would employ a dink secretary. Not to mention one who'd go braless while wearing a sweater tight enough to clearly show the outlines of large nipples crowning rounded-cone breasts—

"Gentlemen," Yevgeny Maximov said, "permit me to introduce Dr. Suzette Nguyen. She will be accompanying you to Cleveland and, if necessary, to Chicago."

CHAPTER
EIGHT

"Something up ahead, McKay," Sam Sloan said, craning forward to peer through the ESO's vision block. Spring was the season of storms in the post-Holocaust world. The Midwestern rain was getting the better of the wipers again.

Billy McKay sighed. "Are we gonna have an adventure, here?" he asked. "How the hell many adventures have started off with those four little words? *Somethin' up ahead, McKay.* Jeez."

Casey laughed. Nguyen looked at him as if he was crazy. *Well, that's an improvement. Usually she looks at me like my willy's hanging out.*

"When I was a kid I always thought it would be totally balls to grow up and have lots of adventures," he said, hauling himself out of his fold-down and wincing at the crackling noises his body made, stiff from hours of inactivity. "Now I'm as grown up as I'm likely to get, and I have adventures for a living, and you know what? It's a royal pain in the ass."

"You're a romantic, my friend," Vesensky said.

"Well, just don't you start getting romantic ideas about *me,*" McKay said.

The Russian laughed. "Have no fear. You aren't my type."

Nguyen shifted in her own fold-down and crossed legs McKay couldn't have turned better on a lathe in woodshop. "Must you be so disgusting, Lieutenant McKay?" she asked. Her English had enough of an accent—French—to be sexy as hell.

"Yes." He moved forward through the red glow of the interior lights.

"Cleveland's somewhere up there, not too far ahead," Sam Sloan remarked. "Or at least the suburbs. I'm not sure where the city proper begins."

"Looks like the Interstate Eighty overpass," Casey said. "There're, like, people up there."

"Slow down."

"Tank, Billy," Rogers said from the turret.

56

"Slow *way* down."

He didn't like driving right straight up to a tank. On the other hand, they were passing through a built-up but seemingly abandoned area, another of the clots of urbanization interspersed with countryside none of them had seen too clearly. They could always ditch suddenly to one side or another if things looked ugly.

Right now it could be important to find out just who might want to park a tank next to the main road in.

"See if you can get the reception committee on the horn," he said, sticking an unlit cigar stub into one side of a not particularly happy expression.

The vehicle crawled forward. The rain hammered on the top deck. The radio said nothing to Sam's muttered inquiries.

Though it wasn't later than midafternoon it was black outside except for occasional random strobings of lightning. Gradually McKay caught site of a tangle of barbed wire strung from embankment to embankment of the overpass, with men in what looked like standard American military uniform clumped soddenly behind it. It wasn't much of a roadblock by postwar standards—until you took the squat, angular bulk of the M1 Abrams parked behind it into consideration. The long finger of the 105-mm cannon was pointed unthreateningly off to one side of the divided highway. Given how fast the blocky turret could traverse it was small reassurance.

Casey started decelerating again, to give the defenders the idea they didn't mean to try running the roadblock, which was no lie. "Shit," McKay said. "I have to go out in this, don't I?"

"Rank hath its privileges," Sam said.

"I oughta make you do it, navy boy. You're the expert at the rubber ducky stuff."

"Typical marine. Griping about getting your feet wet."

"That was low," McKay said in disgust, and reached for his boonie hat and a poncho. "All right, Case, might as well stop it here."

He opened the side hatch. It was as if somebody'd left a bucket of water balanced atop the door. He was instantly soaked, hat and poncho notwithstanding.

"Hey, shut the door!" Sloan exclaimed. "You trying to drown us?"

McKay snarled something the storm swallowed up, slammed the door, and trudged forward.

"Halt and identify yourself!" a voice called from behind the wire.

"I'm Billy McKay. We're the Guardians. We tried to call you."

"Radio's out. Come on inside the wire. Your buddies can wait inside where it's dry. Lucky bastards."

There was a man-sized path between the wire and the sloped cement face to his right. McKay took it and was greeted by an officer whose uniform was plastered to a tall, skinny form, and whose face was lost in the shadow of his Fritz helmet.

"I'm Captain Furnier, Ohio National Guard." A penlight stabbed out of the murk, briefly illuminating McKay's name stenciled on the breast of his cammies. "I don't mean to piss you off, but how do I know you're actually one of the Guardians?"

"I know all the secret handshakes." McKay reached under the poncho. A couple of troopies poked M16s at him, one with a bayonet on the end of it, for Christ's sake. He gave the man a sour grin and produced his all-purpose packet of bona fides from President Jeff, fortunately encased in plastic in case the elements started to get like this.

When he saw the presidential seal on the packet, Furnier summoned a troopie to hold a poncho over the proceedings while the handyman with the penlight gave light to his CO. McKay stood and looked at the other soldiers. They stared back.

They were a sorry, soggy lot, slouching with weapons mostly slung. They didn't act real pleased with the state of the world. Interstate 80 overhead didn't seem to be helping that much to keep them dry, since periodical gusts of wind blew the rain almost horizontal. But to McKay, who'd spent a lot of his own life as a wet disgruntled grunt, it seemed they had something more on their minds.

Furnier came back shaking rain off his coalscuttle helmet. "Look okay. Of course, I guess you could've whipped them up at any print shop in North America, provided the Xerox machines weren't melted and you could get power in."

"Hey, you caught me, you're too smart for me. Electricity was no hassle. You'd be amazed how much voltage you can get from a dink on a ten-speed."

Furnier grinned joylessly. "Well, I've always admired you dudes and all, so I really hate to tell you the answer's no."

"Say what?"

"You're headed for Cleveland, right?" McKay nodded. "Well, Cleveland's quarantined. Nobody gets in."

" 'Nobody' don't include us, bunky. We're on a mission from the president."

"I don't care if you're on a mission from God. You're not going into Cleveland."

McKay took off his hat and wrung it out, in lieu of wringing Furnier's scrawny neck. He stuck the hat back on his head, which wasn't any wetter for having been bared for a moment or two.

"I don't think you understand—"

"I don't think *you* understand, Guardian. There's some kind of disease loose in there that's killed maybe twenty, twenty-five thousand people in a couple of days. It's like the fucking war all over again; it's like a suburb of Hell. I've been in there. I've *seen.*"

McKay sighed. The man was genuinely afraid, shit-scared. "We got orders to investigate what's going on in there. That's the only way we're going to be able to find out how to deal with it."

"What's going on in there is *death*, mister. We have qualified personnel investigating. Until we get a line on the situation, we're not letting outsiders go tramping around, picking up Christ knows what kind of contagion."

"Washington—"

"Screw Washington. We take our orders from Governor Pautz. He says nobody goes in until our experts say it's okay. That means *nobody*. You included."

McKay looked over the knot of troopers and the glistening bulk of the Abrams. The men still slouched, but their attitude now was sullen defiance, not the apathy of chill and nervous exhaustion.

"You ever hear about your buddies in the Iowa National Guard?" he asked.

"Rotten traitor renegades. No buddies of mine. I hear you kicked their asses good over in Luxor, and more power to you. But listen up, Mr. High-and-Mighty Guardian: we're patriotic Americans. We fought looters and Effsees and road gypsies and New Dispensation crazies. We've fought floods and fires and eighteen different kinds of disease already. And if you try to go in there, and risk spreading this epidemic and killing twenty thousand more innocent people, we'll fight you, too, no matter whose name you got on a piece of paper."

"They used to say a second lieutenant with a map and a compass was the most dangerous thing in the known world," McKay said, shifting his ass around on the fold-down. The seat was thinly padded, and it felt as if his soaked-through jumpsuit was starting to give him diaper rash. Just what he needed. "But the biggest pain in the ass is a goodamn weekend warrior with *orders*."

Captain Furnier had his orders, all right. And he wouldn't budge from them, no matter how much McKay bellowed and blustered. Since the M1 trumped any card McKay held in his hand, unless the blocking detachment were willing to be sports and let him clamber back into Mobile One for an Armbrust antitank rocket, the Guardians were in no position to force the issue.

After a lot of racket Furnier had agreed to pass the word along up the chain of command to Governor Pautz. He doubted it would make any difference.

"You Americans are undisciplined," Nguyen said in her overly precise foreign way. "I cannot see why you resisted the efforts of the Federated States to restore order to your country, selflessly and without concern for the sacrifice. With our help you might have overcome this anarchy you now suffer."

McKay made a noise like a rusty hinge. Sam swiveled his ESO chair. "Pardon me, Doctor, but it looks to me as if the problem here's too much discipline. The captain's following his orders."

"So did the Nazis." Nguyen sniffed. "Don't think you can confuse me with such sophistry, Commander. The *problem* is clearly that your people have insufficient respect for properly constituted central authority. They follow the dictates of their local warlords instead of their president. Of course, perhaps they have right at that, since your so-called president is a usurper—"

"Yeah," McKay said roughly. "I seem to remember the North Vietnamese teaching their former Vietcong buddies a few things about proper central authority, starting about '75."

Nguyen's full lips compressed to an angry line. Her father had been a VC district commander. He'd been executed, and his family forced to flee, when the NVA began to purge the Vietcong immediately after the fall of Saigon. Suzette was five at the time.

She and her family had been fortunate. An expatriate uncle living in Paris had wangled entrance visas to France for them. There was no drifting in a boat until the South China Sea sun, thirst, or pirates did them in, no festering in a squalid refugee camp. It had been a nightmare, just the same.

McKay's crack had the effect of squelching the conversation, which was fine by him, no matter how reproachfully Sloan eyed him. Nguyen had been yapping like a terrier with a cat up a tree since they'd bid farewell to the lovely and talented Yevgeny

Maximov and left Okie City. He'd never thought with a girl that cute he'd fantasize a lot more forcefully about strangling her than porking her. Just went to show how much progress the world had made toward Hell.

He glanced across the compartment. Vesensky sat next to the FSE scientist, as oblivious to her presence as if she were on another planet. *He would be. Homo.* The KGB defector had a loop of fishing line and was making cat's cradles with it. The almost invisibly-fine line fluoresced slightly in the instrument glow, creating an eerie laser-light show effect apparently in midair.

Vesensky glanced up, saw McKay watching him, produced a microscopic smile. McKay's mouth tightened. *What if he winks at me?*

He closed his eyes and let the back of his head fall against the cargo compartments molded into the V-450's hull. The voices of wind and rain lulled him away.

It was well past sunset—not that it made that much difference in this storm—when the radio burped and started talking in Captain Furnier's voice, apologizing for the delay and explaining that their commo gear was still twitchy and that they'd lost a lot of phone lines in the storm.

"Yeah, yeah," McKay grumbled. "So what did His Nibs say?"

"No."

McKay felt his face turn red. The blood was rushing into it so fast and hard it felt as if it was just going to swell up like a balloon and bust.

"Let me," Sam said, hurriedly cutting his boss out of the comm circuit.

McKay glared at him for a few sledgehammer heartbeats before he let himself realize Sloan had a point. He was in no mood to win hearts and minds. And that damned Abrams made tough talk look pretty sick.

But Furnier's fly wasn't any easier to catch with Sloan's honey than McKay's vinegar. "Criminy, what *is* this guy, a loan officer?" Sloan asked the air at one point, prudently dumping his own mike.

Nguyen got up and moved forward, purposeful and tiny as a toy train. "Let me talk to him."

Sloan flipped his eyes to McKay. McKay shrugged. "Maybe if she offers to go around the world for him—"

Sloan turned dead-white. Nguyen glared at McKay, obviously not catching his drift but not liking it anyway. Sloan handed her a microphone.

"Hello, Captain? I am Dr. Suzette Nguyen. I insist on speaking to your medical authorities at once. . . ."

Nguyen's black-almond eyes went wide. "No? *No?*" She threw the headset down.

"They refuse me! I tell them I must examine bodies of victims of the plague. It is necessary. It is rudimentary courtesy to a fellow scientist. And they tell me no!" She shook her head violently. "They do not even disclose symptoms. Can you imagine?"

"Yeah," McKay affirmed around an unlit cigar stub. "They're pissants, on G.P.'s"

Sloan shook his head. "Not that simple, McKay. What could the harm be in cooperating to that extent?"

"Like, what could they have to hide?" Casey asked.

"Perhaps they're afraid of something," Vesensky said.

McKay squared his shoulders. "All the more goddamn reason to go in there and see what's really goin' down. Bring up that map of the area on the nav display, navy boy. Anybody know anything about a back way into Cleveland?"

"You should have sent me, McKay," Vesensky's voice said over the intercom as the rain cut loose with a fresh snare-drum solo on the top of the turret. "Without prejudice to Commander Sloan, I'm not without experience in this sort of business."

McKay grunted. "Yeah. Like I'm really gonna let a Russian spy out of my sight."

"Anything I say will sound like 'trust me.' " Vesensky laughed mirthlessly. "But you have no choice but to do exactly that. We're stuck with each other. Besides, you have to sleep sometimes, as the saying goes—and you have, since we left San Antonio."

McKay peered at the gouache of rain smeared across one of the one-man turret's vision blocks. Outside was a lot of black nothing. "Yeah. But I've had somebody to keep an eye on you at all times, too."

Vesensky only laughed again. McKay was mainly pissed off at him because he was most likely right.

They'd all four gone through the incredibly intense Guardians training together. They were fully qualified in a range of skills from small boat handling to interrogation to small unit tactics to infiltration and scouting. At least, that's what it said right here.

The brutal fact was that experience was where it was at. And McKay and Rogers—yeah, and Vesensky—were the ones with the most experience in snooping and pooping through hostile terrain. Sure, Case and Sam had gotten some under their belts since the One-Day War—more than most special forces types, to be honest. But it wasn't their field of expertise.

Which was part of the reason McKay had sent Sam Sloan to scope out a possible path into Cleveland through the suburbs on the northeastern heights of the plateau on which the city rested. Tom had spoken to him about it back in San Antonio, even before the latest crisis came down. The representatives of navy and air force needed more work on the ground, to hone their skills and maintain their confidence. McKay and Rogers weren't always going to be available when scouting had to be done.

This seemed like a good confidence-builder for Sloan. McKay had never had a high regard for the weekend warriors of the National Guard—though he did respect them, and the dangers of an unknown and partially rubbled urban area, enough not to lead with the chin and just go rolling on in with Mobile One. He figured Sloan could handle this.

But up here alone with the sound of rain and the smell of lubricants and sweat he was beginning to have second thoughts. He didn't need any help from a commie fruitbar assassin for that.

"*All right, McKay,*" Sloan's voice said out of nowhere. "*I've scouted ahead a klick or so. I'm in a shopping mall. You've got a clear shot in—no serious obstruction, no signs of activity.*"

"Roger that. You got that, Tommy? Roll 'em out—Sloan'll talk you in." He popped the feed tray cover on the Mk19 as the heavy V-450 lurched into motion like a dinosaur roused from sleep, making sure the linked belt of 40-mm grenades wasn't tangled. They gleamed dully in the faint pilot light glow, little blunt, smooth R2-D2s.

Hot white glare lanced through the viewslits as Mobile One rocked to sudden impact and a noise like a board the length of the Brooklyn Bridge being broken in two.

CHAPTER
NINE

The whole universe seemed to shake. It took McKay a heartbeat and a half, or roughly forever, to realize Mobile One was trucking on in a hell of a hurry.

Someone was screaming. "LAW, Billy," Tom Rogers said from the driver's seat. If the words hadn't been vibrated directly into his skull via his bone-conduction phone, McKay would never have made them out.

"Yeah." He jammed his thumbs down on the firing switches for both the Mk19 and the M2 .50-caliber mounted alongside. The double muzzle flashes were almost as bright as the Light Antitank Weapon's blast had been, and they shook the car damned near as much. But it was a reassuring sort of hell they raised.

He was firing blind, just busting caps—the two best defenses against AT rockets, aside from not being seen in the first place, were to keep moving and make the missile boys pull their heads down, and even if the rocketeers weren't in the direct paths of the guns, they were liable to be impressed by the sound-and-light show.

"Goddamn you, Sam," he grunted. He flicked on an infrared sensor with pickups on the front of the turret. When the small screen inset in the hull above the guns came alive he cursed again, soundlessly, as he saw bloblike heat signatures flitting through what he knew were bare trees to either side of the broad street ahead. He distrusted the fancy high-tech stuff, and so he tended to forget about it, even when it would come in handy—like tonight, when even passive IR saw farther than his eyes in the dark and the cold rain.

"McKay? What's going on?" Sloan's voice asked.

The IR image faded as the onboard computer automatically turned down the gain to keep the sudden novas of muzzle flashes from burning out the screen. Bullets clattered off Mobile One's titanium-alloy skin like ultrahard hail. Acceleration was pressing McKay back into the padding of the gunner's chair as he sent a burst of .50-caliber at a clump of heat signatures.

"Ambush, Sam," Rogers replied.

"That thing break through the hull?" McKay demanded. Through the forward viewslit he caught a glimpse of a face lit bright white by the M2's flame, and then the thumb-thick bullets bowled the face's owner away.

"Negative, Billy," Casey replied from the ESO seat.

Yellow-white light plucked at McKay's peripheral vision. Out a side vision block he saw another LAW drawing a line of fire across the night. Servos whined as he tracked the turret to bear on a cloud of white backblast smoke, which wind and rain weren't dissipating quickly enough for the continued well-being of a soldier in National Guard uniform desperately discarding his empty launchtube. The man vanished in a blossoming of white phosphorus smoke and HEDP flashes.

"Then who the fuck's sniveling?" He could hear broken sobbing welling up from the belly of the giant car.

"Uh, Dr. Nguyen's having, like, a tough time," Casey said.

Fucking great, McKay thought. *We're stuck with a bimbo who comes unglued—*

"Turning, Billy," Rogers said.

McKay grabbed stanchions and clung on as the former Green Beret cranked them around a corner of two wheels. As they blew through the dense white smoke-starfish from the 40-mm burst McKay had just fired, McKay heard the rattle of automatic fire from within Mobile One's hull, and he caught the dance of a muzzle flash. Vesensky had clearly opened fire from a firing port.

Good for him, McKay thought.

He tracked the turret forward in time to catch sight of a whole line of blobs bobbing in the IR screen. *Fuck this,* he thought, *they sure as hell know where we are.*

He punched up the million-candlepower spot mounted coaxially with the turret guns. A file of National Guard troopies was trotting along the sidewalk with their M16s at high port. The .50-caliber shattered them like bottles in a Hollywood bar fight.

Sam Sloan lay on his belly in the ruins of a burned-out boutique and felt like hell.

The weather of more than six hundred days had leached out most of the stink of ashes, leaving a wet mustiness that surrounded Sloan like a fog. An apparently intact roof kept some of the rain away, but he wasn't willing enough to trust its structural integrity to get back too far beneath it. He was wet, cold, scared—and convinced that he'd fucked up.

McKay was right, he thought with bitter certainty. *I'm not cut out for this kind of work. How on earth could I have missed a force that size?* Even through the storm he'd heard the door-slam thuds of explosions, the crackle of small-arms fire, and the pounding of Mobile One's guns like some giant distant carpenter at work.

He peered into the rain-shot night until it felt as if he were going to force his eyeballs out of their sockets. It was so black he could barely make out the bare trees in their planters sunk in paving their own roots had started to buckle about them, could only see them because of the restless motion of their limbs in the wind. The self-luminous night sights of his M203-mounted Galil provided a friendly glow, but he refused to be reassured.

This was all going wrong. *Should I be in NBC gear?* From the reports they'd heard the plague had been contained in the inner city, Cleveland proper, but those reports had been fragmentary at best. What if the National Guardsmen were right, what if Sloan was already contaminated, what if the Guardians themselves were about to become a vector, what if—

A flicker of lightning betrayed movement to his left. Hard training and harder experience took over; he snapped himself out of prone position, coming to one knee and bringing his grenade launcher-rifle combo to bear.

A second flash. There was a figure standing scant meters away, looming, ready to strike. He clamped his teeth shut against a rush of sour vomit and yanked back the trigger.

"Stop the car!"
Rogers had them headed balls-out away from the ambush, angled away from Sloan's hiding place so as not to lead pursuers to him. The pucker factor was high for McKay riding alone in the turret. Going this fast risked plunging headlong into ambush, but when you knew there were bad guys with rocket launchers in the vicinity, that was clearly a lesser evil.

The sudden command had come in Vesensky's accentless English. Rogers complied without hesitation, cranking the wheel left, bouncing up over the curb with a crunching of curb giving way beneath the big cleated tires, onto the sidewalk, crowding against the brick face of an elementary school with a rusting corpse of a car to give them partial cover.

"Cover right, Billy," Rogers's voice said through the intercom. "Big Victorian house diagonally accross that intersection. Three men."

McKay felt the side door open and shut, not much faster than a heartbeat. "What the fuck, over?" he asked. His throat was dry.

Rogers didn't answer. It had been one of those—what did you call them?—rhetorical questions anyway. McKay trusted Rogers's judgment, and there wasn't even any room to feel resentful he'd followed "orders" from a fucking Russki spy.

A flurry of motion caught his eye. Vesensky had faded back ten meters from the car and was racing across the street bent low over his little AKR assault rifle. A muzzle flare jittered abruptly from the inset doorway of the old gable-crusted house. Vesensky went down.

McKay's thumb tightened on the M2's firing switch. The Soviet came up in one continuous motion, fired a burst from the hip, dashed the rest of the way across. McKay relaxed. Fucking Vesensky was one of the good guys here, if only pro tem. Hell of a note.

The Russian maneuvered down the facades of the buildings across from Mobile One, ghosting effortlessly from a doorway recess to a skeletal tree to a trash can standing like a lonely decommissioned robot. McKay could keep him in sight only because the renegade Soviet agent wasn't trying to screen himself from him. The sucker was a real professional—a real artist. McKay had to give him that.

He'd have to be, to have given the Guardians so much grief over the years. McKay felt a weird tingling-tightening in his guts. This was all too screwy to him, backing a play for a man who'd devoted most of his waking hours for almost two years to trying to kill him in person. . . .

Whoever was in the building had too many nerve endings for his own good. A figure jumped out of the big house's doorway, leveling an M16 from the hip.

"*No, McKay,*" Vesensky said, his borrowed communicator piping the words right into McKay's close-cropped skull. He dropped to a knee behind the husk of a Volvo and fired a quick burst. The figure spun, discharging its M16 into the low belly of the clouds, and went down with a rubber-jointed sprawl that told McKay he wasn't likely to be getting up again short of Judgment Day.

Vesensky was up at once, racing across the intersection, dodging between cars parked on the blacktop apron that surrounded the house, which apparently had been converted into an office building of some kind. Gunfire flashed from the house, raking the street, nowhere near the Russian.

"Wow," Casey murmured. "Dudes must be panicking." There were no targets in this direction except Mobile One, and those little 5.56s wouldn't even raise a rash on her hide.

Vesensky had his back plastered to the wall beside a pilaster that framed the doorway. Holding the assault rifle in his left hand he back-handed an object into the door with his right.

Light erupted, blue-white and dazzling. A second-fraction later McKay heard the high-pitched *crack* of a stun grenade.

The standard move at this point would have been to roll around through the door and hope nobody inside had been looking away when the flash-bang went, or would unload half a clip out the door in reflex. Instead the Soviet eeled up and through an old-fashioned counter-weighted window right above his head that fortuitously happened to be standing open—sign that the building had stood mostly derelict through the chill of winter.

It was a good move, because as he disappeared a frantic burst crashed out from the doorway. Despite himself, McKay grimaced. *That would've caught him right in the guts—*

Another stun bomb cracked off inside the house, throwing a man's stark scarecrow shadow across the pavement. There were shots, and screams. And silence.

The Guardians waited. The rain slacked to a limp dribbling on the car's upper surfaces, though a rainspout puked a steady stream of water onto the rear deck. McKay kept his eyes moving from block to block, turning to look through a whole 360, trying to see everywhere at once. Apparently, they'd run into a few stragglers from the ambush team—but he hadn't lived to the middle of his thirties by trusting to appearances. There might be more bad guys out there, and even if there weren't the ambushers had to've heard the shooting, and would be heading this way with bells on.

"You think, like, Ivan got hit, Billy?" Casey asked.

Characteristically, he sounded more concerned for the fucking Russian than for the fact that some loose asshole might happen by with a LAW at any moment and Shake and Bake the lot of them.

"I'm fine," McKay heard at once. He glanced toward the house. Vesensky was trotting forward, bent under the weight of a limp form held in a fireman's carry.

"Case, get the door."

McKay felt the door open, felt vibration through his tailbone as Vesensky laid his burden inside on the deck, then climbed in after and shut the door.

"Intelligence" the Georgian declared.

• • •

"Yeah, I think we can pull the car in here all right," McKay subvocalized, studying Sloan's trashed-out boutique with a powerful hand flashlight—Mobile One's coax spot would throw too much glare onto the clouds' underbellies, definitely a Bad Thing when it looked as if they'd managed to give their playmates in the National Guard the slip.

He frowned, twitched the light back to something he'd tracked it thoughtlessly across a second before. "Sloan, did you by chance happen to shoot about half a dozen holes in this mannequin?"

"Uh—" Sam said.

"What the fuck, Sloan?"

"It went for me."

"Jesus."

He guided the car as it crunched into the shop, waving his flashlight like one of those dudes who guide airplanes up to park at terminals. Case left the computer monitoring radio freaks for nearby traffic and climbed up into the turret. Rogers stayed at the wheel, ready to boogie or battle if and as circumstances demanded, while Vesensky emerged to help McKay and Sloan mask the vehicle with junk scarfed from nearby stores.

Anything of any real value had long since been scarfed by local scavengers, and lots of useful stuff like cardboard boxes had simply melted in the rain. But they were able to scare up some plastic and fiberboard partitions, which when propped up against the V-450 and garlanded with a bolt of ugly Mylar-like cloth that had gotten lost in the clutter underfoot—or that had just been too tacky even for hard-up foragers to trouble with—served to break up the distinctive silhouette of the armored car.

"That'll do it," McKay said, surveying what now looked like just another heap of debris with a professionally critical eye. "Not as secure as I'd like. Rather have some walls between us and the bad guys."

"If you want walls you have to go deeper inside the mall," Vesensky observed. "Might be easier getting in than getting out, especially since it's too dark to reconnoiter very well. Better to keep the option of a quick getaway, yes?"

"Yeah," McKay said. He glanced sidelong at Vesensky. *Shouldn't keep being surprised at having to agree with him,* he told himself. *Gonna have to watch him close, all the same.*

He took a last pull on his cigar and flipped it regretfully into the musty-smelling crud at his feet. "Let's put out some Claymores, in case the bad guys find us, and go see what the little friend you found us has to say.''

Inside Mobile One it was close and cool. Feeling self-conscious about the incident with the mannequin, it took Sam a few moments to become aware of a sense of wrongness. He frowned, trying to identify it.

McKay had a new cigar—unlit—clamped in his jaw and was hunkering over a youthful trooper in a sodden National Guard uniform who was laid out on an air mattress next to the turret root. Nguyen was crouched over the soldier, looking small and somehow feral as she glared at McKay.

"It was a breach of ethics to sedate him," she said, in that crisp, curious English Sam found so enticing. She was beautiful, really breathtaking—like some kind of perfect porcelain doll. It reminded him that, unlike McKay who'd been fending off women with both hands, and Casey, who'd been busily expanding the horizons of the formerly virginal Sister Light, he hadn't gotten his ashes hauled in some time. "Now you want me to give him a stimulant on top of it?"

"What, you used up your quota for busting the Hippocratic oath?" said McKay. "Look, you do it, or we do it, take your choice." He shook his head. "I've about had it with you anyway, sis. The way you freaked out during our little firefight—"

"Back off, McKay," Sloan heard himself say.

Like the true Guardian that he was, Sloan had a pretty low fear coefficient—but also like a true Guardian he wasn't dumb, and mouthing off to McKay when he was in a surlier mood than usual was a reasonably quick way of getting one's head unscrewed. Fond as he was of letting his fists do his talking for him, he'd never offered physical violence to any of his teammates. But it was that famed first time Sam was leery of.

McKay just looked at him and cocked one eyebrow.

Vesensky sat on a fold-down overlooking the proceedings. "Do it," he said, quietly but firmly.

Nguyen flashed almond eyes at him. "But—"

"Do it," he said. "You're under discipline, Comrade Doctor. Need I remind you?" His voice was silky as a strangler's noose.

Sloan recoiled internally. Intellectually he knew Vesensky had tried in the past to kill them—would almost certainly try again, if they happened to survive the current crisis. But he'd never known the Soviet as a face-to-face antagonist. McKay had met him in the concealed reactor at the Galves plant, and Casey had actually seen him through the high-tech scope of his sniper's rifle, when he came within a finger's width of canceling Vesensky's account in Washington. But for Sloan, Vesensky the antagonist was just a name.

Whereas the flesh-and-blood Ivan Vesensky was an intelligent, charming man, a man who could talk about something besides football, beer, and getting laid, not to contrast him to Billy McKay or anything. And Sam Sloan, affable country boy as he was at core, found himself warming to Vesensky right off.

Now he'd gotten a glimpse of a different Vesensky: a genuinely sinister son of a bitch. The man who'd been ace hit man for the KGB's Department V-for-Victor, in charge of what they used to call "wet work."

"Wet" as in blood, of course.

Sullenly Nguyen was busying herself obeying Vesensky. McKay had rolled the young trooper onto his side with the titanium-reinforced toe of a combat boot; nylon restraints secured the captive's wrists. Nguyen had a water-squeaky sleeve rolled up one of his forearms, probing for a vein. She found it and pressed a compressed-air injector against the clammy bluish skin.

Whatever it was she'd injected it hit pretty fast. The youngster's eyelids began to flutter and he made small noises in the depths of his throat.

McKay let him fall back onto his back. "Got some questions for you, junior."

The soldier rolled his eyes for a few moments before his mind sorted the words into sense. "Fuck you," he slurred. Drool ran from a side of his mouth, into pale stubble.

Vesensky caught McKay's eye, raised a questioning eyebrow. McKay shrugged.

A knife appeared in the Georgian's hand. The boy's eyes rolled more vigorously and he shied away like a horse from a sidewinder as the bare blade approached his face.

Vesensky's hand flashed out and caught the soldier's ear, dragging his face around. "You're going to answer our questions," he said, "sooner or later. Sooner would be easier for you." Gone was the perfect Midlantic English; in its place was a harsh accent, jagged with menace, pure B-movie Russian.

The blade touched the soldier's lower eyelid, dug in. Blood started around the tip. The captive squealed like a piglet and thrashed.

"Don't fight," Vesensky warned in a hissing whisper. "If you struggle the eye comes out. Like *this*."

He dug with the knife. Even in the poor light Sloan could actually see the eyeball's surface dimple from the pressure of the knifepoint. He looked around in horror for his comrades to restrain the Soviet. Rogers paid no attention, and McKay just squatted there with his hands on his thighs like some kind of idol.

Sam caught Nguyen's eye. Her full upper lip curled, and her shoulders moved in a slight shrug before she looked away. He could almost read the thought: *undisciplined American. He deserves what he gets.*

The captive started to sob hysterically, tears diluting the blood that streamed from his violated eyelid. Vesensky let him go for a minute, then snapped a couple of fingernails backhand across the bridge of his nose.

"Enough. Now talk."

"I'll tell you anything—just don't put my eye out, please! *Not my eye!*"

Vesensky tested the edge of the blade with a thumb. "That depends on you, doesn't it?" He smiled.

"Just what the fuck were you doing, trying to ambush us back there?"

"It was Morrigan. H-he called our commanders. He knew you were here."

McKay looked at Sloan. Sam tried to speak, but his throat and lips were too dry. He swallowed and licked his lips and tried again.

"That's absurd, son," he said, trying to sound friendly and nonthreatening, and realizing at once he was slipping into the good cop to Vesensky's bad. "We've been monitoring radio frequencies all night. Unless your commanding officers and this Morrigan share a scrambling code."

The boy shook his head. "No, no, it was the phones. He called on the *phone.*" He stared at Vesensky. "Don't let him hurt me, please. I'm telling the truth!"

"So what the hell did Morrigan say?" McKay asked.

"He said if you got into Cleveland he'd wipe out the rest of the city. He'll release the virus again!"

CHAPTER
TEN

Sam Sloan sat in the cover of a gutted desk from the boutique's office, keeping an eye on the apparently abandoned suburb across from the mall as it became visible, particle by particle, in the slow-growing light of dawn. The rain had stopped during the night, and the clouds glowing pink and canary over the eastern horizon were breaking up into clumps.

The houses were wood siding or solid brick, at this range showing no visible damage. There were plenty of trees, the skeletal outlines of bare branches just beginning to soften with the green growth of spring. On the whole the picture had a pleasant, comfortable bourgeois feel to it, if a little too urban for Sam's tastes.

He felt a pang of nostalgia . . . and it was all illusion, he knew. It would be dispelled for good and all, he knew, once he started poking into those placid houses—the first time he saw the skeleton of a child sprawled on a rotting carpet, perhaps with a doll lying neglected an inch or two from tiny bone fingers. How many would it take: One? Two? Half a dozen?

Or maybe the flesh would still be on the bones, just starting to soften—maybe some of the plague victims they'd come to look for were lying right there, waiting to be discovered. Waiting for them to pick up the infection and carry it away with them. . . .

"Sloan."

He started, turned. McKay was standing right behind him with his hands sunk in the pockets of a cammie parka.

"Shoot. Shouldn't sneak up on me like that." It always amazed him how silently a man of McKay's bulk could move, even across rubble ready to creak and crunch when the slightest weight came down on it.

McKay grimaced, staring off toward the silent homes, maybe feeling a little nostalgia of his own—and maybe even the dislocation, the eerie, lonely emptiness Sloan had been experiencing a few moments before.

"Sloan," McKay said without looking at him. "I didn't want to come down on you in front of the others." His breath came visible in puffs of condensation in the cold morning air. The lack of the accustomed echo in Sloan's skull told him McKay's pocket transmitter was turned off. "How the hell could you just cruise on past that ambush force like that? Are you losing your touch?"

Leaving his Galil propped on a plastic pole covered in scratched and faded Mylar that had obviously been used as some kind of decoration, Sloan spread his hands. "I don't know, McKay. I was being as careful and observant as I know how." He bit his lip. "No excuses."

"Yeah." McKay stared a little longer. "Maybe this shit's starting to get to you. Maybe it's starting to get to all of us."

"And maybe you're being unnecessarily harsh on your team-mate," a newly familiar voice said.

The two wheeled around, Sloan grabbing for the Galil/M203 combo, McKay's hand gravitating to the black rubber Pachmayr grips of his .45. Ivan Vesensky stood next to the amorphous heap of trash that was Mobile One. The barrels of the Mk19 and the .50-cal. looked silly as hell, festooned with shiny cloth, but you'd never recognize them from any distance.

"I didn't hear myself asking for your opinion on the subject," McKay rasped.

Vesensky grinned. "Sometimes you don't hear very much at all, my friend," he said. McKay colored. "I thought you might be going to confront Commander Sloan about his apparent care-lessness. With emphasis on *apparent*."

"I already said, no excuses," Sloan said. His own voice didn't roll out as smoothly as he would have planned.

"Have it your way. But did you stop to consider that the ambush-ing force almost certainly infiltrated to their blocking positions *after* you'd already gone past?" He gave a little sidewise toss of his head and turned back to slip through the hidden door of the car.

"Son of a bitch," McKay said.

"Yeah," Sloan said, carefully not looking at his superior.

Vesensky's explanation was almost too attractive, the way it let him off the hook. But once it was stuck under his nose it was almost certainly true, and McKay obviously saw it, too.

But maybe it was small comfort, after all. Why hadn't the possibility occurred to either of them? Vesensky was as expert as anyone alive, but so were they. Could it be McKay was right when he said the constant strain was starting to get to them?

It wasn't a comforting thought. Because the stress would get worse before it got better. If it ever did.

Incongruously Sloan realized what had felt wrong inside the car the night before. The V-450 had been their home for a long time—over a year for this vehicle, the second to bear the designation Mobile One. Now it had intruders in it, not just temporary tenants like the prisoner, back under sedation until they figured out what the hell was going on, but outsiders who'd nonetheless been with them long enough to make an impression with their smells, their feel, their presence.

A mighty strange pair of outsiders at that, Sam had to admit.

"Tom'll spell you in a few, let you get some rest," McKay said, as if none of the last couple minutes had ever happened. "Little later we'll try to pull a recon on foot. Full NBC gear. Our intelligence says we're still a good ten klicks from the affected area, but we can't be too careful with this shit, at least until we have some idea what it is we're dealing with."

"Billy," Casey said in McKay's ear. He sounded sleepy. *"Got something on the radio. Like, maybe you better hear it."*

McKay frowned at Sloan and reached up to change the setting on his communicator. "Got it, Case. Put it on the horn."

"—from now on," a dry, slightly scratchy voice was saying, "citizens will be held responsible for listening to these broadcasts. We need to re-establish a sense of national community of purpose. Of discipline. Nothing's more important than discipline."

Sloan looked at McKay. "Morrigan."

"No shit."

"It's, ah—" A quick smoker's cough. "It's come to my attention that agents of the renegade Jeffrey MacGregor, who's posing as president of the United States, are right now in the Cleveland area, defying a ban on entry imposed not only by myself but by Ohio Governor Pautz. These men call themselves the Guardians.

"This act is clearly a violation of the Constitution, as well as a serious threat to the welfare of the residents of all of northern Ohio, who have been unequivocally warned of what will happen to them should my directives be disobeyed. But, after all, what else can we expect from a man who murdered the last legitimate president, William Lowell, to put himself where he is now—"

"Jesus," McKay said, "is this guy for real?"

"I don't know," Sloan said. "He's obviously disturbed."

"He's a fucking nutbag!"

"What I said."

"—chance to redeem themselves. It's not a chance I give lightly, but after all, the citizens of Ohio aren't entirely to blame for the irresponsible acts of MacGregor and his hirelings. My offer is this: destroy the Guardians within twenty-four hours and I won't, I say again, *will not* release the virus—unless I'm compelled to do so by continued defiance of my rule.''

A pause. "I know my measures seem harsh. But history will vindicate me. Our country cries out for a strong hand, and that hand is mine.

"It's really all for everybody's own good. Morrigan out.''

"I'm going along," Suzette Nguyen stated flatly.

"Bullshit," McKay said. "Get out of that damned monkey suit and sit your ass down."

He, Rogers, and Vesensky had struggled most of the way into their bulky Nuclear, Biological, Chemical protective suits, tiger-striped with brown and tan camouflage patterns. They looked like space commandos with their faces peering out of the close-fitting hoods.

"I'm going," the Vietnamese biochemist repeated, determinedly pulling on her own almost miniature suit, which was glaring white. "This is what I came for. This may be my only chance to examine plague victims."

McKay frowned at her. "There may be shooting, sweetheart."

"I don't care. I have a duty."

"You just about let go of your bladder last night when the hammer came down.''

Her cheeks went pink. "That was different. I—I sometimes have nightmares about being under bombardment, when I was a child. And last night I was confined in a very visible, very vulnerable vehicle, totally at the mercy of men whose competence I have no reason to repose very much faith in. I apologize if my composure slipped.''

"Uh," McKay said. As a matter of fact, he didn't feel much better that she did about riding around in a big can of high-octane fuel, no matter how well armored it was. He was a grunt; he liked to feel the ground beneath him when the bullets started cracking, and especially when AT rockets started popping off. He'd *seen* what happened to AFV crews when their luck ran out: Krispy Kritter time.

"Ought to do something about that white suit," Tom said.

McKay sighed.

"Is this the right thing to do, McKay?" Sloan asked. His hair was rumpled from a too-short nap on the other air mattress, next to the prisoner, who was also awake now and staring at everyone as if they'd come out of a UFO. The captive was gagged; he'd started moaning about his wife and mother and how they were going to die, and it got on McKay's nerves.

"Is what the right thing?"

"Well, this. Should we still be messing around here? This lunatic Morrigan says he'll wipe out the rest of Cleveland unless we clear out. Is it worth the risk?"

"Listen, Sloan. If he does Cleveland, he does Cleveland. We got to find out how to stop him before he wipes out the rest of the goddamn country." He smiled sourly. "Besides, he didn't say he'd grease the place unless we cleared out, he'd said he'd do it unless we *died*. You want us to just off ourselves here and now?"

"*Billy,*" Casey said from sentry duty outside.

"*Now* what?"

"*I think we have trouble.*"

McKay paused just long enough to pull his M60 out of its brackets on the way out. He joined Casey face-down in the gritty muck that had accumulated on the floor of the boutique, peering across the parking lot.

A crowd was moving slowly toward the mall from the residential area across the way. "Who are these assholes?"

"No idea, Billy. But I have this kind of feeling they know we're here."

McKay stared at them a moment longer. "Shit. Sam, get up in the turret. Tom, get ready to drive. We could have problems."

Vesensky dropped down beside them. "They're coming this way, it seems."

"I didn't hear myself giving you any orders to deass the vehicle," McKay said. "Listen, I know you're Chairman Max's right-hand fairy, but I'm the ringmaster for this circus, and from here on in you better follow my orders."

The Soviet looked at him, green eyes unreadable as marbles. "Very well," he said quietly. "What do you want me to do?"

"Shit, I don't know. Tell me what you make of this crew."

Vesensky raised a pair of binoculars. "Civilians. Or not in uniform, anyway. A few guns, a lot of clubs, hand tools—"

"Molotov cocktails," said Casey, who was peering through his fancy scope.

"Fuck us."

"I believe that's what they have in mind, Lieutenant," Vesensky said.

The crowd petered to a halt several hundred meters away across an expanse of cracked blacktop largely empty of car-corpses. Vesensky touched McKay on the arm. In response to his outraged glare he pointed.

A man stood a little before the bulk of the mob, cupping his hands around his mouth as if trying to call to him. Wherever the midmorning wind was taking his words, it wasn't to them.

"Sloan, can you get the shotgun mike on this dude?"

"Roger, McKay, he's in my line of sight. I'm not sure how well it'll work through all this trash, though."

"Can't Tom fiddle with the computer and filter that out or something?"

"I'll give it a try, Billy."

Several moments passed, then: " —in there. Are you in there, Guardians? You were seen to go in there. Answer me, Guardians."

McKay looked at Casey and then at Vesensky. Casey pursed his lips in a silent whistle.

"Yeah. Tom, patch me through the loudspeaker."

He left the M60 with its bipod down and stood up, stepping forward out of the ruined boutique.

"I'm Billy McKay," he said, then ducked and winced as his own words boomed out in his ear, monstrously amplified. He stepped aside until he was no longer in the bullhorn's direct line of fire.

"I'm head of the Guardians. Who are you?"

"That doesn't matter." It was funny to hear the distorted, tinny, black-accented voice in his skull while he was scarcely able to see the speaker. "All that matters is you got to go."

"You heard Morrigan's broadcast."

"Yes, sir."

"He said he wants us dead."

"We figure it'll be enough if you just leave. He doesn't want anybody poking around Cleveland. If you go away he won't have reason to kill us."

McKay reached up and hit the *squelch* button on his communicator. "Dream on," he said, without his words booming out in instantaneous echo. He released the button.

"We got a job to do in Cleveland. We need to examine plague victims and report to the president of the United States. That's our duty."

"Then we got to fight you, Guardians. We've got a duty, too.

To our wives and children. To everybody trying to build a life out of what the war left us.''

McKay stood there with the wind whipping his bulky NBC suit against his calves and his big hands gradually balling into fists.

"Show your strength," Nguyen's voice said in his ear. She'd obviously found her way to the ESO seat. *"They're just civilians. Show what you can do."*

"But they're barely armed," Sloan said, shocked. "They're *Americans.*"

"Then you won't have to fight. They'll run away when you demonstrate your power."

"I doubt it, ma'am," Rogers said.

"What's your answer, McKay?" the unidentified speaker asked. *"Destroy them, then. You have guns!"*

McKay drew a finger across his throat. Case relayed the signal to Tom, who killed the loudspeaker. "Doctor, it ain't that simple. There's a thousand people out there. There's who knows how many more thousands in there waitin' for us, and they may not be so damned ready to trust Morrigan's better nature."

"Are you afraid? Do you think they can hurt you with bare fists against steel?"

"They got Molotov cocktails, and you damned well better believe those can hurt us. But, yeah, even bare fists can take us out, if there're enough of 'em, and enough of their owners are willin' to die."

"What's your call, McKay?" Vesensky asked softly.

"Reel in the claymores. I'd rather we were moving than penned in here."

"Well, McKay, what's it going to be?" the spokesman persisted.

McKay waved the loudspeaker back up. "Give us a minute. We gotta think this out."

"We don't have many minutes. It'll take time to convince Morrigan not to wipe us out—if you leave here alive."

Vesensky was moving toward the car with his arms loaded with disarmed mines. McKay was trying to think up a good answer when earth and asphalt fountained out of the parking lot a hundred meters away and a blast wave almost punched him off his feet.

CHAPTER
ELEVEN

"Mortar, Billy," Tom reported, as McKay tried to find his balance in a hurry. *"Four-deuce."*

"Our friends in the National Guard appear to have found us, too," Vesensky said, reeling in electronic-detonator wire and coiling it around hand and elbow.

"Roll 'em out, Tom!" McKay bellowed. His ears felt as if they were stuffed with cotton. Even with the little high-tech earplugs they wore, to cut out the hearing-destroying frequencies of guns being fired, a big round going off so close did a number on his ears.

Across the parking lot a lot of the crowd was making love to the pavement, and a number more were running off into the barren trees and empty houses. The spokesman still stood fast. He seemed to be waving his arms and yelling, but McKay was no longer real interested in what he had to say.

Mobile One exploded out of its mound of trash. Vesensky stood in the open door, holding a hand out to McKay and Casey as the car slowed for them.

"This really sucks," McKay remarked as Vesensky helped him aboard.

Vesensky struggled with the long sniper's rifle while Casey clutched the doorframe and grabbed for the handle of the wildly swinging door. Another 4.2 inch mortar round landed in the mall. What remained of the boutique's roof caved in behind them.

"Where're we going, Billy?" Rogers asked.

"The hell away from here."

Rogers steered them around light poles and through the fraying fringers of the mob, right toward the center of Cleveland. "Hell, Doc," McKay said, peering out the viewports, "maybe you were right about these people not having the guts to take us."

She showed him a smug look across the compartment. It was a little strained and white, and her lips looked like fingers pressing together hard enough to strain the joints.

They burst out of the parking lot onto a commercial street lined with the cadavers of Kentucky Colonels and Payless Shoe Sources.

"Crowd up ahead, Billy," Tom reported.

"Take a different route."

They made the suspension moan going around a corner past a Daihatsu showroom. Several cars still sat inside, with the doors and hoods opened and everything of value stripped from them—tires, headlights, wiring, even the seats. They looked like dead cockroaches after the ants had been at them.

A shot smashed into the vision block right in front of McKay's face. The laminated glass and plastic armor was designed not to spall, but McKay jerked back in sudden reflex. "Jesus Christ!"

All at once the street was full of bodies, swirling around the car like a river at flood. Tom drove the brake pedal in like a stake through a vampire's heart. The huge car fishtailed, and screams beat like fists on its underbelly as its cleated tires smashed half a dozen people to pulp.

"What's happening?" Nguyen shrieked. Overhead the two heavy weapons in the turret cut loose like a thunderhead with a spastic colon, jarring McKay's back teeth. The navy boy was going to be going through shit changes over firing up a bunch of unarmed civilians—except he couldn't hit anybody anyway. They were too damned close for the barrels to depress far enough to get at them.

With fewer scruples than Sam about shooting unarmed Americans, Vesensky jammed his stubby Krinkov out a firing port and triggered a burst. McKay was yanking open a compartment set into the inner hull. "Tom! Can you get through 'em?"

"Street's packed ahead," Sloan reported from the turret.

The Super Commando was more than capable of grinding forward, mashing any number of bodies warm or otherwise into Port Wine Cheese Food Product Spread, but McKay thought about how many of those bodies were undoubtedly carrying around bottles of Super Unleaded with them. The Molotov cocktail was the oldest and humblest of antitank weapons. But it still worked. Especially against light armor like Mobile One.

"Try to back us out." McKay pulled a can-shaped grenade out of the open compartment, jerked the pin, cranked open the overhead hatch aft of the turret. He let the CS grenade clatter down the flank of the car and yelled at Nguyen to hand him another *pronto*.

After a millisecond's hesitation she complied. He heard his first grenade pop and start to hiss outside as she pressed another into his hand with fingers cold as ice. They sure didn't want the stinging tear gas in the car with them, but he wanted to lay another couple of grenades on their friends outside before sealing up again.

He stuck his hand up and let the second CS grenade go. Somebody latched onto his wrist and pulled.

"Well, shit." He grabbed a stanchion and pulled back. Hard. Somebody's beard-stubbled face crashed into the hatch rim. Tooth fragments pelted him like scattered hail. He smashed his newly liberated fist into the face. It went away.

He groped outside for the hatch. Somebody else promptly grabbed his arm again.

The prisoner, who'd been acting semicomatose, jackknifed off the air mattress and threw himself against McKay's legs, sweeping his feet out from under him. For a moment McKay hung in air in the compartment, suspended only by whoever was clamped on his arm.

The prisoner bit his ankle. He yelped, from fury more than pain—the leather of his boot took most of the sting from the bite. He cocked his other foot and kicked with all his strength. He felt an impact on his toe, heard a muffled crack. The prisoner's weight went away from him.

"This shit's gotta stop," he said. He hauled out his .45, clicked off the safety, and poked his gun and upper body out of the hatch.

A chubby man was clinging to his arm as if he were drowning and it was a lifeline. He opened tightly clenched eyes just in time to look straight down the barrel of McKay's Colt.

"*Nooo!*" he squealed.

"Wrong answer," McKay said, and fired. The man's face kind of collapsed in on itself. Juice and various chunks of stuff went flying. The man let go of McKay's arm and rolled off the deck. McKay fell back inside, coughing on tear gas, hauling the hatch with him.

Tom had the car reversed. He laid rubber and took off back past the Daihatsu place, across the street and over the curb with a thump that threatened to knock all McKay's interior components loose, into the mall parking lot again.

Half a klick away an old M60 tank approaching from the east fired its 105 on the move. The crew wasn't real strak—otherwise they would have been in Europe for the ground fighting preceding the One-Day War, and either been dead or part of the FSE's armed forces by now—so that HEAT round missed Mobile One's squared-off stern and sailed on to vaporize eight members of the crowd coming from the other direction.

"What the hell was *that?*" McKay yelled in response to all the noise.

"Tank, Billy," Tom said.

"Jesus *Christ.*"

"Yeah," Casey said. "These people sure have a hostile attitude, man."

Each time they tried to cut west they found their way blocked by impenetrable crowds. Once McKay ordered Tom to try to bust through anyway, and they found themselves busting cinderblock walls on either side of an alley too narrow to pass them while McKay hung his body in the way of a lot of stray lead passing overhead and sluiced flaming gasoline off the front glacis with a fire extinguisher.

Meanwhile, the Ohio National Guard was advancing from the east and southeast. They'd made a try at breaking through them, too. The weekend warriors had tanks, LAWs, recoilless rifles, and more mortars, so that didn't pan out too well either.

"Where were all these heroes when the Effsees were squatting on us?" McKay demanded as a junked panel truck ate a rocket meant for them and went up in a big orange ball—Tom wasn't as brilliant a driver as Casey, but there was nothing wrong with his hand-eye coordination and his judgment was impeccable.

"Hiding," Sam Sloan said from the turret, sending a spray of 40-mm grenades back in the direction the LAW had come from. "Scattered. They look pretty tough to us in terms of numbers, but the Effsees had a thousand troops to every hundred of them."

"Maybe they collaborated with us," Vesensky offered, slamming another red plastic banana magazine into his AKR Krinkov. "We might even have provided them with the arms they're firing at us now."

"Great."

"They're herding us, McKay," Sloan said.

"No jive. And the way they're herding us—"

A jeep came boiling out of a side street. Tom hit it broadside at sixty kph. He never had a chance to swerve.

Not that it mattered. The ten metric ton mass of Mobile One didn't run down the smaller vehicle. It simply butted it out of its way with a squealing crash. McKay saw the jeep fly through the air, spilling uniformed bodies, and carom off a building. Nguyen screamed.

''—we're about to run shit out of land. We're headed straight for Lake goddamn Erie.''

McKay's prediction panned out all too quickly. Pressed by mobs and Guardsmen they shortly found themselves in a gritty industrial suburb whose name they couldn't exactly be bothered to call up on their nav screen. Beyond it was nothing but gray water and paler-gray sky.

A shellburst hit in an old self-storage lot, scattering little prefab metal sheds with pitched red roofs like toys from the foot of a giant brat. ''That didn't sound like a four-deuce,'' McKay remarked.

''One-oh-five, Billy,'' Tom said matter-of-factly. ''They got a howitzer battery somewheres.''

Casey was humming an old Crosby, Stills, Nash, and Young song under his breath, working the controls on the ESO console and not showing much sign of interest in the external world.

''Pretty poor shots,'' sniffed Sloan. Once the gunnery officer on the cruiser *Winston-Salem,* he had little tolerance for sloppy artillerists. ''They're not within three hundred meters of us.''

''Weekend warriors,'' McKay said.

''They probably have no forward observers,'' Vesensky said, sipping a cup of herbal tea from the little onboard microwave, ''at least, who can see us. They're firing blind, to keep us running scared.''

''Yeah, well, it's working. What the hell's that smell?''

Sip. ''The prisoner. I believe you broke his neck.''

''Oh, well.''

'' 'Oh, well,' '' Sloan's voice burst outraged from the compartment speakers. ''You casually kick a man to death, and that's all you can say? 'Oh, well'?''

''Yeah. He was trying hard to get me killed. I offed him. What's the big deal?''

For a moment Sloan couldn't talk, which was fine with McKay. A salvo *whomped* off a klick or so away. *Russki's right again.*

''At least have Dr. Nguyen examine him,'' Sloan said.

''No joy. She's freaked out again. Curled up in a knot making these little kitten noises.'' He sniffed again. ''Right. Life's too short. Tom, slow down a moment so we can get rid of the deader.''

"You mean to say you can actually just open the door and kick the poor kid out?'' Sloan said.

"Actually, I thought Comrade V could open the door, and I could kick the poor kid out,'' McKay said, and that thing happened.

"Billy,'' Casey said. "We've got radio traffic getting close.''

"You just never give me any good news, do you?'' McKay said, checking plastic Australian ammo boxes for his M60. They were shaped like half-moons and held half a belt of linked 7.62 ammo, fifty rounds. They kept the belt from tangling, making an assistant gunner unnecessary. "What do they have to say?''

"It's code. But since it's all, like, 'Foxhound to Hunting Cap, we're closing in on the bunny,' it isn't too hard to figure out.'' He started humming again.

"Subtle,'' Vesensky said, with a little laugh.

McKay glared at him. "Cold-blooded motherfucker, aren't you?''

"Of course. And so are you; you simply enjoy being dramatic. We are lifetakers, McKay. We've long ago had any illusions about leaving this world alive knocked out of us. It's the game, and the game is all.''

McKay flared his nostrils and shook his head. He couldn't think of anything to say.

"But I can see the pressure's affecting you some. You didn't refer to me as 'fatherfucker,' and I haven't noticed you passing up any earlier opportunities to refer to my sexual preferences.''

"Jesus. You're disgusting, you know that?''

"Yes, in fact. Though most people, I think, would find my being a professional killer more repellent than my homosexuality — hadn't we better get off this street?''

Abruptly McKay turned a glower on Casey. "If you keep humming that damned 'four dead in O-hi-o' song I'm gonna twist your head off your skinny neck.''

"Sorry, Billy.''

"Besides,'' Vesensky observed, "there're six of us.''

"I hear a chopper,'' Sam chimed in.

"We're just not catching any breaks, are we?'' McKay said. "Let's duck in this plant thing up on the right, here.''

A cluster of looming khaki structures like Great Cthulhu's own building blocks perched on a two hundred foot sheer fall-off to choppy, gray, miserable-looking water. Whatever it was, it was big, and looked as if it might offer plenty of strongpoints to defend—and room to play cat-and-mouse with attackers until it got dark and they could exfiltrate on foot.

"Do we want to be pinned down, man?" Casey asked. He usually didn't contradict McKay, or offer much of any opinion at all, but as a former fighter jock he was pretty obsessive-compulsive about keeping mobile.

"Not really. But this ain't a goddamn Fighting Falcon. We can't outrun the bullets. We're going to have to fight this one out with our wits."

"We're doomed," Sam Sloan said.

The sprawling plant was surrounded by a three-meter chain fence topped with a helix of razor tape and mounted with sensor posts at ten-meter intervals. The gate was open, which made the heavy security a bit silly. But right now it meant Mobile One could get in without being too obvious about it; driving a ten-tonne armored car through a chain-link fence wasn't hard, but tended to leave pretty distinctive signs.

Just what the damned place was all about wasn't any clearer when they got inside. There were long rows of heavy equipment, yellow paint not much faded by the elements—dozers, carryalls, all that stuff, so many that only a few showed signs of being stripped by scavengers. There was simply too much booty here—and in a fuel-poor postwar environment, there was maybe not that much demand for humongous tracked earthmovers.

"Where to, Billy?" Rogers asked.

"Hell, I don't know. What about that big building there, looks like a hangar or something."

"As good as anywhere else," Sam said under his breath.

Suzette Nguyen seemed to have recovered her composure once they got under cover, with at least psychological distance between them and the noise of the battle trying to seek them out.

"So, how are we going to defend this place?" she asked, briskly rubbing her hands together. It was cold in here among the rows of parked forklifts and trucks.

Her words chased each other around the high I-beam rafters like squirrels. McKay just looked at her and laughed.

"Sweetheart," he said, "you gave me a company of marines and some rocket launchers, maybe a mortar or two to call my own, and Casey to snipe, I could hold this place against the whole

Ohio National Guard, as well as whoever we left on their hind
legs among their buddies over in Iowa. We're talking Stalingrad,
for sure.''

"We held off a lot more in Texas," Casey said dreamily. "Ten
thousand *Cristeros,* man.''

"With a couple hundred Texicans to help us hold the line.
Yeah. What we got here are four hard-core heroes—five, if you
count fags—plus one bimbo doctor who twitches out when a fire-
cracker goes off.''

Nguyen went pink. "That's not fair! I—can't help my reaction
to shellfire.''

"Yeah, but you sure talk like Rambette when the shitstorm isn't
coming down. But the point is you ain't much help. Hell, we ain't
even got enough stiffs to play *Beau Geste* worth a fuck. Maybe
we shoulda kept that dead troopie.''

"We got good lines of fire in all directions," reported Rogers
via communicator. He was off with Vesensky and Sloan scouting
their position. *"Pretty good sight lines, too, if we get up on one
of these buildings around here.''*

"Yeah. If we just had people to put on them buildings.''

"I can get up in a good lookout and keep watch," Casey said.

"Yeah. That's gonna be our best bet. Vesensky, you know how
to use an M79?''

"I was *spetznaz* qualified, remember? We learned how to use
enemy weapons, just as your own special forces do.''

"Yeah, I forgot. You can probably hit a roof rabbit in the ass
at five hundred meters.''

"Effective range of your M79 launcher is four hundred.''

"Yeah, so I was just checking. Sloan, get him the spare Vest
o' Grenades.'' It was their private joke, to talk about the special
canvas vests with a dozen pockets to hold 40-mike mike rounds
as if they were something from Gary Larson's *The Far Side.*

"Okay, Comrade, you go with Case and watch his ass—just
not too close. When they find us, you can get a look at the hand
we're dealt.''

He swept his gaze through the gloom of the cavernous garage.
"And then we can figure out how to play it.''

CHAPTER
TWELVE

The building shook to the enormous hammerfall of a shell landing right nearby. Dust drifted down from the rafters.

"Troops moving across the street, Billy," Casey reported from his vantage point on a neighboring structure. *"Like, I think they know we're here."*

"Maybe not," Sloan said. He was sitting on top of Mobile One's turret with his legs dangling inside the open hatch. "They're probably planning to check the place out and are willing to waste a few shells prepping it to make it easier on their boys in case we are in here."

"Probably," McKay said around his cigar. "But it don't matter shit, since they're gonna find out real soon we really are here."

Nguyen kept moistening her lips, over and over. Her eyes darted around like small animals seeking shelter. "Perhaps we could hide from them."

"They'll find the vehicle and seal the area off, Billy," Rogers said.

"Yeah. It'd be best if we could hide. But they can bring in enough troopies to smoke us out. They could trot out every last survivor in the Greater Cleveland area, if it comes to that. These people're willing to stand up to an armored car, they're gonna be positively coming at the prospect of just having to *look* for us. Anything to keep Old Man Morrigan and his bad germs away." He rubbed his jaw and spouted smoke. "Shit."

"What about waiting for nightfall?" the doctor persisted.

McKay checked his watch. "Even at this latitude and time of year, it's just too far away. I don't think we could hide out that long."

She faced him squarely, her square-cut bangs drooping almost to her eyes, looking more angry than scared. "How long can we hold out if we fight?"

"Damned if I know."

"They're spreading out along the perimeter, Billy," Casey said.

"Keep an eye on 'em. Don't fire 'em up yet." His mind was

racing like the tire of a car stuck in sand, and doing about as much good. Instinct, training, and bitter experience all told him that in a crisis, action—even erroneous action—was vastly preferable to just sitting still.

"Should we try to break out?" Sloan asked. His normally road-tanned face was pale, but his square jaw was set. "Moving target's harder to hit."

Rogers shook his head, very slowly. "They got too much depth to their defense. They got enough people so they don't have to cordon us with a thin line."

"Yeah," McKay grunted. "A whole city full of people. All of who'd rather eat bullets than have the invisible creeping cruds get them."

"Wouldn't you?" Vesensky asked. He sounded amused, there in the back of McKay's head.

"Yeah. That's what bothers me. These people ain't gonna boogie if we say boo."

"In the Orient, they, like, call it 'living as one already dead,' " Casey said. *"Means they haven't got anything left to lose."*

"Casey, I'm so glad you chose to share that little philosophical tidbit with me. But we *do* got something to lose. We're supposed to be saving the United States of America from some detached asshole named Morrigan and his AIDS-in-a-Drum. And we ain't gonna just roll over and play dead."

A not-too-distant crash echoed his words. The oil-spotted cement floor shook beneath their feet.

"Close one," Casey said casually. He was all the way into his supercool Chuck Yeager fighter jock mode now, just as imperturbable as Rogers. *"They're starting across."*

"Right. Fire 'em up; go for noncoms and radiomen first, then officers. Vesensky, you can play, too."

He stooped and picked up his Maremont chopper, which was resting on buttplate and bipod like the foldout in the latest *Soldier of Fortune.* A shellburst bulged the concrete wall to their left.

"This is no time for *machismo,*" Nguyen said. Tears streamed down her perfect face, but she was mastering her urge to run and hide and cower with visible effort. "Think what's at stake."

He worked the bolt to cock the MG. As if in response small-arms began to snap, crackle, and pop outside.

"I know what's at stake, sister. And maybe it is macho bullshit, but right this second I don't know anything to do but fight it out and see what goes down."

"Yo, gentlemen," a voice called. "Maybe I can be of assistance before anybody, like, does anything rash."

McKay turned to stone. He and Tom Rogers, the Ultimate Professionals, had been snuck up on like a couple of conscript sentries jerking off and smoking dope behind some adobe wall in Libya. Im-fucking-possible.

But it was all too possible, he knew in a sick sledgehammer moment of realization. The place was just too big for the five of them to secure. And with the whole goddamn army marching toward them in neat little rows, nobody thought they'd have to contend with getting creepy-crawled.

Slowly he turned. "Say there, my man, just please don't be pointin' that Sly Stallone in my direction. I got what you call a nervous constitution."

Reluctantly McKay let the barrel of the M60 drop. After all, if their new visitor had wanted their asses, a quick spray of full-auto fire while they were all standing around making speeches at each other would've had them.

"Who the hell are you?"

What he was was peculiar enough. McKay saw a very black man, five eight or so, with a wiry-strong kind of build—not gymnast, exactly, but in that neighborhood. He had on black Keds, black and green cammie pants, a black turtleneck with leopard-skin cuffs, and a flak jacket with some kind of little flag patch on it that had black and red and yellow horizontal stripes and a small white circle with some kind of design smack in the center of it. Heavy gold pierced-ear rings, a gold lamé headband, and iridescent red sunglasses rounded off the apparition. He was holding a Smith & Wesson 300 riot shotgun in one hand.

"Terry Achemba's the name, and right this minute saving your honky asses is the game."

McKay glanced to the car. Rogers had unobtrusively slipped into the vehicle. Sam still sat up top with his teeth in his mouth.

"Is this guy for real?" McKay subvocalized.

"Who knows?" Sloan replied.

"Now, I can see what you really want to do is stand there admiring my excellent taste," Achemba said, "but it might be more appropriate to haul butt, don't you think?" He showed horribly white teeth.

"Can we trust him?" McKay wanted to know.

A new barrage landed outside. Tools clattered off hooks on the walls. "Next one liable to land on our heads, and shit," Achemba said. He didn't seem real upset at the prospect.

"Do we have a choice?" asked Rogers, who by now was almost certainly covering the intruder from the depths of Mobile One.

"No," McKay said aloud. "What do you want us to do?"

Achemba grinned wider. "That's more like it. Why don't y'all just pile back in that car and follow me."

"What, you think we're gonna be bulletproof all of a sudden just cause we got a spade with a gold garter on his head with us?"

"McKay!" If it was possible to subvocalize a groan, Sloan did.

"Naw. I be takin' you out the back way, unless you got your honky heart set on playin' John Wayne at the Alamo and shit."

"Nope. That was last month. *Case, Vesensky, give em a couple more to remember us by, then form up on One ASAP."*

The next barrage didn't land right on their heads. It fell farther away, out in the heavy-equipment park. Casey and Vesensky came pelting in while the debris was still ricocheting off the outer walls of the hangarlike garage. A bullet ricocheted off the doorframe as they entered, red-cheeked and blown more from excitement than exertion.

"They spot you?" McKay asked, peering unhappily out into the watery daylight.

"Come on, come *on*," Achemba urged, showing nerves at last. "You dudes can socialize later."

They piled into the car, except for Achemba and McKay, who planted his butt on the front glacis and cradled the M60 across his chest. The black nodded vigorously, jumped up next to the ex-marine, and slapped the armor slope.

"Let's go. Took you long enough."

At close range McKay could see that the design in the middle of the flag patch was some kind of fuzzy-head bird. "What, you belong to some kind of black radical group or something?"

" 'Or something,' " Achemba agreed. "Get the lead out, okay? This way."

Taking over the wheel, Casey drove to the rear of the garage. A loading-bay door stood open, large enough to accommodate the fat V-450. As they rolled outside a file of men in semimilitary drag were filing in through the human-sized door next to it, carrying backpacks and cheap suitcases.

"What the fuck, over?" McKay asked, lighting a new cigar.

"Friends of mine. Be settin' up a nice little surprise for the dudes who're looking for you. I *like* surprises. Don't you?"

He guided them between piles of cargo containers and detached truck trailers and clumps of mechanism fenced off with barbed wire. "Jesus, what was this place?" McKay asked.

"Did a little bit of everything," Achemba said, not very helpfully. "Hey, tell my man to turn left here, past this generator thing."

A gully ran through the lot, lined with cement for part of its course. Achemba pointed a finger like carved ebony to where it passed through the perimeter wire, which had been cut away in a sort of half-moon above it.

"Right this way."

"What, are you nuts? That's right off into space."

More incoming mail whistled in. This package crashed right into the middle of the garage, now two hundred meters behind them. Achemba looked back as McKay raised his head from out of the fur collar of his parka.

"Hope the dudes got clear. Yeah, Lieutenant McKay, you sure figured it right out. I done rescued you from your little predicament back there so's I could have you drive you 'n' me and ever'body off a cliff. Who-*ee*, but you smart."

"All right, all right. Go for it, Case. But remember: this boat still ain't got wings."

McKay hung on for dear life as the car lurched out and over. It nosed down a steep slope, and for a heartstopping moment McKay thought it would just keep tipping forward, somersaulting all the way to the lake and launching him and this smartass nigger into space.

Ten meters down the gully bottomed into sort of a ledge. A very rude path led away from it, switchbacking down the face of the bluffs. "Hey, Billy, look at this!" chirped Casey.

"Yeah," he said grimly around his cigar. "But it ain't on the NASCAR circuit. Keep it in mind."

Mobile One waddled down the path. The cleats of the tires gave good traction, but the packed-earth surface kept crumbling under the car's ponderous weight. McKay resolutely refused to look overboard, ignoring the gray lake, which seemed to be surging and leaping below like a pit full of hungry Dobermans.

"So did you people build this little stairway to heaven?" he asked sideways. Whoever *you people* might be. It didn't seem the right time to ask.

"Path been here a long time. People been addin' to it over the years. We just done our part." He was leaning back smoking a cigarette and apparently enjoying the view. No accounting for taste.

To McKay's astonishment there was a boat bobbing at a small concrete pier at the foot of the path. It looked like some kind of river tug. A Browning M2 .50-caliber poked out of an improvised mounting atop the cabin. A sturdy-looking corrugated metal ramp led from its flat rear deck to the pier.

A white man in a CPO jacket with a long black FN-FAL slung across his back waved and pointed from the taffrail. McKay looked back up the cliff to see the dozen or so men who'd been going into the garage as they came out jackrabbiting down the precarious path on little knobby-tire scrambler bikes.

Casey halted the car on the little shale beach the pier stuck out of. "Go ahead, man," Achemba urged. "Drive on aboard. Ramp'll take her weight, no problem. We transported shit like this before."

"Now, just a minute—" McKay began. Something made him turn and look up at the top of the bluffs instead of continuing.

A red-orange mushroom cap of flame was swelling into the sky from the mysterious plant. A moment later the soundwave hit, a low, rolling rumble that built like an avalanche, so that it was deafening before you really thought it was loud at all.

"What the fuck, over?" McKay hollered when there was a point to it. The bikers swept past whooping like Comanches and hotdogging their bikes up the ramp into the boat.

"Among other things, this place up here was researching use of methane as fuel," Achemba said. "Had big ol' tanks of it buried ever'where. Scavengers must not think it's worthwhile to scarf gas you get off rotting shit. But it sure do burn nice, don't it?"

He dropped to the shale. "Anybody get hurt?"

"Oat Willie got his little finger shot off," a bearded man called. "Otherwise, it went smooth as fuckin' a baby."

Achemba raised his glasses and blinked surprisingly small eyes at him. "I guess it depend on your perspective, Lou Blue," he said. "Okay, my man, tell Lieutenant Wilson to drive this baby on board and we can shift on to greener pastures."

That reminded McKay where he'd left off. "Not so fast, dude. What makes you think we're goin' anywhere with you?"

Achemba reached under his flak jacket, brought out something the size and shape of a small flowerpot, and planted it on the armor face right over Sloan's ESO seat.

"This," he said. "It's your basic state-of-the-art Soviet RKG-7 antitank hand grenade, with a magnetic shaped-charge head capable of penetrating two hundred millimeters of armor. But no need to look so uneasy, because it's been modified to be detonated by *this*—''

He held up his hand. "A man of your background will easily recognize an electronic hand-detonator. A clacker, right? Only this one's rigged as a dead man's switch. I relax my grip''—he held up his other fist, opened it explosively—''boom.''

"What the hell's going on?" McKay rasped.

"In the name of the sovereign city-state of Detroit, and of the Motor City Madman, may his name ring forever, I hereby take you all prisoner."

CHAPTER
THIRTEEN ────────────

Lots of guns were abruptly pointing in McKay's direction. He raised his hands, letting his M60 hang from its long Israeli-style sling.

"You hear that?" he subvocalized.

"Got it," Sloan said. *"What should we do?"*

McKay noticed the fat tube of a LAW resting on a brawny shoulder, pointed generally in his direction. Achemba had backed a few paces away.

"Nothing," he said aloud. "Don't do nothing."

Achemba nodded happily. "Smart man. I hated to play it this way, you know? But we ain't got time to mess around." He glanced up toward the top of the bluffs. A fat pillar of black smoke was worming its way into the pale sky. "Now, may I cordially invite you and you friends aboard the Love Boat?"

Billy McKay stood by the rail of *Dreamboat Annie,* as the field-expedient gunboat was named. He could feel its enormously powerful motor, which occupied most of its space belowdecks, throbbing through the soles of his boots. It left little room for crew and a raiding force that called itself the Suicide Mechanized Unit, not to mention half a dozen involuntary passengers. Most of whom were huddled inside Mobile One, which was lashed to the afterdeck with heavy chains, out of the chill, spray-impregnated air.

The lake's motion wasn't as bad as he would have expected from looking at it. He'd had more than a little experience dicking around in small boats, so it would have taken quite a bit to get to him; none of the Guardians was very susceptible to seasickness. Still, he wasn't going to complain that the ride wasn't rougher.

He pulled out a lighter and stoked a cigar. Achemba came back from the cabin, rubbing his hands together. "Shit, it's too damned cold up here. I wish I'd moved to Florida."

"That makes two of us," McKay said. He pointed with his smoke off northwest along the lake's length, where a low, long, dark silhouette glided through the haze that clung to the turbulent surface. "What the hell's that?"

"Bulk carrier, bro. Prob'ly hauling iron ore from the Michigan mines, maybe some choice items of scarf. Effsees left us a couple warehouses full when they boogied. Choice stuff. Real fine."

"Didn't think the Effsees'd be that generous with their loot."

Achemba grinned. "They didn't intend to be. We talked 'em into believing it's more blessed to give than to receive, 'specially when what you're receiving is bullets and Molotovs. So we send that shit off and the carriers come back loaded with coal from Pennsy. We don't like to use that stuff much, 'cause it's real dirty, you know? Makes acid rain and shit. But it comes in handy, and it ain't liable to be no problem for a few years yet."

"Thinking like that's how acid rain got started in the first place," said Sam Sloan, wandering up from the stern, where he'd been swapping shoptalk with a crewman with a stocking cap and a cataract eye.

"Thinking other ways is how folks go cold and hungry," Achemba said levelly.

"Yeah, I remember the good you eco-freaks did back in Pittsburgh. Steelworkers got to breathe clean air while they starved to death."

Achemba held up hands freighted with heavy gold rings. "Now, hey, be cool. Let's all be friends."

"You're a hell of a one to talk about friendship. You kidnapped us."

"After rescuing your honky butts from those National Guard boys. For which you ain't exactly been dripping gratitude."

"Goddamn it, Achemba, we're on a mission from the president," McKay said, turning red.

"And we're on a mission from the Motor City Madman, to bring back any interesting info on this plague shit. Which we're doing."

"What do you have?" Sam asked.

"You." Sam blinked. "What else would dudes like *you*'ve been messing around in Cleveland for? Especially for some dink snatch scientist."

"Well, we're sure as hell going to be a lot of help to this Motor City jerkoff," McKay said, "since we turned up exactly jack shit."

"We know that. And what you was gonna turn up next was dead." He patted McKay on the shoulder. "Chill out, bro. The

Madman just want to talk to you. Maybe pool some resources, figure out a way around this Morrigan cat."

"How did you know where to find us?" Sam asked.

"Well, my man Morrigan been announcing your general location to the world for a lotta hours now. And we got us some nifty radio gear on this boat, including RDF equipment, so we was able to just follow the bouncing ball as the Guardsmen chased you dudes. Fortunately, you picked a place to hide that we'd scoped out pretty good."

"You certainly seem to have a line on things," Sam said.

"That we do," Achemba said. He gazed off after the bulk carrier, which was almost invisible now, out where sky blended seamlessly into water. "Madman, he figure the way things gonna be in this country for the next few years, water transport gonna be where it's at. Trade and commerce, you dig? And here we got ourselves astride the finest waterways on the continent."

He swept a hand around the horizon. "We got boats all across Erie, Huron, Michigan, even Ontario. We have trading rights on the Ohio and clear up to the St. Lawrence to Montreal, where the Russkis bombed it and blocked the channel. A year, two at the max, we'll have gunboats on the Missus Hip." He shook his head. "Madman, he act pretty flaky sometimes. But everything he does he got a reason for, you can bet to that."

"Gunboats," Sam repeated. "So people don't exactly have much choice about trading with you."

"Hey, they're just to protect our interests, Commander."

"That's how empires usually get started, I understand."

Achemba shrugged. "What's so wrong with empires, man?"

McKay spat a fleck of tobacco into the sea. "Empire, my bleeding piles. This is the United States of America. Anybody says otherwise is fooling himself."

"United States gone the way of the buffalo soldiers, bro," said Achemba, meeting the full force of McKay's scowl.

Have to give him credit for guts, Sam thought. Even though the Detroiters had numbers and all the guns, Billy McKay's mean look fell into the category of natural phenomena like hurricanes, twisters, and seismic sea waves. Even in his better moods he looked like somebody who could take a bite out of Rambo.

"I think we're about to pass into Canadian waters," Sam said, thinking it might be a good idea to shift the conversation to a different topic.

"Not no more. These Detroit waters now." Achemba smiled.

"Shoot, if I'm gonna be uptight about anything I should be uptight about that, since I'm actually a Commonwealth citizen."

"Say what?" McKay said.

Achemba patted the flag patch. "See this? I'm from Uganda, bro."

"Right. You sure talk like it."

"Hey. My old man was a diplomat. He was with some kind of industrial mission to Detroit, back when Big Daddy was the main man in Kampala. I grew up in the Motor City."

"Your father served under the Idi Amin government?" Sloan asked.

"Until he decided to overlook an order to come home to sorta talk about things. He thought his head looked better on his shoulders than setting on a shelf in my man Idi's icebox, you dig?"

A Suicide Mechanized troopie with a Fritz falling over his eyes came out of the pilot house. "Got a broadcast from Chicago comin' in, Terr." He grinned. "Seems our guests made the early news."

Achemba made a circular motion in the air with fingers like carved ebony. "Share the wealth, my man. Let's hear it."

"You getting this, Case?" McKay subvocalized, and received an affirmative as William Morrigan himself began to speak from a loudspeaker stuck on the rear of the cabin.

"My congratulations to the people of Cleveland," he said. The cheap speaker gave his rich-rough voice a tinny cast, as if it were really a Mel Blanc impersonation. "And to the officers and men of the Ohio National Guard, for wiping out a blemish on the American body politic, as well as earning a reprieve from a severe punishment I sincerely did not want to inflict."

He paused, hoping for dramatic effect. "So, out with it, mo-fo," Achemba called. His troopies clapped and shrilled catcalls.

"Governor Pautz and Cleveland city officials have confirmed that at 1027 hours this morning, Eastern Emergency Daylight Time, the terrorist group known as the Guardians were apprehended and destroyed by elements of the Ohio National Guard. Our nation owes a debt of gratitude to these brave men. That is all."

" 'That is all?' " McKay echoed incredulously. "Did he watch *MASH* reruns too much, or what?"

Achemba laughed and slapped his arm. "And you say I never did nothing for you! See? I killed you!"

•   •   •

Bright—or at least partly cloudy—and early the next morning
the *Annie* put into a former marina near Alfred B. Ford Park,
across from Belle Isle, which had gotten overgrown and looked
like Guam. It was a short hop to Jefferson and then straight downtown to where the Madman hung out in whatever passed for imperial splendor hereabouts.

The Guardians got to drive themselves and their two temporary
allies. Achemba had switched the deadman detonator on the
magnetic mine with a radio controlled unit, and just for good
measure clamped a second device to Mobile One's stern. This one
aimed straight for the guts of the engine compartment.

"This way you can drive yourselves, feel right at home,"
Achemba said, with one foot in the open door of the command
car he'd transferred to. "Just be sure to follow us real close."

McKay was eyeing the charges dubiously. "Just how well
shielded are those fuzes, Achemba? I mean, if somebody drives
by with a Mr. Microphone, do we get to meet Jesus?"

Achemba smiled and bobbed his head like one of those little
terriers geeks used to have in the back window of their cars, the
ones with the little lights in their eyes that blinked when you
signaled for a turn. If his eyes did that, you couldn't tell for his
shades.

"Naw, it's cool, man. They're shielded." He pulled the shades
down and squinted over the tops of them at the explosive on the
V-450's front armor. "Just the same, maybe you shouldn't follow
too close, if you know what I mean."

"You're all heart, Achemba."

Detroit had taken two bombs—well, Hamtramck had sucked
one, and Hamtramck was kind of an autonomous enclave that
used to contain twenty thousand or so blameless citizens and a
couple of Billy McKay's Polack cousins he had to admit he didn't
miss too much—and gone through the usual round of plagues,
riots, and other hassles that here as elsewhere had taken more
lives than the thermonuclear bombardment proper. In addition, it
had been the scene of vicious fighting during the months of FSE
occupation, as Achemba and his crew had indicated in a lot of
their little byplay—and by the way they handled themselves and
their weapons, it looked like a good bet they'd been in the thick
of it.

All things considered, it looked about the way you'd expect a
city to look that used to have a population of eight million, even

after the industrial belt exodus of the eighties and nineties, and would today be able to turn out a fifty percent overflow crowd for Michigan Stadium over to Ann Arbor, if you herded out the kids and crippled folks.

Still, twenty months had gone by since the war, and as the Guardians had seen time and again, life goes on. They saw a fair number of people doing people things. Maybe they were a little shabbier, and their activities less energy intensive, than what you'd have seen back in the old days—but the same old people going to work, kids cutting school, people chasing dogs, hanging out the wash. *Stuff.*

"Maybe it's my imagination," McKay said, "but people seem a lot less uptight here than they did down in Okie City."

"Is that any surprise?" Sloan asked. He kept trying to sit to one side, so he wasn't directly in the line of fire of the shaped charge on the other side of the armor. "In Oklahoma City if you think the wrong thought too hard the Brothers of Mercy are liable to come through the door and take a blowtorch to you."

"I thought people in Oklahoma City were very well behaved," Nguyen said.

"You're a naive little creature," Vesensky said.

Casey was craning to peer around as he drove. "I don't know," he remarked. "It sure doesn't *look* like an empire."

"What does an empire look like?" McKay asked.

"You should know, my friend," Vesensky said.

"Hey, is that another commie put-down of America?"

Vesnesky laughed. "Hardly. I used to belong to a subject race of the other great empire of our epoch."

"You used to belong?"

"We used to be subject. Now we and the Great Russians are in the cesspit together."

CHAPTER
FOURTEEN

There was a very large man wearing a robe that looked like a gold shower curtain, playing the grand piano at the foot of the well-like atrium that ran up through the fifty stories of the almost brand-new Hyatt Regency on Gratiot downtown. Above the mezzanine there was no light except what filtered through rooftop skylights high overhead, giving the atrium a cathedral feel that was at once airy and oppressive.

The mezzanine was vaguely lit by ceiling fixtures and clamp lights. The song was "Lady Madonna." It wasn't being played particularly well, but it was played *con* the kind of *brio* that didn't give a particular damn whether it was good or not.

Terry Achemba rapped his knuckles on a white cylindrical planter that looked a lot like the ashtrays dotted around at strategic locations, except that it was bigger and had a plant in it. "Your Excellency. *Excellency*. Yo. You got company."

The pianist finished up with a flourish that consisted of mashing huge fingers down on as many keys as they reach at once, and popped up as if he were spring-loaded.

"*Damn,* but I love that," he said, putting hands on hips and stretching. He turned and came down the two steps from the dais where the piano sat, hand extended. "So you're the Guardians. Pleased to make your acquaintance."

I hope every two-bit self-named head of state who figures the United States ain't bigger than him anymore ain't bigger than me, McKay thought. The Motor City Madman was tall—not as tall as the president of the Republic of Texas, but broad, and a good thirty years younger; say an inch and fifteen pounds over Billy McKay, but also about six years. He had a broad square head and a mashed nose and auburn hair streaming down to shoulders that could shrug like Atlas. His beard was neater than you'd think and picked out with gray, especially in two lines descending from the ends of a wide and surprisingly full-lipped mouth. His eyes were gray. He wore blue jeans and some kind of stretch garment that from the blue shimmer of it was probably the visible upper half of some kind of Danskins.

Nothing too unusual for one of the best-loved professional wrestlers in America at the time the balloon went up.

McKay took him in and said, "I guess they don't call you the Motor City Madman for nothing."

Sam Sloan could feel his heart drop right down through his boots and the floor and the lobby below *and* the parking garage. Hearts and minds had never been McKay's strong suit—he even had a T-shirt that read "Give me your hearts and minds or I'll burn your damn huts down," which was one of the few things in Creation that could make Tom Rogers, who was an ex–Green Beret and took that sort of thing seriously, roll his eyes—but talking back to a self-proclaimed emperor, not to mention a self-proclaimed *madman* . . .

The Madman said nothing. McKay took hold of the proferred hand. Sloan's relief died a-borning as he realized his esteemed leader was *playing the knuckle game*.

Sloan felt sweat start up near his hairline. He turned his eyes sideways. Tom was impassive as ever, but Vesensky's long green wolf's eyes had widened ever so slightly. Casey, wearing a Radiators tour cap, was oblivious, and so, thank God, was Suzette—Dr. Nguyen. She wasn't as tough as she liked to pretend, that was obvious, but Sam had also kept noticing she wasn't as brittle and superficial, either. . . .

What he was trying not to notice went on for a whole minute. His horrified eyes watched the muscles of the Madman's forearm rippling under the shiny fabric—

And then the Madman lunged forward and threw an arm around McKay's shoulders in a crushing hug. "Well, all *right!* You're everything you were cracked up to be."

He turned to the others, deftly extricating his hand from McKay's grip. "You're Sloan, aren't you? Hero of Sidra Gulf? A pleasure." He had the sort of baritone that comes out of a chest like an oil drum and a voice box that's been pounded on some, by fists and forearms as well as booze and cigarettes. "And you must be the infamous Casey 'Top Gun' Wilson."

Casey's mouth rumpled up. "Uh, Miramar's for naval aviators, like," he said. "I'm an air force *pilot.* Uh, sir."

The Madman stuck out his jaw. "You spent time there, though?"

"Well, yeah, I did TDY as an instructor there after I got back from the Med."

"I knew that. I knew that! The Madman knows everything. And you, of course, are Thomas Rogers. I owe you a tremendous debt of gratitude, sir."

"Beg pardon, sir?" Tom said softly. It was maybe the third time Sloan had ever seen him caught by surprise.

"You organized a very efficient—and very nasty—resistance movement in these parts, last spring and summer when the Effsees were in town. Mostly to draw attention away from that secret base down in Iowa, or so I assume. But your people gave the Expeditionary Force black eyes on a regular basis, and in the fullness of time a lot of them found their way here to work for me. You trained me some damned fine fighters, Lieutenant."

"Thank you, sir." Tom sounded as if he meant it. But then he always did.

"And you, fair lady—" He turned and captured Nguyen's hand. She recoiled as he bent down, seemingly afraid he might bite off a finger or four, and her eyes went wide as he kissed it instead. "You are—?"

"She is Dr. Suzette Nguyen, late of the Sorbonne," Vesensky said.

"She's a very fine biochemist," Sloan added.

"*Enchanté.* And yourself?"

"Colonel Ivan Vesensky, late of the KGB. I'm a spy."

The Madman's eyes went wide. He held out a hand. "If you'd be so kind as to join me for lunch? My chef does a hell of a clam linguini. White *or* red sauce."

The Madman patted the last traces of crumbs and red sauce from his beard and took a slug of wine. "I always figured one day I'd retire from the square circle and never have to eat in a hotel coffee shop again," he said. "Then I found out I'd done it so long I *like* eating in hotel coffee shops." He belched.

The coffee shop was stashed to one side of the mezzanine, behind pierced-wood screens and potted ferns. Achemba and the Suicide Mechanized boys he'd escorted the prisoners in with had made themselves scarce. If the Madman had any security on hand— and Sloan wasn't such a downy chick as to doubt he had—they were distinctly not in evidence.

The waitress caught Sam's eye as she cleared his platter. She was black, or rich brown, anyway, and looked like a fashion model. She contrived to hitch her black skirt high enough to make it clear the stockings beneath were supported by a garter belt before turning away. Sloan watched her sway toward the kitchen, then caught himself, chided himself for being a sexist boor, took a sip of white wine, and cleared this throat.

"I beg your pardon, ah, Excellency—"

"M.M., please. We're all friends, here."

"You seem to be an educated man. Would you mind telling me—"

"Telling you why I became something as gauche as a professional wrestler?"

Sloan turned beet red. "I don't mean to be judgmental. I know you were an Olympic Greco-Roman wrestler. But still—"

"But professional wrestling wasn't exactly the *real world*, was it?" The Madman laughed. "Well, winning a bronze at Montreal didn't exactly prepare me for the real world. Neither, I blush to admit, did my college career. Would you like to know the only thing more unemployable than an Olympian Greco-Roman wrestler? An Olympian Greco-Roman wrestler with a degree in history. *And* a minor in an obscure Central Asian language."

"Hell, you could of got a job as a translator for the CIA," said McKay, taking a pull at his beer.

"Not when the language is Tocharian A. Or B, for that matter. Nobody was going to pay me to sit in a windowless trailer somewhere in Turkey to listen to a language nobody's spoken for thirteen hundred years, Lieutenant. Not even the CIA."

"Perhaps the KGB would have," Vesensky said, "had your father been sufficiently important."

The Madman traversed his big head to bear on him. "You're not exactly the way I'd expect a KGB colonel to be."

"You're not exactly as I'd picture a former professional wrestler and rock and roll musician who's made himself dictator, either."

"No, I suppose I'm not. Though I don't like to think of myself as a dictator. *Madman*'s actually my title. Self-conferred, though, I admit that." He drank more wine. "But I'd think you'd at least defend your system more enthusiastically."

Vesensky smiled. "Your country was bourgeois and decadent; our ideologues were right about that. But I can't very well carry on about the superiority of our system, inasmuch as we lost. If not by much."

Nguyen shifted in her seat. "Really, I don't see how you can waste time with small talk in a situation such as this. How many lives are being lost while we sit here?"

"Well, none, little lady, unless our friend Morrigan has gone back on his word and let his bug go. Which seems unlikely, since those pinheads in Ohio convinced him and themselves that you're dead."

"But we are speaking of a disease, a contagion. You cannot turn such on and off as if it were an electric light."

He rubbed his chin. "But I understood strains of virus or bacteria could be specially bred—or gene-engineered—to retain their virulence for a limited amount of time. Though only so many generations, or whatever—hell, I'm not a biochemist."

"So much is obvious," she said, leaning forward. "Otherwise you would see that pathogens cannot be controlled so precisely. Not in the real world."

Everybody was looking at her hard. *She may be exquisite and tiny as a china doll,* Sam thought, *but she could sure give McKay some bull-in-the-china shop lessons.*

"Perhaps you should speak more respectfully to our host," Vesensky said, with an edge.

She shot eye-bolts at him like something out of a video game; if you looked close, you could just about see "20,000 Point Bonus" at the edge of the screen. Obviously, a bearded goon who dressed the way Superman might if he lost his fancy longjohns and had to go shopping at Goodwill didn't qualify in her mind as Legitimately Constituted Authority.

A pity she hasn't a clue just how much her revered boss Maximov would love to get drunk with a man like this.

"Actually, our charming doctor has a point," the Madman rasped, pushing back his chair. "We have serious matters to discuss. I insist on allowing a proper period of digestion—no point in spoiling a splendid meal *post facto,* eh?—but after that, to business. Definitely."

Sullenly Nguyen coiled up to carry on, ignoring a warning glance over the rim of Vesensky's glass of mineral water. The Madman looked past her toward the entrance to the coffee shop and his pitted ugly-handsome face lit.

"Ho. And now I have the privilege of introducing my consort—"

Sloan turned in his chair to see a woman in russet and yellow

Danskins and leg warmers brushing a fern frond out of her face.
Her hair was streaked honey. Her face and body were so beautiful
it hurt to look at them. Also quite familiar, though Sam had never
met their owner in his life.

''—Merith Tobias.''

Only the most famous woman in prewar America.

CHAPTER
FIFTEEN

With a final grunt McKay shoved the Olympic bar up to the full extent of his arms. He held it for three heartbeats, locked arms trembling, muscles standing out on his thick throat, and then gratefully let the spotter guide it into the pressing bench's brackets.

"Five hundred pounds," he panted, swinging to a sitting position. He felt as if he'd been drenched in motor oil. "Not bad for a light workout."

One of the perquisites of being an emperor, even a small-scale one was that you to got to live as high as you wanted, even in a post-Holocaust world of forcibly diminished expectations—as the Motor City Madman kept reminding his guests. Looked at in that light, an ultramodern hotel made an appropriate choice for imperial palace.

The Madman wasn't all guff and calculated tackiness—even McKay picked up on that. He had, for example, worked it out for himself that the guerrilla campaign Tom Rogers masterminded against the Effsees last year had really been intended as a giant diversion to get their minds off the top-secret Heartland complex— and Jeff MacGregor, being held prisoner inside awaiting execution of a death sentence. A hotel was a logical command center, possessing extensive administrative facilities—especially with the five bottom floors converted to office space—and plenty of barracks space for troops, plus it was designed to support a large number of inhabitants in comfortlike conditions.

But the Madman had a fine eye for perks, and it was always open. Among the features that had recommended the new Hyatt to him was that it possessed a humongous gym, complete with free weights and Nautilus equipment and an indoor swimming pool—a real, genuine, honest to Christ half-length Olympic pool, too, not one of those wading pools shaped like an internal organ that were so popular in fancy hotels.

After lunch the Madman had indeed wanted to talk business. He was primarily interested in getting President MacGregor to recognize his claim to authority over Detroit and dependent ter-

ritories—meaning the land he'd grabbed since the Effsee collapse—and in concluding trade agreements.

Sometimes even now Jeff MacGregor struck McKay as a liberal
wimp. But there was not the chance of a single snowflake in Hell
that he was going to ratify the Madman's partial dismemberment
of the United States. He hadn't come close to doing so for LaRousse
and the Texicans, who had a lot more overtly legitimate government and a better claim on sovereignty. But he could work out a
modus vivendi with the Madman, as he had with the Republicans,
that would permit them to deal with each other on a reasonably
amicable basis and leave weighty questions of ultimate authority
for a time when they were a bit more realistic to consider. The
Guardians were ideal go-betweens in such negotiations.

It was the sort of job Sloan and old cadreman Rogers excelled
at. It was the sort of dealing that tended to piss McKay off, so
he excused himself as his two buddies and the Madman made
their way to the Madman's penthouse suite.

Nguyen, who'd been working herself up to a tantrum because
nobody was discussing the virus, got sent off with a pat on the
head to play in the city-state's database, which was extensive; as
consolation she was given access to any or all of the Madman's
scientists, who were told her word was for the moment law—the
Madman didn't look like the type who'd have scientists working
for him, but he did.

Casey, who was about as much use in negotiations as a carp—if
not actively obstructive, like McKay—had let himself be escorted
to VIP visitor quarters, where he was meditating or listening to
rock from the Madman's personal library, which was digitalized
and also stored in the database. A man who'd stolen his *nom de
guerre* from Ted Nugent was liable to have a pretty extensive
collection, especially when he was an absolute potentate.

For his part McKay decided to work out. He needed the exercise,
and besides, this didn't strike him as a handy time to get shitfaced,
which was his other main mode of attitude adjustment.

Having gotten a good pump McKay wandered to the martial-arts
exercise area, where Vesensky, who was not exactly invited to
join in the discussions upstairs, was working out.

He had on a borrowed set of black kung fu pajamas and slip-
pers—trust Vesensky not to soil himself with grimy sweats when
there was something better at hand. He was just finishing up a
complicated *kata* with a Chinese sword; he nodded to McKay and
laid down the sword, then beckoned over one of the Madman's

black-belted attendant-instructors for some light sparring.

The Detroiter was good. He was taller than Vesensky, and bulkier. It was also apparent at once he was utterly outclassed.

The Soviet stayed in constant motion, carefully keeping his movements arrhythmic, unpredictable, as he flowed around the mustache black belt, elusive as mercury, launching attacks from the most unlikely postures and angles. The Detroiter seldom landed a blow, in fact rarely unleashed a strike or kick Vesensky had to parry; the KGB renegade was simply *not there*. At the same time Vesensky scored regularly with fists and elbows, even high kicks to the face—light cheekbone-tappers—that were the classic downfall of the overconfident martial artist.

Before he got into the Guardians McKay had never had much interest in the Oriental fighting arts—the Jap martial artist whose style most closely matched his natural approach was Godzilla. Major Crenna, mastermind of the Guardians and Project Blueprint, imported the top experts from all over the world to his Arizona training camp, and McKay's head got turned around: there *was* a point to all that fancy ballet shit, after all. He acquired at least a nodding familiarity with most of the major schools and styles, and polished his own approach a bit. Of course, his own style was still pretty much *Gojira-jutsu*, but at least he had a clue.

To his semieducated eye Vesensky seemed to be using the no-style style of long-dead movie martial artist Bruce Lee, *jeet kune do*. He seemed to exhibit much the same grace, the same barely credible speed and control and flexibility as the greatest of all celluloid chop-sockey heroes.

"He's good, isn't he," a voice said at his side. A throaty and feminine sort of voice.

McKay instantly felt warmth spreading through his lower belly. It was a familiar feeling, a good feeling. A predatory feeling. It was also a feeling that could be hazardous to his health.

"Yeah," he said. He let himself look sideways. She was wearing her exercise togs still. She had a red headband holding back hair streaked in shades of honey, wheat, and pale amber. A mist of sweat sheened her perfect face. Her lips were slightly open. She watched Vesensky intently with eyes that were gold and green and hazel. "He's fast. His form's damn near perfect."

She glanced up at him then. "From your tone of voice, it sounds as if you think you're better."

"I got more power. He'd need several good shots to take me down. But if I connected once—" He shrugged.

Vesensky's opponent was tiring. He was also clearly getting pissed off. He was getting sloppy-aggressive, taking too many chances. Now was the time McKay anticipated Vesensky was going to fake weakness long enough to get the black belt to commit to a whirlwind attack, then clean his clock for him. It was the sort of trick that made you look good.

Instead, Vesensky broke off, said something to his opponent about a sore heel that was beginning to trouble him, slapping him on the arm and smiling before bowing away. The black belt bowed back and grinned, a little confused.

Vesensky nodded to McKay again as he walked past. He ignored Merith Tobias as if she didn't exist. He went over to a set of gymnastic equipment, stripped off his shirt, and began to work out on the parallel bars.

For the first time in his life McKay thought about what a man as totally physical as any athlete might be like if he had no trace of *machismo* in him. If the proposition had been stuck under his nose he would've said "wimp" by reflex. But instead he felt sudden understanding as to why Ivan Vesensky was such a stone-lethal sonofabitch.

The woman drifted after the Soviet. McKay followed, aware that he hadn't let himself be led around by the dick this way, with absolutely no chance of ever getting anything, since he was fourteen.

But she was *Merith Tobias*. *The* sex star of the nineties.

For Billy McKay, anyway, the American cinema (as Sloan might call it) had undergone a renaissance in the years before the war. With the HIVaccine series driving a stake through AIDS, and Wild Bill Lowell a lot more concerned with going toe-to-toe with the Russkis than what people did with their clothes off—unlike some of his conservative predecessors—sex had come back to the movies with a vengeance. Merith Tobias had been maybe the main standard bearer of that revolution.

Billy McKay had never put much store in sex stars, anyway. If he wanted to see screwing he preferred to go for the hard-core, instead of waiting for the coy gauze screw scenes they were always slipping into cops'n'dopers Miami Mice melodramas or plunking down money that might otherwise be spent on serious drinking to see a lot of jiggle bunnies in some turdbrain teen sex quickie. Also he couldn't hack most of what they tried to pass off as sex stars. He'd hated Farrah as a kid, and later on thought of Bo Derek as the kind of girl you'd pick up at an adult book store for

$19.95, bike pump not included. Phoebe Cates wasn't bad, but after her—forget it. The big message of the late eighties was Sex is Bad, and, sure enough, sex with the frog-faces and Baby Boomers past the bloom they were trotting out *would* be bad.

Ah, but Merith Tobias. She never went the triple-X route, and when she flashed the parts that used to make Ed Meese mad she did so judiciously. But she exuded sex. She *was* sex.

A buddy of McKay's had put it best, after he went back to the corps from SOG-SWAC. "She can do more for your cock with just her voice," he'd observed, in a crummy tent in the Qattara Depression, "then most girls can with their mouths."

Oh, yeah. He came and stood next to her, head full of thoughts that were going to do him *no* good at all. He'd seen the way she melted against the Madman when he hugged her, back in the coffee shop—if she'd done that to *him,* they'd have had to use a paint scraper to get his skivvies off him.

And if he'd thought humping President LaRousse's daughter was a good way to get killed—

Tobias stood hipshot, watching Vesensky perform his evolutions with immaculate skill. "He's beautiful," she said.

McKay chuckled sourly. "Don't waste it, Ms. Tobias. You're not his kind."

She glanced at him. "I can admire a champion racehorse without wanting to sleep with him, Lieutenant McKay." She walked off and left him standing.

They knocked on his door in the middle of the night. He groped for his .45, then remembered he'd been relieved of his armaments way back in Cleveland.

"Shit," he said to himself. He remembered the hard-core line he'd handed Merith Tobias that afternoon, about what a *baaad* dude he was *mano-a-mano*. He hoped he wasn't about to have to put up or shut up.

Not that he had any reason to distrust the Madman, who'd been a perfect host, aside from not letting them leave or have their guns or armored car back—and the understanding was they'd be free to go in a couple of days. It was just that he had no reason to trust him, either. The world McKay knew hadn't been all that nice a place *before* it went to hell.

He pulled on a pair of pants and padded to the door. A spade aide of the Madman's was waiting outside with a trio of troopies dressed in the usual assortment of K-mart cammies, army surplus, and

Effsee castoffs that were standard paramilitary battle dress from
Maine to Baja. They carried weapons slung.

"Beg pardon, sir, but the Madman would like to see you in his
suite as soon as it's convenient."

McKay bleared at his wristwatch. "0215 ain't what I call
convenient."

"Sorry. It's an emergency."

"Gimme a minute."

The Motor City Madman's suite gave you a better appreciation
of what the word *palatial* was all about. Tonight he was holding
court as he often did in his bedroom, the walls of which were
plastered with photographs of him posing with professional wrestling luminaries of days gone by: Hulk Hogan, André the Giant,
the Junkyard Dog, Doctor Death. There were a couple of posters
of Merith Tobias, including one you never would have seen at the
Hallmark store in the mall—amazing thing, garter belts—and,
above the bed, a big poster of movie critic Joe Bob Briggs, personally inscribed: *To the Motor City Madman—A Drive-In Kind of
Guy.*

Beneath Joe Bob sprawled a gigantic waterbed with burgundy
coverlet and sheets. The Madman himself sat propped up by pillows. Sort of clinging to him was Merith Tobias, lying atop the
coverlet in a burgundy robe that had fallen open to reveal a stretch
of smooth-muscled thigh. McKay had a mental flash of what that
gold-pink body would look like lying fully exposed on that maroon
background waiting just for him, and reckoned it would kill him
if it ever came to pass.

The other three Guardians were there already, none of them
looking as dragged as McKay felt. Well, they should be getting
used to it by now; every time anything went down in this emergency
it was at oh-weird-hundred in the morning.

The door opened and Vesensky came in with Nguyen. Vesensky
looked as if he'd slept eight hours and had his morning coffee—or
herb tea, in his case. Nguyen looked more pissed than usual.

The Madman stroked Merith Tobias's hair. She stared intently
at him, a strange, sad look in her eyes. He kissed her forehead.

"If you'd excuse us, honey," he said softly. She nodded, rose,
and walked out. Every man in the room tried hard not to watch
the way her ass moved under her robe, except the Madman, who
got to, and Vesensky, who didn't have to try.

When the door to the leaving room was shut, the Madman

lowered his head to his hands and rubbed his face. His robe was midnight-blue trimmed in white.

After a moment he raised his shaggy head again. "Gentlemen — Doctor. I have to admit I haven't been entirely candid with you."

No one said anything. Nguyen looked as if she had plenty to say, but from the look she gave Vesensky, McKay guessed he'd had a little talk with her.

The Madman drew a deep breath that set the waterbed to rocking. "The reason I brought you out here wasn't just to find out what you knew about the plague in Cleveland. Nor was it to open a channel of communication with President MacGregor. I brought you here because, frankly, I need help."

"You got an empire, Madman," McKay said. "What do we got to offer?"

"Your expertise. Your resourcefulness. This afternoon I mentioned how useful men trained by Lieutenant Rogers were to me. Think how much more useful the man himself can be — to say nothing of his equally able comrades. Colonel Vesensky and Dr. Nguyen included."

"We're here in the service of the president of the United States, sir," Sloan said gently. "And our associates serve Chairman Maximov. I think Scripture has something to say on serving two masters."

The Madman frowned, and his gray eyes flashed, and for a moment Sloan was afraid they were going to get a more explicit demonstration of just why he was called the Motor City Madman. Then the bearded lips twisted and the big head shook.

"I'm not in a position to threaten you. As a matter of fact, we're all threatened already. I think you know by whom."

"You've heard of Morrigan," McKay said.

The Madman nodded. "He's been demanding my submission since he went public with the plague threat five days ago. I've been putting him off."

He pushed off, rolled over the rail, stood up, and started pacing. His bare feet were splayed and hairy.

"I know you think I'm nothing but an unpatriotic opportunist. Well, you're right. Unpatriotic I could argue — I fought the Effsees with these hands, gentlemen, bled and saw my friends die when the United States was officially *allied* with the invaders, so maybe I can be forgiven if the letters U.S.A. leave a bad taste in my mouth."

"Hell, no," McKay rasped.

The Madman regarded him for a moment, then resumed pacing. "That's your privilege. And as I say, I am an opportunist. I admit it. I've been rich and I've been poor, and being an emperor, even a penny-ante one, beats the ass off any of it.

"But I don't think I'm bad for my people. I've brought them order, I'm opening trade, I provide for the sick and hungry, and I take a damn sight less in taxes that Uncle Sugar used to grab. I think they do better under me then they could expect to under Morrigan. If you've listened to his broadcasts I think you'll agree."

He turned and faced them. "But one thing's for damned sure. I didn't build an empire to hand it over to that genocidal son of a bitch."

"So what's the story?" McKay demanded. "Or did you just haul us out of bed in the middle of the night to practice acting on?"

"You're one ballsy son of a bitch, McKay," the Madman said. "I like you. But don't push me.

"A courier came from Morrigan. An hour ago. He says there's no more time. He wants my answer in twenty-four hours. Otherwise—" He shook his head. His powerful hands opened and closed as if of their own accord.

"What'd Morrigan send a courier for? He's got a radio. He's on it all the damned time."

"There's more, McKay. He's come to take something back with him. Some *one*."

"Us?" Sam Sloan asked. "I thought he thinks we're dead."

"He does. He's demanded I surrender Merith Tobias to him. He wants her for his consort."

CHAPTER
SIXTEEN ────────

"In this corner, *laaay*dies and gentlemen," the emcee shouted, "weighing in at two hundred forty pounds, it's tonight's mystery challenger: the *Masked Mauler*."

The crowd jammed to the rafters of the remodeled Civic Center booed lustily. The emcee was a stout black man in a tuxedo encrusted all over in silver glitter. McKay didn't think they were booing his taste in clothes.

He looked up through the eyeholes of his mask into the dazzle of floodlights and wondered just how the hell he'd wound up in this mess.

He didn't have to wonder *much*. It was all his fault.

It started when he opened his mouth and said, "I have an idea." It just popped out, there in the Madman's bedroom in the early hours of this morning. The Madman looked at him and asked him to explain, so he did.

You couldn't blame the Madman. He'd had the proper response: "No. Never. Under no circumstances."

So McKay, peckerhead that he was, had to argue about it. And Tommy and Sloan, brownnoses that they were, had to back him up.

Come to think of it, it was their fault. *They* knew what his ideas were like. He wasn't sure how it was possible to have an idea without using your brain, but he'd sure done it. It'd been their duty to point the fact out. They'd let him down.

So finally the three of them, with the help of that goddamn faggot pinko Vesensky, had convinced the Madman that McKay's scheme might work. But he didn't like it.

So finally he raised his head and grinned a not very pleasant grin, and said the fatal words: "You got it, McKay. *On one condition*."

"And in this corner, weighing in at two hundred ninety-five pounds, *evvvv*'rybody's favorite: the Motor City *Madman!*"

The crowd lost it completely. And *heeere* came the One Condition, vaulting the rail, bouncing around the ring like a jack in the fucking box, holding his hands clasped over his head in a champion's salute.

The Madman was in full regalia: goggles, a short gold cape, red trunks over gold tights. His vast chestnut-furred chest was bare.

McKay stood there feeling dazed. He was totally out of his depth. His mask made his nose itch, and he was too self-conscious to try to scratch it. The last time he'd seen a crowd this big it was a *Cristero* army, which didn't reassure him.

The emcee was reciting the rules for the match for the benefit of the crowd. McKay knew them already; they amounted to No Permanent Damage. McKay had agreed to let the Madman call the shots in handling Morrigan if he lost the match, and he wouldn't be much use saving the Detroit despot's bacon if he were in a body cast. For his part, he wasn't too happy with his prospects for a long and happy life should he break any important parts off the local dictator.

So what's the sweat? he asked himself. *You ain't got that much to lose—just a shot at trying the dumbest plan you've come up with in your entire life.* Of course, he knew it wasn't that easy. Even in the choreographed prewar professional wrestling matches things could get out of hand and people could get fucked up. He and the Madman were both winging it, and the Madman had racked a lot more hours in this particular cockpit.

What he was mainly worried about, though, was a danger he'd never faced before in his life: being made to look like a weenie, in front of about ten thousand people screaming their lungs out for him to be made to look like a weenie.

The emcee handed the mike to his boss. The Madman waved a hand for silence. He got it.

"Who's the maddest?" he yelled.

"The Madman!" the crowd yelled happily.

"Who's the baddest?"

"The Madman!"

"And who's the Ruler of the Rubble, the Lord of the Lakes, the one and undisputed Master of the Midwest?"

"Madman! Madman! Madman!"

The emcee accepted the microphone and poked it at McKay. "Any words for us before we begin?"

"Kill 'em all, and let God sort 'em out."

"Strong words from the challenger," the emcee commented, and climbed out of the ring. A striped-shirt referree with a whistle climbed in. The crowd fell silent.

McKay caught a glimpse of his buddies, all except Nguyen, who'd refused to have anything to do with this fiasco, sitting front and center. In a half-assed try at security they were tricked out in silk robes and masks of one sort or another, as if they were part of a Mysterious Wrestling Family or something. It made them look like the wallflowers at a dance at a school for ugly girls, or maybe aspirants for the role of Jason in *Friday the 13th Part XII*.

An airhorn blew. The Madman began to circle counterclockwise. McKay shifted left toward the rope barrier, blocking him.

The Madman grinned. "Good. I was afraid this was going to be too easy."

He flew at McKay in a sprawling lunge. McKay didn't want to meet him head-on, so he decided on an aikido-type move, in honor of the absent Doc Morgenstern. He grabbed a wrist, pivoted his hips, and steered the huge wrestler past him in a rush.

The Madman pirouetted, went backward into the ropes, used their spring to catapult right back past McKay. He stuck a brawny arm out and clotheslined the Guardian.

McKay fell on his ass. The crowd cheered frantically.

Well, I got him just where he wanted me with that last move, he thought, picking himself up. He half hoped the Madman would rush him them, since he knew some nasty tricks for that set of circumstances, but the Madman was strutting around the ring holding his arms in the air receiving accolades and giving McKay a shot at his back.

Since McKay couldn't be sure he *wasn't* that dumb, he took the offered shot. He launched himself in a flying tackle.

Sure enough, he wasn't that dumb. What's more, he'd timed McKay perfectly. As McKay lept, so did he, right up onto the ropes. McKay landed on his face.

The Madman fell backward on top of him.

The air blasted out of McKay's lungs. The Madman was instantly grappling for an immobilizing hold. McKay drove an elbow into his kidneys. The Madman grunted and rolled away.

Score one for the dwarf, McKay thought. They both got to their feet, eyeing each other.

The Madman advanced again, with suprising speed for his size. McKay was quicker. He grabbed his opponent's biceps with both hands and wished like hell he could bring up his knee hard.

The Madman grabbed McKay's elbows and threw his weight backward, surprising McKay and dragging him off balance. He took a step backward and turned, whirling McKay around like a ball on a string and releasing him. McKay flew back into the ropes any which way, was propelled forward again before he could regain control.

The Madman leapt straight into the air, twisted, and slammed both boots into McKay's face in a double kick.

McKay discovered he was lying on his back again. He heard his teammates yelling from ringside. He hoped they had the decency to be cheering for him.

The Madman dropped on top of him again with his arm across his throat, caught his wrists, tying to pin him. "Give up?" the wrestler panted.

McKay's knees snapped up and clamped on the Madman's head. With a gut-tearing spasm of effort he flung his opponent off him, rolled back to the ropes, used them to pull himself up.

He knew what the problem was. In a straight, dirty street fight he could have cleaned the Madman's clock a couple of times by now—he'd won the knuckle game, after all, and the fights he'd had in the past hadn't primarily been fought against foes whose main interest was to put on a good show without getting hurt so they could collect their paychecks and go get drunk.

But here he was constrained by *rules*. There were no rules in the Pittsburgh bars or the alleys of Port Said. The Madman knew the rules, knew how to use them to his advantage.

He and the Madman started circling each other. He caught a glimpse of Merith Tobias sitting in the front row. Her body was strained forward, as if she didn't want to miss a moment of this—but the look on her face was sheer misery. He wondered if she knew what exactly was at stake.

Here came the Madman again like a red and gold and hairy avalanche. He flung himself to the side. Madman hit the ropes and once again used them for a flying direction change. McKay dropped as his opponent flew at him, rolled into him and swept his legs out from under him.

Instead of grappling, pitting his strength against his enemy's bulk, he jumped up again. The Madman got to his feet, a trifle slowly, launched another attack.

McKay dodged. He went into the ropes deliberately this time, using them to shoot him out of harm's way as Madman charged again like an angry rhino. The Madman changed direction and lunged. McKay dropped a shoulder and rolled past him.

Furiously, breathing like a bellows, the Madman came after him. McKay kept dodging, so that they were bouncing all over the ring like a pair of Ping-Pong balls. The crowd shrilled fury at McKay for refusing to stand and fight.

But there was another difference between the two men, beyond that one was big and the other was bigger, beyond the fact that one was in his element and the other most definitely out of his. McKay was in his thirties and had been leading an active, dangerous life. The Motor City Madman was a man in his forties who'd been living like a king. He hadn't been neglecting that gym beneath the hotel, obviously, but between the burdens of his office and the pleasures of the flesh he'd found other things to do than work out regularly.

"Damn it," he gasped, hanging on the ropes in a corner, "you can't run forever."

McKay gave him his finest shit-eating grin. "Can't I, now?"

The Madman bellowed and charged.

McKay started a bellow of his own—at the same time he started to pivot. He brought it up out of the center of him, with every bit of energy left in his own massive frame, channeled it through his sweat-covered body and down a pile-driver leg in a spinning back kick that took the Motor City Madman right in the solar plexus.

The Madman folded. McKay grabbed him by the cape and ran him headfirst into a pole. It was padded, but the Madman hit it hard.

McKay hammered an elbow vertically down into the Madman's kidneys. The Madman dropped straight to the mat. He lay on his belly, moaning, struggling to get up.

McKay kicked him in the side to make sure he didn't get any of the air he was gasping for. He knelt, hauled a brawny arm around his neck as if to help his fallen foe to his feet. The crowd, which had shrieked itself hoarse, fell into an expectant hush.

McKay rose, hoisting the torpid Madman into a fireman's carry. He straightened, hunched briefly forward, and then with a grunt and spasm of effort pressed his opponent directly over his head.

For an instant in which he thought all the muscles were going to rip right out of his arms, McKay held him there. Then he dropped him.

The crowd went beserk. The referee stood staring down at his fallen master with his whistle hanging out of his mouth. McKay staggered to the ropes and collapsed, hanging like laundry on a clothesline directly over Merith Tobias.

"Pack your bags, sweetheart," he managed to wheeze. "You're goin' to Chicago."

CHAPTER
SEVENTEEN

One thing you could say about Lake Michigan, Billy McKay reflected, puffing on a cigar from the Madman's private stash of Havanas. It looked just exactly like Lake Erie.

Then he stepped out on the deck of the *Manitowoc Fancy* and saw the slight figure standing by the rail with a few strands of hair the color of honey escaping from the hood of her coat, and thought, *well, maybe it looks just a* bit *better*.

The *Fancy* was a little round-sterned, one-stack cargo vessel that resembled nothing so much as the *Lentra*-class AGI "freighters" the Soviets used to use to infiltrate *Spetsnaz* teams into the U.S. The unlikely party had boarded her that afternoon in Benton Harbor near the west end of the base of the stubby dick that was the Michigan peninsula for an overnight trip, bypassing arteries that were still virtually impassable for fifty klicks in any direction from Chicago, choked with a plaque of cars stalled for almost two years in the Last Traffic Jam. The *Fancy's* captain, a Detroit merchant mariner, hadn't wanted to take her out at night on the Lake, but Morrigan's courier had insisted, and he had a warrant from the Madman himself that said what he wanted, he got.

Another figure stood by the rail a few meters down from Merith Tobias. This one wore various oddments of military dress and a black H&K 91 slung over its back. Its Fritz helmet had red, gold, and white ribbons tied around it—the Madman's personal colors, marking the wearer as a member of the elite unit sent to safeguard Detroit's tribute to its new master.

Eyes watering slightly behind lightweight brown contacts, McKay went to stand next to him. The troopie nodded and touched a finger to the helmet's Kevlar brim.

"The last time I had on a helmet was in Afghanistan," said Colonel Ivan Vesensky, who'd taken a reduction in grade for this mission. "Never occurred to me when I rotated out that the next one I'd put on would be one of yours."

"You go in with Papertin in '79?"

"Good lord, no, that was well before my time. I was rotated through as part of my *Spetsnaz* training. Live firing exercises with the Afridis, that sort of thing."

"How'd you do?"

"They kicked our asses."

"Good."

Vesensky laughed.

McKay moved down the rail to stand next to Tobias, pausing to straighten his Green Beret—and hadn't Tom been pissed about *that*, the more since he had to wear a Fritz like the rest of the grunts.

She glanced up at him as he leaned his elbows on the cold rail, which was beaded with condensation and spray. "Sergeant Dubrowski."

He grinned and nodded. "Ma'am. Just wanted to be sure everything was all right with you."

"As well as could be expected."

He glanced around the deck. There was no sign of Whitlock, Morrigan's man, a bloodless little man with a long nose that dripped perpetually.

"Haven't had a chance to talk to you about this," he said in a quieter voice. "I'm sorry to put you through this. It's all my plan. The Madman was dead-set against it."

Fuckin'-A straight he was, he thought ruefully. His words came slurred because his mouth was still puffy, and the right side of his jaw ached ferociously under its two-day stubble of beard from the Madman's two-footed kick.

She smiled sadly. "Don't worry about it—Lieutenant. I got used to doing what I have to do a long time ago." She brushed hair back from her face.

"Before the war, as a matter of fact," she added, so softly he half thought he'd imagined it.

He didn't know what to say, and before he could think of something a small, hooded figure approached from behind. "Mistress Merith, Mr. Whitlock says you must come below. He doesn't want you taking a chill."

"Thank you, Li," Tobias said clearly. She turned and walked toward a hatchway.

Dr. Suzette Nguyen turned McKay a furious look and followed. McKay grinned and shot her a thumbs-up. She never saw it.

• • •

For reasons unknown the *Fancy* carried a lot more berthing space than you'd normally expect on such a dumpy little cargo ship. As commander of the security attachment, ''Sergeant Dubrowski'' rated his own closet-sized stateroom. It wasn't much, but it beat hell out of an air mattress in the back of Mobile One—which was parked in the garage beneath the Madman's Hyatt headquarters, programmed to self-destruct in case the Detroit ruler's techies got too inquisitive.

A knock on the hatch brought him awake. *I shoulda known better than to expect a decent night's sleep,* he thought. *I ain't had one since this slam-dance began.*

He padded to the hatch, his .45 held behind his right buttcheek. Sidearms were among the few items of Guardian gear that got to go along with them on this pleasure cruise. Another was their neat pocket communicators, though when they were out and abroad they just used them as high-tech walkie-talkies, without benefit of larynx mikes and bone-conduction phones that might serve to indicate they were anything you couldn't pick up at Radio Shack for a couple hundred bluebacks.

Out in the gangway a diminutive figure stood. The dim lamp illuminated a pale twist of hair spilling out from the hood of a bulky jacket.

''May I come in?'' a voice like slightly fermented honey asked softly.

McKay blinked. ''Yeah. Come in.'' He waved absently with the pistol.

The figure slipped inside. He shut the door. The Colt automatic felt unnaturally huge and heavy in his hand. He felt like an idiot for holding it.

He flicked on a light. The feeble glow it emitted couldn't have put much strain on the engines. She was unzipping the parka. Beneath it she wore a man's red-plaid shirt, ludicrously large and stuffed anywhichway into blue jeans. He wasn't sure where there was room in them to accommodate the spare cloth; the jeans fit like dermis.

He stepped past her and stuffed the .45 back into its holster tucked under the mattress. ''There some kind of trouble?''

To his amazement she was sitting on the edge of the bunk undoing the Velcro fasteners of her hiking boots. ''Can I stay?'' she asked, through a faerie-gold curtain of hair.

''What?''

She was standing again, the jeans unbuttoned, sliding down smoothly curved flanks. She wore nothing beneath. Her pubic hair was dark blonde, darker toward the center.

"I asked if I could stay," she repeated, pulling the oversized shirt off over her head without unbuttoning it. Her breasts were large for her size, though they didn't overwhelm the fine-muscled sleekness of her body. The nipples were pale pink. McKay stared at them and moistened his lips and remembered the fantasies that had roiled in his mind, seeing those tits bouncing a hundred times the size of life across a movie screen.

"What the hell is this?" he croaked.

She approached him, hesitantly, coming onto tiptoe, tilting her head back. "Don't talk now," she said huskily. Her upper lip strayed from the lower, displaying white even teeth.

He had to bend his knees to reach her mouth with his. His hands roved across the incredibly silkiness of her skin, down her back to her ass, up across the furrows of her ribs to cup her breasts, while she flowed against him in a gentle rhythm that made his blood boil.

She broke away with their mingled saliva glistening on her lips. Her eyes fixed on his, burning like lamps. He grunted and tried to crush her against his bare chest. She flowed through his grasp like oil, dropping to her knees, lips just brushing the ridged muscles of his chest and belly.

Her hand slipped his shorts down his thighs. His cock fell like a drawbridge and bounced, its tip brushing her cheek. She rubbed her face against it, gaze still locked with his, then with excruciating slowness enveloped the glans with her flawless lips.

McKay groaned and sank his fingers in the golden cascade, her hair.

She wasn't content with bringing him off, explosively, in her mouth. She kept at him, teasing, sucking, while pleasure danced on pain's keen edge and he fought with the twin desires to pull away and to drive on and fuck that gorgeous face in the ultimate fulfillment of a hundred sweaty fantasies in a popcorn and grease-scented artificial night of a hundred movie theaters.

When he was all the way hard again she flowed back up him like a vine, urging him back on the bed, straddling him, impaling herself on him while he gasped with the suddenness of it all. They thrashed together, a furious wrestling match, now one on top, now the other, and he realized with what was left him of conscious thought that he was horny as if he'd been celibate a month.

When they finished this time both were legitimately exhausted. For a while they just lay there intertwined, breathing each other's panted breath.

As he started to recover McKay wondered why it was all these women were sneaking into his bed who didn't belong there. Not even he had the balls to say that to Merith Tobias, though.

But still, this was just too weird. She wasn't just the lust-object of every straight male in prewar America—and postwar, too, when you got down to it. She was the Motor City Madman's woman. Who at least to all appearances was being shipped off like a prize racehorse to be the woman of the self-proclaimed Marcus Aurelius, in hopes of preventing him from bringing down the Madman's house of cards with a weapon invisible and insubstantial as air, and deadlier than a hurricane. No way was she Billy McKay's woman.

It took him a while to figure out how to phrase it.

Eventually he just decided to blurt it on out: big surprise.

"What made you decide to jump in bed with me?"

"The Madman's strong," she said, rolling onto her back. "You beat him; that means you're stronger."

"Huh?"

"I figured it all out, after the bombs quit falling. The only way for someone like me to survive was to attach myself to the strongest man around."

McKay had had his share of alpha-male fantasies—and a lot of other people's shares, too—and was accustomed to women being turned on by the fact that he didn't know the meaning of quiche. But this was pretty bald.

"What happens when we reach Chicago?" he asked.

She rolled onwards to face away from him and didn't answer. He admired the muscles of her back, well-developed under pink-tawny skin. The feeble light of the bedside lamp turned her all to shades of gold.

"I'll do what I have to do," she said throatily. "Don't worry about me."

That wasn't exactly what he'd meant. He was about to try asking again a different way, when he felt her hand steal back and begin playing with his cock.

"Hey!" he exclaimed. "What, do you think I'm still nineteen, or something?"

She glanced over her shoulder. "*Part* of you does," she said archly.

And she began to rub the head of his stiffening glans slowly up and down the crease between the perfect cheeks of her ass, and he forgot all about talk.

CHAPTER
EIGHTEEN

"This is never going to work, McKay," Sam Sloan sub-vocalized. As if to punctuate his words a bullet bounced off the iron skin of the M113 somewhere near his head, the impact audible even over the clatter of treads and engine grumble.

The APC driver looked back over his shoulder. "Told you boys it'd be a rough ride."

"Twenty-two long rifle," McKay said, lighting a cigar. "You call that rough?"

"It is if I make you get out and walk," the 113 jock said darkly.

"Yeah, your man Morrigan'll be real happy if you don't bring us to him just like he ordered. Likely give you a medal."

"Say, you mind not lighting that rope in here?"

McKay blew out greenish smoke. "Yeah.

"Piece of cake," he continued for the benefit of his buddies. They'd unobtrusively slipped mikes and bone phones back into place when they'd clambered into the can, away from the gimlet gaze of Whitlock, who'd squired Merith Tobias and her "maid" into an armored Lincoln limo back at the harbor. *"We changed our silhouettes. Don't look nothin' like we did on the cover of* Parade. *Except for Ivan, and nobody knows what he looks like."*

He chuckled and blew smoke at the shaved back of the driver's neck. *"Besides, we're dead. Nobody's going to identify dead men."*

The Guardians' intensive and comprehensive training regimen, carried out in Arizona beneath the single watchful eye of Major Crenna, had covered any number of skills for which the Guardians couldn't see any use — or occasionally even imagine any. Comments to that effect tended to elicit questions about how much time the commentater had pulled post-Holocaust — meaning that the program was meant to give them the best possible preparation for circumstances both unforeseen and unforeseeable, and shut up and soldier, soldier.

Even with all the various kinds of trouble they'd been in since the One-Day War, they still hadn't used all the skills Crenna had insisted they get grounded in. One of those skills was disguise. Until now, that is.

The changes in their appearance were subtle; that was one of the first principles of effective disguise, as it was so many other things: Keep It Simple, Stupid. It meant less maintenance, less chance of a flaw showing.

So McKay had darkened his hair and eyes and his beard had grown out into a Ringo Starr-Yasir Arafat stubble. Rogers's distinctive shark-gray eyes were brown now, too, and he'd acquired an army mustache. Sloan also had a mustache, and his hair had been darkened from brown to black, giving him the appearance of an Old West gunslinger that secretly gave him a charge.

Casey, on the other hand, had his blond hair shaved to an almost silvery plush—the first time, McKay reflected, studying him through the gloom of the armored personnel character, that his hair had been a decent length since they got out of training. Without his inevitable yellow Zeiss shooting glasses and rock-band baseball cap even McKay could hardly recognize him. Sitting there with his H&K assault rifle between his knees—Tobias's bodyguards hadn't been disarmed, even though they weren't privileged to ride with her—and his ears sticking out so far his Fritz seemed to rest on them, he looked like nothing so much as a frightened teenage conscript.

More bullets hit the hull, a cluster of them this time, more authoritative than before. This burst seemed to strike right behind Vesensky's head, which he'd tipped back against the green-painted metal as if taking a nap.

"Nine millimeter," he said without opening his eyes. "Uzi, by the rate of fire. These bandits don't have any antitank weapons, I trust?"

"Naw. They're just rubble runners. Scum. Street People, we call 'em. Only laws they got's what we lay on 'em." He glanced back again, smirking at his own wit as he took a corner. "Not unless you consider Molotovs serious AT."

"They can do the job."

"This Morrigan's sure done a hell of a job of pacifying his own turf," McKay said. "I thought the Loop was his backyard."

"Yeah," Sloan said. "It's never been safe to walk the streets around here, but this is ridiculous."

"Very funny. I notice he's got you Detroit bastards all running up to kiss his ass."

"Yeah," McKay growled, "and unless you'd like to kiss mine, maybe you better shut the fuck up and drive this dune buggy."

Ivan Vesensky flipped a thumb at the blunt barrel of a *Fabrique National* automatic grenade launcher poking from a sandbag emplacement next to the gate, as the M113 rattled and slowed beneath them. It was similar in concept to the Mk19 Mobile One mounted, and fired the same 40x53-mm rounds; the Europeans had finally quit futzing with rifle grenades and got with the real world.

"Nothing but the best for the Chairman's friends," he said with a grin. He spoke aloud; the fancy mikes and earphones had gone back into buttoned pockets.

A couple of blocks back the driver had given them the all clear to pop the hatches and ride up top if they wanted. McKay suspected it was more to get rid of the cigar smoke than because the area was suddenly free of snipers—and maybe the little rat-faced bastard hoped it wasn't, at that. But the small-arms hailstorm had stopped a couple of minutes back, so the Guardians climbed up into a briskly pleasant morning to get a look at their objective.

McKay looked around and nodded sourly. *Ain't gonna be an easy nut to crack,* he thought. He didn't have to say it aloud, because he knew his buddies were thinking it, too.

In the last half of the twentieth century the city was a talisman. It meant *centralization:* uniformity and control. *City planning* was a mantra for generations of social engineers.

But the herd wasn't so pliable in real life as it was in geometrically tiered city planning and sociology classrooms, where the air was processed like individually wrapped slices of plastic cheese and the sun never intruded. People began to drift from the gleaming Hive Centrals the planners envisioned, into the suburbs—even out of the Industrial Belt, at various times.

The planners went berserk. You could have seen the core-death of city as something evolutionary, something natural. But you didn't say *natural* to the Plan Minds. *Environmental impact* was a buzzword, they grasped that, and anything with *eco-* stuck in front of it. But not natural.

So they fought back. With the stick of regulation and taxation. But with the sweet, too. Because what they could pull in in taxes they could squirt out in bribes like soft ice cream, to developers, to your better class of apartment dwellers.

The Citadel was one such bribe. A complex of spiffy apartments on one side of the street, complete with offices and a small medical clinic, and an exclusive mini-mall on the other, linked by underground passages, implanted in a decayed section of the Loop like a concrete and tan stone Jarvik heart. It was designed as a bastion for the New American Class, the bureaucracy and its upper middle class satellites, including the planners themselves—even people who'd had any sense of irony cut out of them in grad school couldn't be wholly comfortable directing the rebirth of the inner city from Kenilworth ranch-styles. So they built themselves an enclave.

It was Morrigan's now. The wire perimeter made it his, and the sensor posts, and the claymores, and the machinegun nests backed with mortar pits, and the one block kill-zone that had been scraped clean of rubble and living buildings alike by FSE Expeditionary Force plows.

The limo driver said a few words to the gate guard, who snapped to and saluted Whitlock. The Lincoln crawled through. A squad of guards in identical cammies trotted out and lined up to either side of the M113.

An officer with a fresh-minted look to him stepped out. "I'm Lieutenant Hospers. I have to ask you to surrender your weapons and climb down from the vehicle."

"Our weapons?" McKay said. "No chance, junior. We're here to guard Ms. Tobias's body till we turn her over to Morrigan. That means we keep our weapons."

"You're in the Citadel now. Ms. Tobias is under our care now. And outsiders aren't permitted to carry weapons in the compound. So, if you please—"

"No way."

Hospers shrugged. It was as if the pleasant masked slipped away, showing sharp teeth. "Have it your way."

The Guardians and Vesensky found themselves looking down the barrels of twenty M16s.

McKay sighed. "If you're gonna be that way about it." He nodded. His four men lowered their H&Ks by the slings to troopies who stepped up to collect them.

McKay dropped to the ground. "Sidearms, too?" Hospers nodded.

"We get receipts for these?" Sloan asked, passing over his service-issue Beretta. His and Casey's big Magnum revolvers were considered too distinctive; Case had traded his .44 for a P7 like Vesensky's.

Hospers laughed. "M.A. may give 'em back to you when you leave. *If* you leave, that is."

McKay wheeled, threw out his chest. "Ten-*ho!*" he bellowed in his best Parris Island DI voice. "Ri'*face*. Ho'ard *harch!*" And he marched his little detachment into the compound.

The Lincoln crept along, obviously to allow them to keep pace, and so they filed into Morrigan's stronghold like a mother duck and her ugly ducklings.

"Eyes right, McKay," Sloan said out of the side of his mouth.

"Got it, Sam." McKay had spotted it the instant before, huddled behind a cement plant thing near the base of the high-rise: a 90-mm recoilless rifle emplacement. Ostensibly obsolete, in fact death on light armor, and when it fired special beehive rounds, capable of sweeping the cleared killzone of life like a giant broom.

Another was mounted atop the lowest level of the multitiered mall, likewise aimed along the street toward the gate. Odds were good others just like them were set up to bear on the entire perimeter.

"Impressive," Vesensky murmured.

"We had a setup this good," McKay said, "we would've kicked the ass off your *Cristeros* down on the Gulf—worse than we did, that is."

The limousine stopped in front of the apartment building. Several troopies in black berets bustled over, opening the door, helping Tobias and a sullen Nguyen out, snapping salutes.

A thin man in khaki pants and tan windbreaker came out of the apartment with his hands stuck in the jacket's pockets. It took Mckay a moment to recognize William Morrigan. He didn't look much older than the photo they'd seen in Okie City, but he was taller than McKay had figured.

A retinue of aides in mufti came spilling out a few steps behind the man who called himself Marcus Aurelius. McKay was aware more troopies were materializing around them. The flashes on their berets showed a mailed fist clutching a rose: Morrigan's personal insignia.

Morrigan stopped before Merith Tobias. She looked incredibly small beside him. He reached down, caught her hand, raised it to his lips.

"Welcome to my castle, dear lady," he said. He had a gift of projecting his voice so that even the wind, blowing faster here between buildings, couldn't dampen it.

Tobias raised her eyes to his. Slowly she kneeled. A moment later Nguyen followed her example, moving like a marionette whose joints were seizing.

Marcus Aurelius smiled. The crowd applauded. And a hand grabbed McKay right above the elbow.

"What's the matter with you?" a bass voice growled. "On your knees, asshole."

Without moving his eyes from Morrigan, McKay wrenched his elbow free and drove it backward with all his strength. It met resistance, sank in. Right on target in the solar plexus, if the grunt and blast of alcohol-flavored breath that washed over the left side of McKay's face was any indication.

Bolts clicked. Soldiers closed in like piranhas around an unlucky steer. From the corner of his eye McKay saw Sam and Case go pale. Vesensky stood with a half smile on his face, flexing his hands from blade to claw, ready.

A rifle butt rose. McKay felt the cord of his scrotum yank taut, gave the rifle boy a make-my-day grin. *Maybe I overplayed our hand,* he thought, *but fuck it.*

"At ease," Morrigan said. "At ease!"

His bark arrested the rifle in mid-descent. The troopers backed away from the five "Detroit" soldiers.

McKay led them to within five meters of Morrigan, stopped, and saluted. "Sergeant George Dubrowski, in command of City of Detroit security detail. You're Morrigan?"

The inverted-triangle head nodded slowly. The eyes were unreadable.

"Delivering Merith Tobias into your custody as ordered, sir. But our orders don't say one damned thing about bending the knee. Sir!"

The troopies behind them growled like a pack of feral dogs. A man in camouflage fatigues pushed forward. He had a red-blond beard and a potato nose. He was about McKay's height—hey, at least it was somebody who wasn't taller. Or he would have been McKay's height if he hadn't still been kind of hunched over his gut.

"You ain't gonna let him talk to you like this, boss?"

Morrigan smiled. "This is Major Llewellyn, my chief of security, my dear," he said to Tobias. She nodded gravely.

"Well, Sergeant—Dubrowski, is it?"

McKay nodded. He *hated* the name George.

"You have spirit. If your fellow Detroiters had half your spirit you wouldn't be in this ignominious position now. I salute you and your men."

He fired off a regulation salute, which McKay and company returned. McKay was firmly in the millions-for-defense-and-fuck-a-bunch-of-tribute camp, but even so he was thinking the folks in Detroit'd more likely have half his *brains* if they flat-out defied a man who could swat them all as if they were a fat, tired fly. Even he could see a call for subtlety sometimes. Hell, that *was* why they were in this position.

Morrigan's hand came crisply down. Past the billowing sleeve of his jacket McKay saw Llewellyn glaring at him with bloodshot blue Poland China hog eyes that promised to settle accounts ASAP. McKay swallowed a psycho laugh.

Shit, this could be fun, he thought, *if we don't fuck up and die and get the world destroyed.*

CHAPTER
NINETEEN

"Can you believe this shit?" McKay asked out of the corner of his mouth. "A *ballroom?*"

"Why not?" Sam Sloan said. He sipped his Perrier. "Ballroom dancing was all the rage when the war broke out."

"Yeah, but in an *apartment?*"

Sloan shrugged.

They were standing with their backs to a wall hung in red, white, and blue bunting, to avoid having anyone come up to eavesdrop from behind. Before them glittering couples swayed across a polished hardwood floor. A ten-piece band wheezed swing on a low dais.

McKay sipped his beer and said, "*Mad Max* was never like this."

Casey drifted over, chewing on a bagel from a spread laid out on half a hectare of gleaming white tablecloth over by the wall. "In here it's just like the war never happened, man," he remarked, waving the bagel for emphasis.

"Well, set your mind at ease," McKay said. "It happened."

"Have you spotted Dr. Carter?" asked Sloan, referring to the head of the Chicago biochem lab that was part of the Blueprint for Renewal.

"No. But, like, isn't that that Cromartie dude, hanging out with Morrigan?"

Morrigan was dressed in a midnight black uniform; pretty eye-catching, but it made him look like the American Nazi poster boy. Next to him a short oil-drum body stood balanced on spindly, slightly bowed legs, with the distinctive balding head of Dr. Cromartie stuck directly onto it without the intervention of a neck. Cromartie had a piece of cake on a napkin. He was spilling crumbs down the front of a bottle-green tuxedo and chewing with his mouth open.

"You got it, Case. What do you want to bet Doc Carter's holding up a patch of pavement somewhere?"

134

"Perhaps he's part of the cold cuts you were punishing so severely a few minutes ago," Vesensky said, approaching. "How you carnivores can bear to eat the meat of your fellow creatures is beyond me."

"Hey, I thought dudes like you did that all the time," McKay said.

"McKay," Sloan said.

"Cut the small talk." McKay pointed with his chin. "Look who's comin'."

It was Merith Tobias, playing the role that had made her a star. She wore a white gown that plunged all the way to just above her pubic hair, and clung on for dear life on the way. Her hair was done up in some kind of elaborate design, and McKay wondered if Doc Nguyen, tagging along looking demure as hell in clingy blue silk pajamas frogged in black, had quit her bitching about being forced to play serving maid long enough to reveal an unsuspected talent for hairdressing.

Morrigan turned with a skull's smile on his face, caught the hand which Tobias extended without seeming to. She wore white gloves to the elbows. He kissed her hand, letting his lips linger and his eyes rove free. Looking at her, McKay felt a twinge in his groin that was so severe that last night—and the early hours of this morning, for that matter—might never have happened.

"Don't burn your eyes, bud," a bass voice growled in McKay's ear.

He glanced around. "Major" Llewellyn hovered behind his left elbow like a big meat cloud. The Citadel security head wore a tan uniform blouse the breast of which was splashed with ribbons, some of which McKay was fairly sure Llewellyn had no right to wear and some of which he guessed Marcus Aurelius Morrigan had made up on his crazy own, unless maybe Llewellyn had served meritoriously in the army of Zambia or Mongolia or somewhere. Stranger still, he had on a kilt of some predominantly red tartan—knowing it was called a *tartan* exhausted McKay's knowledge of the subject; he had no clue as to what it might signify—and one of those hats, tam-o'-shanters he thought they were called, that looked like a plaid gland.

McKay took out a cigar, unwrapped it with provocative slowness. "I had plenty of time to look on the trip out, Jack."

"Well, don't do it no more. She's M.A.'s woman now. Absolutely off-limits."

He glared and blew the fumes of Morrigan's expensive scarfed bourbon into McKay's face. "If I thought for one minute you had the balls to've done more than look, your ass would be grass this minute."

McKay couldn't *even* think of anything to say . . . just as well. *If only you knew, asswhite. If only you* knew.

The security chief turned away. A couple of ribbons swung beside his pussy little tail of bleached-blond hair.

"Hey, is 'Llewellyn' a Scotch name, or what?" McKay asked Sloan from the side of his mouth. Not for the first time he missed the communicators which allowed them to communicate even in a crowded room without others overhearing. *We should be so lucky that this is the most I'm gonna miss 'em.*

"I don't think so," Sam said, chewing. "And they like to be called 'Scots.' "

"Who gives dick what they like? I'm just thinking what people always say they got under them kilts. *Nothing.*" He pitched his voice loud enough so the Citadel officer *might* have heard. But Llewellyn, striding away through the mob, gave no sign.

"That's not exactly what they say," Vesensky said thoughtfully. "And besides, it's not true. I can attest to that."

"Jesus, you're disgusting."

"Sergeant Dubrowski?"

McKay turned. A flunkie stood there next to him, with flunkie molded in every contour line of his black face and every line stitched into his uniform, having arrived as quietly as only a flunkie could. Sometimes McKay wished he could catch a whole bunch of these dudes, turn them over to Tommy Rogers to whip into one mother of an infiltration force. No one would *ever* know they were there.

He lit his cigar. "Yeah? What can I do for you, junior?"

Irritation did not disrupt the flunkie smoothness. It doesn't.

"Colonel Morrigan would like to speak with you in private, Sergeant."

McKay looked around. Merith Tobias stood by the buffet, looking fifteen and radiant and somehow innocent in that fundamentally indecent outfit. Her eyes met his; he gave her a grin, but her gaze swept on like a searchlight that had missed him, though he knew she had to have seen. *Oh, well, she got to play her role.*

Nguyen hung back doing an acceptable imitation of Kato. Magnus Cromartie was rooting through the spread like a hog looking for half a Mars bar in a garbage bag, but the big man himself was nowhere to be seen.

"And you're supposed to take me to him?" The flunkie nodded. "Do that thing."

The walls of Morrigan's office were paneled in a dark oaklike veneer—might even have been oak. They were hung with an assortment of hand-colored prints of old-time military costume, Guards and Hussars and Uhlans and people like that. Standing at attention, McKay ran his eyes across them with a certain amount of interest. When he was a kid, he used to love to look at pictures of soldiers in their funny old uniforms. Only thing he liked more was pictures of naked ladies.

Come to think of it, maybe he hadn't changed that much. Though his primary reaction at looking at some of the prints was to be glad he didn't have to fight standing fifty meters from the enemy with a wig crammed over his ears, a bright red jacket, and big white belts crossed right over the aim-point to put you away for good.

"I admired your display of spirit this afternoon, Sergeant," Morrigan said, studying the way a curl of cigarette smoke broke up into turbulence. "Spirit is the most valuable attribute in a fighting man, after discipline."

He looked up with his head tipped to one side. It made him look boyish in a way McKay hadn't expected. "I'm looking for men with spirit. It's a rare commodity. I'd like you and your men to join me."

Whoa, baby, McKay thought. *Is this a setup? Has this psycho puke made us?*

It was almost too perfect. The plan had mainly been to get them inside and wing it from there. Morrigan was known to be recruiting mercenaries, heavily, had been for weeks. The hope had been that he'd pitch to the disguised Guardians—but still, to have it come this baldly, this cut and dried—

"I appreciate the offer, sir," he said, keeping his eyes locked with the redcoat he'd been looking at earlier. The Limey looked worried, as if maybe he figured there might be a Yankee farmer drawing down on him from behind a rock wall, somewhere out of sight.

McKay sensed Morrigan's frown. Marcus Aurelius wasn't a man who was used to anything but instant obedience. "It's a chance to go with a winner," he said, with just a dash of acid.

McKay was no actor. He knew this. So he'd worked it out in advance: the only way to play was to Billy McKay it.

"I think you forgot to mention something earlier, sir. There was discipline and spirit. But there's also loyalty, sir."

"You're a mercenary, aren't you? I'm prepared to offer generous terms."

"Even to a man who'd switch sides the first time somebody offered him a bribe? Sir?" He was pushing it, he knew; sweat ran down the back of his neck into the collar of a uniform blouse that was still too stiff and new. The problem with this gig was, he'd never been that great dealing with superior officers in real life.

Morrigan laughed. "Touché. You pass the test, Sergeant. With flying colors." He leaned forward and knit his fingers together on the old-fashioned green blotter paper. "But tell me, just how far does your loyalty to the self-styled Motor City Madman extend? He rolled over and played dead, man. He even sent me his woman, for God's sake."

Morrigan lit another cigarette. "Is that any place for a man like you? Serving a man like that?"

McKay shifted his weight from boot to boot, feeling as uncomfortable as the role demanded for entirely different reasons. *I shoulda set things up so Sam pretended to be the foreman. He's the one who can handle this shit.*

"The Madman trusted us with a real important mission."

"Which you discharged fully and well. How much further does duty go?"

McKay licked his lips. "Well, I heard you talking earlier when you mentioned going with a winner. But I got to, uh, got to talk to the men."

"Certainly. The Madman said he was sending five of his best, and I can surely make room for you all."

Morrigan gazed past McKay at the wall. "And don't worry about what your former employer will think. If he'll give up Merith Tobias, he'll never give you boys a second thought."

He should have expected it by now. There were worse life-patterns to fall into, but sometimes even a hard-core hero needed his sleep.

She was short, maybe five foot nothing, so full-bodied that she might have been five, six inches taller, and then compressed. Not saggy or cellulite pocked, but voluptuous to the max. Immense knockers, swaying inside a sheer blue chiffon negligee as she shut the door of the upper-floor apartment he had to himself. Her aureoles were broad and dark, her pubic hair a trim, prim wedge and darker still.

McKay dialed down the table lamp beside his bed, which he'd punched on once he'd seen her silhouette against the light from the corridor outside. It was a good thing he'd been right about the two A.M. intrusion; he hadn't even bothered to go for his .45.

She walked toward the bed, swinging her wide hips. She had full lips and a fleshy nose with a mole beside it. She was the sort you expected to see attached to the arm of a banana republic dictator. Attractive in a coarse kind of way. Not Billy McKay's type.

Of course, she *would* have been if Merith Tobias hadn't damned near sucked the marrow from his bones the night before.

She slid onto the bed with him, smooth as oil. "I'm Imelda."

"You would be."

"I beg your pardon?"

"Never mind." His eyes kept being drawn to her huge breasts, which wasn't surprising since she was sticking them in his face. "Old Marcus Aurelius believes in old-fashioned hospitality, huh?"

She dropped her eyes. "The colonel is a great man."

"Yeah, uh. Hell of a guy." He was shifting around under the covers. She had a clean fresh-soaped smell to her. Her skin looked surprisingly smooth. And maybe he was more of an iron man than he'd thought.

"Do you not like me?" He noticed the dark smudges beneath heavily outlined black-almond eyes. "I can have someone else sent up from the harem if I am not to your taste."

"From the *harem?*"

"Of course. Marcus Aurelius maintains a talent pool to service his officers and honored guests."

"And you go for that shit?" He was surprised at being so shocked. He thought he was the last real male chauvinist in America.

She shrugged. "It's a fairly easy life. We have privileges, not like the laborers. And it's better than being given to Dr. Cromartie." She shivered. It caused interesting chaotic events a few centimeters from McKay's flaring nostrils.

Imelda flipped down the sheet and ran her hand down McKay's chest and muscle ridged belly. "And sometimes," she purred, "the job's a lot of fun."

• • •

Later he lay on his back, staring up at the gray oblong of the ceiling and figuring that if they ever got Project Blueprint all put back together he could maybe rent out his services as a stud. You wouldn't get shot at so much, and it *had* to pay better than being a Guardian.

Imelda lay curled up next to him like a kitten. He couldn't tell if she was asleep or awake, as he usually could. He guessed that might be a useful talent on her part.

He sighed. *Back to work.*

"You awake?" he asked.

Even as he spoke her eyes opened. For a not terrifically pretty woman she had great eyes. He was in a frame of mind to notice that now. She nodded.

"You said something about not wanting to be given to Dr. Cromartie. What the hell does he do with women? Torture 'em?"

He meant is as a joke, but she nodded. "But only sometimes, and only for play—you know, velvet whips and that sort of thing. Mostly we don't want to go to him because he and his technicians are pretty creepy. Especially him. And kinky, you know? And if you don't like to play he experiments with you."

" 'Experiments?' "

She swallowed. "That's right. Injects you with some kind of virus, makes you breathe some chemical. It's how M.A. executes criminals, too."

Great guy, McKay started to say. Then it occurred to him the room had to be bugged; Imelda probably wasn't going to say anything his prospective employer didn't want him to hear.

She rose from the bed and walked to the bathroom. "I feel like a shower. Care to join me?" She struck a provocative pose in the doorway.

He really *was* too worn out by now. "No, thanks, I—"

The words ran down the drain of reality. He caught the look in her eye. "Uh, yeah, I guess I'm feelin' a little grimy, too. Exercise does that to you."

She made him soap her first. Damn it, he started to get hard again. This was almost beginning to worry him.

She stood with her face held up to the shower—quite a luxury in the post-Holocaust world—for a long moment before turning to him.

"That little Chinese girl you brought with you," she said huskily. "Merith's maid. Gorgeous but real uptight."

"I know the one," he said.

"Shh." She held a finger to his lips. He grimaced. M.A. probably had filters that could take the shower's white-noise right off a tape, but he didn't see much point to mention the fact if she was in the mood to play I've Got a Secret.

"Cromartie wants her," she whsipered. "He's got, like, the ultimate hots for her."

"Shit." Suzette Nguyen wasn't high on his list of favorite people, but at least for this mission she was one of the good guys—she was part of his *team*. And he didn't like the thought of one of his buddies chained to some wall while a neckless wonder played worm-in-the-apple with her taut little fanny. "How do you know this?"

She shrugged again. It was really a fascinating process. "Harem talk. You know how word gets around."

"Yeah. Well, we got to do something."

"There's nothing you can do. Cromartie always gets his way. M.A. is . . . he finds him useful."

McKay had the distinct impression she was about to say Morrigan was afraid of the scientist. But about then she hopped up, wrapped strong wet-slick legs around his waist, and bit him on the base of the throat, and he decided to worry about Doc Nguyen in the morning.

CHAPTER
TWENTY ─────────────

He spent the night wondering if his comrades were getting similar treatment, among other things.

At breakfast in the coffee shop down in the lower reaches of the Citadel he studied their faces. Tom was the Great Stone face, per usual. Case was his happy-go-lucky mellow self—in his own goofy SoCal way he was every bit as inscrutable as Rogers.

But Sam Sloan, on the other hand, looked ever so slightly guilty. *Bingo,* McKay thought. Sloan was just the sort to look guilty over getting his ashes hauled, especially as a gesture of hospitality. Some kind of hang-up about using women.

"Have a good sleep last night, Commander?" he rasped around a throatful of coffee hot enough to sear and strong enough to make the dead do the pogo. It was the only thing that was keeping his bones rigid. *Nothing* could keep parts of him that way.

Sam blushed. Tom and Casey looked out the floor-to-ceiling windows at the troops drilling on the street between the apartment and the junior-grade mall.

McKay finished his eggs. Real eggs, not freeze-dried puke: they hadn't seen any chickens in the compound itself, but it seemed some of the squatters and rubble-runners under Morrigan's heel sent them in as tribute. He pushed back from the table.

Vesensky was just walking up with a cup of Red Zinger tea in one hand and a bitten apple in the other. McKay didn't want to know what he'd done last night—though he guessed Vesensky wouldn't be too eager to let M.A. know about his sexual proclivities. Morrigan seemed like an old-fashioned guy in a lot of ways.

"That your whole breakfast?" McKay asked the Soviet.

"Of course. I don't like to weigh myself down to start the day."

"Well, that's good, 'cause we're all goin' for a little walk. Right now."

"You should have wrung his scrawny neck when you had a

142

chance," Sam Sloan hissed, with a viciousness McKay had never heard out of him before.

"Hey, hey, I thought you were a peaceful, love your neighbor sort of guy."

"That's Casey. The son of a *bitch.*" The latter didn't mean Case. Sam was not taking the news of Nguyen's impending fate calmly.

"Well, I thought about it. But if he's got containers of the virus hidden all over like he claims in his broadcasts, just killing him won't help. He just may have followers nuts enough to release the shit to avenge their fallen leader."

They were walking near the perimeter wire, trying to keep the troopies at PT between them and the buildings, keeping an eye out for the shotgun shape of a directional mike pointed their way. It was a horribly insecure form of commo, but there was no question Morrigan's techs would spot the signals if they tried to use their communicators inside the compound.

"Then what are we going to do?" Casey asked

"About Nguyen or saving the world?" McKay asked.

"Ms. Tobias can talk to Morrigan," Sam said eagerly. "She can intercede for Suzette. Refuse to give up her maid."

"Yeah. That might work. But maybe we need to talk about saving the world right now—"

The loudspeaker set on a post ten meters from them burped into life. "—attention, please. Your attention please. The Maximum Leader is about to address the nation. You will be responsible for this broadcast. That is all."

" 'Maximum Leader?' " McKay echoed. "I thought that was fuckin' Stalin."

"Why not, man?" Casey asked. "Hitler's out. Stalin won. Why not use him, for, like, a role model, if you want to be a dictator."

The others stared at him. It was the first time anyone had ever heard him utter a political opinion of any sort. Possibly since he was born.

"Once more, the Georgians lead the way," Vesensky murmured.

"People of America," Morrigan's voice said over their heads, "listen to me. Many of your leaders are heeding the voice of reason. In the last few days I have received the submission of the city of Cleveland, and yesterday afternoon emissaries arrived from

Detroit bringing word that the Motor City Madman has acknowledged my authority; as a reward he will rule the eastern Great
Lakes region as my satrap. I am not an ungenerous man.

"But the self-proclaimed president of the United States, Jeffrey
MacGregor, has refused to concede my authority. He has not
responded in any way, except to dispatch an elite team of assassins,
who were hunted down and crushed by the alert and patriotic
citizens of Cleveland."

"Oh, yeah," Billy McKay said with a smirk. "Tell it, baby."

"My patience is growing thin. Resistance of any sort is unaccept-
able. I now present this ultimatum to Mr. MacGregor: submit to
me, or those areas of the former United States that lie outside my
immediate control will be sterilized of all human life forty-eight
hours from this moment.

"The choice belongs to you, Jeffrey MacGregor. You can grace-
fully accept the inevitable. Or you can be responsible for genocide.
That is all."

"That son of a bitch!" McKay exclaimed. "I should have
wrung his scrawny neck when I had the chance."

The hammer was clearly coming down. Only thing to do now
was accept Morrigan's offer and hope for the best.

How the hell much good can we do in forty-eight hours? McKay
wondered, trudging up a back set of stairs in the apartment, smelling old paint and dust. *Show him what a stud I am so he'll fire
Llewellyn and make me his head honcho? Big fucking chance.*

Maybe, he reflected grimly, it's a good thing he's offered us a
job. Give us something to do after the surrender.

—Because President Jeff was going to give in. Not even Billy
McKay could suggest a way to fight a superinfectious, ultimately
lethal disease. Not that he would have given in himself, no way.
But McGregor wasn't him.

Of course, Jeff could make a show of giving in, while the
Guardians kept boring from within. Then when—if—they found
a way to pop M.A. and neutralize his bug, the president could say
I said I gave in, but whaddaya know? I had my fingers crossed.
Right.

He could practically hear what Major Crenna would say, in a
voice rough as a bad back road but in no other way like William
Morrigan's: *It's okay to lie to terrorists in a hostage situation—for
anybody but the president. He's got to keep his integrity intact,
or looking that way, anyway. Giving in's a sign of weakness, and*

then if he tried to take it back later he'd just look like a cheap crook as well as a weak one. You've got to stop this bastard now.

"—got to stop him *now.*" The words were practically ringing in McKay's ears when he turned a corner and saw Merith Tobias sitting at the next landing, smoking a cigarette.

Her hair hung in her face. She looked older than he'd seen her look before, but so beautiful it made his whole chest cavity ache. She gave him a distant smile.

"M.A. doesn't approve of women smoking. These stairs seem the socially accepted way of grabbing a little *sub-rosa* privacy. So here I am."

McKay nodded. He bent down to kiss her.

She turned her face away, took it on one smooth cheek. Her body language repelled him like the magnetic field that lifted an experimental train.

"Hey," he burst out, "what's the matter? I thought we were—"

"Were," she said. "I'm Morrigan's woman now. What went before—" She blew smoke.

"Morrigan's?"

"He's the strongest. He even has the president at his mercy." She shook her head. "And not even you can do anything about it, Billy McKay."

I'll do what I have to, she'd said, back on the ship. *Don't worry about me.* He hadn't really known what she meant by that until now.

Or maybe he had, all along. Just hadn't admitted it to himself.

He thrust past her, driving hard up the stairs. It was that or break her neck.

"You want me to do *what?*" Suzette Nguyen demanded. The anger was like a cold dead thing inside her.

"You must go with him," Vesensky said in French as flawless as his English. A little additional security; if they were overheard despite his precautions most people wouldn't understand a word anyway, and if anyone heard him speaking that language they'd assume he was a Canuck and think nothing of it. "It's our only chance to get someone into that lab. We haven't much time."

"What's your hurry?" she demanded bitterly. "Why do you care if the American president is humiliated?"

Vesensky's eyes glittered like chips of jade in the merciless light of the fluorescents in the pantry of the more modest of the two restaurants in the apartment's complex's lower floors. "No more than you. But don't you understand, you little fool? This madman Morrigan has the virus dispersed all over North America, or so he claims. How long till there's an accidental release? And if there is, who knows if it will be so conveniently self-limiting as the outbreak in Cleveland? Do you want to take that chance?''

The outbreak in Cleveland—it tugged at her mind; it still bothered her. But at the moment all she could think of were the little greenish encrustations between Magnus Cromartie's teeth, the dirt-speckled pallor of his skin, his hands as cold as frog's feet.

"I can't," she moaned.

He gripped her biceps. His fingers dug in like an eagle's talons, until she winced from the pain. "Think of the lives at stake, you selfish little bitch."

"What do you care about lives? *Killer.*"

He slapped her.

"Have you forgotten that you're under discipline? If you've forgotten your duty as a physician, to humanity, I'd suggest you don't similarly overlook the duty you owe Chairman Maximov."

She sagged in his grasp, hating herself for her weakness. He was right, that she should not think of herself. But what he was asking—

A rap at the door, small and furtive. A moment later it opened. A head stuck in, with short, curly red hair, snubbed, freckle-dusted nose.

"Somebody's coming. You better get out of here."

Vesensky nodded. He released Nguyen and walked away from her, out of the pantry without saying a further word.

The redheaded girl from the seraglio gave him a conspiratorial grin as he passed. She'd arranged the meet with Nguyen, but she'd had a price. His gymnast's body had been very much to her taste.

The sacrifices I make for the Cause, he thought sardonically. *Ah, well. Fortunately she's got a boyish look to her, and if you turn her over . . .*

Nguyen slumped back against a shelf of scarfed institutional-sized cans of food. She glared after Vesensky as if her hatred would burn holes in his back. She would do what he ordered; she had no choice, on any level.

But for the first time in her life she knew what it was like to want to kill a man.

CHAPTER
TWENTY-ONE

A bullet cracked over McKay's head, hit beige brick, and screamed away like a banshee. He hugged rubble behind his beefy black H&K and wished he had his trusty M60 for this little outing.

A couple of hundred meters away the Sears Tower looked like nothing he'd seen this side of nightmare. An airburst had cracked the giant structure off clean, a couple of stories from its base. A long, narrow, red-black slab, it lay with its distant tip partially blocking the Chicago River.

Another bullet ricocheted too close for comfort. McKay squinted through haze compounded by dust and gunsmoke. There—atop a three-story building with an ancient Coke ad faded to hieroglyphics on the side of it, huddling in the lee of a tattered billboard urging voters to say Yes to Proposition 7, as if it mattered now. A face, smeared with diagonal swathes of green and purple paint, peering down the barrel of an M16 from amidst a tangle of matted hair.

The H&K had terrible battle sights for such a high-tech rifle, and McKay hated its too-sharp recoil, but he lined up on the face and squeezed the trigger and ate the recoil. The head jerked, and a quick dark cloud seemed to puff out behind, and then the face was gone. Good to know his Expert Rifleman rating hadn't gone all the way to seed.

A knot of men ran past to the left, bent low as they dodged through the tendrils of smoke grenades. McKay heard a weight come down beside him, glanced back to see Tom Rogers lying there with the Benelli riot shotgun he'd brought from Detroit. For the moment they'd been allowed to keep the gear they'd brought with them from Detroit. The name MOON was stenciled on the breast of Tom's cammies.

McKay gave him a sour grin and a thumbs-up; Rogers nodded.

McKay turned his eyes back to the fallen tower. It fascinated him in a weird way. He could see movement now, among the tangle of pipes and twisted members on the cliff-face the base of the fallen part had become. An extended family of what Morrigan's boys called the Street People had nested in the ruined building, turning it into a hive a third of a kilometer long.

"Good thing they sent us after this bunch," McKay said. "It'd rankle ass to have to mix it up with some of your old Resistance buddies."

Rogers nodded. The Sears Tower nesters were stone-crazy, truly vicious; the survivors and street gangs Tom had helped train had fought them as enthusiastically as they did the Effsee invaders. On the way in their squad had found broken bodies hanging from awning frames, human bones Rogers said had been chewed by human teeth. If they had to fight alongside Morrigan's goons to prove their worth—and they did—this was sure the best bunch they could have picked to mix it up with.

Glad something's going right, McKay thought.

Morrigan had sworn them in himself, then given them a lecture on Discipline. His heart had obviously not been in it; he'd chain-smoked and stared off into space a lot. Maybe he was preoccupied by the approach of his own deadline.

Or maybe he just can't wait to get back to his hot-pants little bitch, McKay had thought.

Once sworn to serve Marcus Aurelius unto death—oh, yeah, and didn't they plan to do just that thing?—they got split up and divvied among various details for evaluation. Morrigan had sized McKay and Rogers up as the two hard-core grunts—which actually gave McKay an ounce or two of respect for him—so they got sent off with this expedition to the west side of the Loop.

Neither McKay nor Rogers had too much idea what they were supposed to be accomplishing here, other than running around and shooting people. One of the men in the squad they were provisionally assigned to said it was a habit of Morrigan's, to send probes here and there to shoot people and find out what was going on around the domain.

McKay was along as a sort of excess-baggage noncom in a short but very pressed-and-polished platoon that was covering the two actually carrying out the attack. It seemed like a strange way to break in new men who had been pitched so heavily by the Man Himself. Maybe they were simply a couple more trophies to score off the hapless Motor City Madman, uninteresting once they were won. He wondered if a similar fate awaited Merith Tobias.

Somehow he doubted it.

The firing ahead rose to a crescendo. McKay squinted through smoke and dust and almost-hot morning sun, but couldn't see much but running figures and yellow muzzle flashes stabbing through the bright haze. He felt weird, dissociated, out of touch.

Battles are always confused. Official histories are usually pretty well made up after the fact, generally by the victor. No one *really* knows what's going on; you can only see so much at once, and that's usually smoke and dust and spasms of confused motion, people running, dodging, falling down—and, as a general thing just when it all gets most interesting, is when you need to seek the low, hidden places to keep from eating a chunk of Hot Metal Death.

Battles are confused for everybody, but they're especially confused for the simple squaddie who has at best the sketchiest knowledge of what is even supposed to be happening. This was McKay's first firefight as a grunt in so long a time it made him wince to think about it.

He missed his buddies, and the neato-keeno pocket communicators that welded them into a single smoothly functioning unit. The Guardians' fights were different from other battles. They were usually in constant touch, fighting a more numerous enemy—which generally had the effect that they knew where the bad guys were better than the enemy knew where they were. They had the initiative to strike where and when they would, or to withdraw if they had to. They had *control*. A battle was still a confused kaleidoscopic adrenaline rush, but you had a line, something to cling to.

Without his comrades' voices in his ears, McKay felt like an amputee.

The platoon was straw-bossed by a lieutenant with a flattop like a slab of blond cement that he must have been proud of, since he didn't wear a Fritz or any kind of cover. He came forward, standing beside the gutted corpse of a Wells-Fargo truck, chewing gum and peering along the street with a pair of field glasses, trying to make some sense out of the magnified confusion ahead.

There was a bass *thrum* and a wet but hard sound, like a watermelon falling on a wooden floor. The lieutenant turned half around, his blue eyes glazing into incurious marbles, blood drooling from his mouth.

There was a meter-long chunk of rebar stuck through his chest. It went in just under his left collarbone and came out somewhere near his right-hand kidneys. A troopie standing behind the long-dead armored car dropped his rifle and began to scream as the lieutenant's legs gave way and he went to the pavement in two thudding impacts, first knees, then face.

"Heroes," McKay grunted as he did a sideways jackknife in the gritty rubble, doubling like a worm to track his hefty rifle left. A weird kind of giant crossbow made from what looked like automotive springs was teetering on the parapet of a four-story brownstone across the street. A couple of scrubs dressed in shredded tweed sports coats were frantically trying to cock the beast, tearing their fingers bloody on its steel-cable string.

McKay flicked the selector switch from Single Shot to Rock 'n' Roll and gave them a quick burst. It was all you could do; even if you were as big and strong as Billy McKay your fire pattern went quickly to hell with one of these mothers. There was no such thing as a truly controllable fully automatic 7.62 rifle.

If he'd had his Maremont, now, he could have greased them with one burst, no sweat. As it was he caught one somewhere high and right and spun him back out of sight and clean missed the other, Expert or not. However, the crossbow went on over and cartwheeled down to the asphalt, and the second nester hung halfway over the parapet to make a grab for it, like a jerk. McKay planted one spang in the middle of his forehead and felt much better.

From behind his boonie hat McKay heard a sliding rush of shoe soles on rubble. Rogers came up to one knee as a figure wrapped in rags soaked in brown stiffness that could only be dried blood and waving a fire axe came charging out of the stairwell which, with the block back wall, was all that was left standing of the building whose rubble they were lying in. The first charge of double-ought buck hit him in a fist-sized wad in the right side of his rib cage, freshening up the blood impregnating his clothes and driving him down to one knee. A second charge scooped off the right upper side of his face like a jumbo dip of Baskin Robbins.

Suddenly they were popping out all over everywhere, pouring like streams of puke from doorways and low windows, crawling up out of manholes, for Christ's sake: nesters, festering, stinking, and mad as Dobermans with their nuts caught in a sliding glass door. "Shit," a soldier with a quick hand on the obvious screamed, "they've flanked us! They're everywhere!"

He jumped off the sidewalk in front of a TV repair shop long cleaned out of anything but a few uninhabited console cabinets with the plastic woodlike veneer peeling off in stiff sheets and started running. A ragged figure stepped out of the repair shop's door, took aim with a snubby revolver held in two fingerless-glove encased hands, and opened fire. The nester bent his elbows at every shot, letting the pistol ride clear up to vertical, far more than the .38 recoil called for. He nailed the troopie between the shoulder blades on his fourth shot anyway, and then Billy McKay knocked him through the gape of the glassless window with another short burst.

The nesters had infiltrated through the sewers and storm drains and were jumping all over the support platoon. The Lieutenant on a Stick wasn't much help, and no noncoms were to be seen. Looked bad for the visiting team.

The old sergeant in McKay kicked in. "Masks," he bellowed, rising to a crouch and pulling a CS can from his web gear. "Masks *on,* goddammit!"

Morrigan's troopies didn't look near so strak when the shit started to fly and the creases started to come out of their cammie fatigues, but McKay hadn't been a Dreaded Parris Island Drill Instructor for nothing. They *listenend* to him.

Letting his H&K91 hang from its sling, McKay pulled the pin on a tear-gas canister and threw it at the ground right at the feet of a charging pack of nesters. They squealed and shied away from it, fearing one of the exploding kind of grenade.

The beauty of CS was that, while it wasn't as likely to mess a body up near as permanently as a frag grenade, it had the capacity to mess a lot of people up *enough,* which in a firefight was what counted. Like most combat grunts, McKay had learned from brute experience that frag grenades weren't anything like the vest-pocket nukes they showed in the movies, that would send baddies flying out of huge clouds of smoke like a berserk popcorn machine.

Morrigan's obsession for discipline was meanwhile paying off. He insisted his troopies carry gas-mask containers, with gas masks inside them, and awful punishment for defaulters. The twenty or so men within sound of McKay's voice were fumbling their masks on, turning themselves into ungainly goggle-eyed alien figures as the cans began to pop and twine thick white smoke around them.

McKay took his H&K up and hosed quick bursts into the nesters who'd spilled out of the surrounding buildings. They were just freaking out, weeping and wailing and batting their hands at the gas tentacles grabbing at them like a fifties movie monster. Nothing like blowing up the world to induce a good case of paranoia; they thought it was some Awful Nerve Gas, and barely even worried that they were getting ripped to shit by bullets.

And shotgun blasts, as Rogers tossed off a couple of his own grenades and added his Benelli to McKay's 91. They stood there and ripped the nesters with tears streaming down the sides of their bare faces.

The mysterious tide of morale had turned. The platoon pulled back together like a film strip of a car exploding rolled in reverse. By the time the troopies from the two units that had pushed ahead to the tower came straggling back, their route home was secure again, held by masked soldiers and the sprawled grotesque corpses of forty or fifty nesters.

They came for him in the shower.

Unlike his buddies, who got moved into more modest apartments that they had to split two and two, as a noncom Billy McKay rated an apartment to himself, even if it was on a lower floor than the one he'd had his first night and smaller. Space wasn't at much of a premium even though the Citadel had several hundred residents.

Along with rank came hot-water privileges. How-water meters were starting to be common features in big-city apartment complexes even before the One-Day War, to make sure the denizens weren't consuming more energy than the government wanted them to. McKay set the timer function of his wristwatch to beep when his allotted time was up; no point in gratuitously pissing off his employers before it was time to blow them up.

—Right. *A day and a half to go,* he told himself as he soaped his hairy armpits, *and we're still spinnin' our wheels.* They just had no clue what they were going to do to stop Morrigan. The straightforward approach was out, and there wasn't time for subtlety. McKay wasn't sure what the hell was left.

There was no way to tell how long they'd pounded on the door before he heard them over the rush of hot water. Cursing, he punched off the stream; his allotment was almost up, and here he didn't have all the soap off him yet. He grabbed a towel, wrapped it around his waist, and marched into the living room.

Uniformed men armed with Uzis were crowded between bare walls lined with good if sterile-looking scarfed furniture. McKay scowled. "What the fuck is going on here?"

His first thought was that it was a railroad job; when his platoon had returned to the Citadel the regular segment had announced his intention to bitch him off to Morrigan, claiming he'd exceeded his authority. Since the man had been awaiting them on arrival—substantiating the claim of several squaddies that he'd booked when the nesters attacked—McKay hadn't been too worried.

So great. Bullshit barracks politics are gonna fuck me up. What else can go wrong?

Then he saw Major Llewellyn himself, bearded and surly, helping himself to one of McKay cigars, and saw the trim athletic form standing behind him, and knew at once things could go wrong he'd never even *thought* about.

The Citadel security chief took his time lighting the cigar. "Nice try," he said, puffing blue smoke. "But it didn't wash, McKay."

CHAPTER
TWENTY-TWO

A fist thudded against the side of McKay's head. It was a very large fist, powered by a very large arm.

McKay barely felt it. His brain seemed to be packed in those little plastic intestine things they used to ship stereo parts in.

Colonel Ivan Vesensky, former operative of the KGB and current traitor, shook his neat narrow head. "Such technique. You'll jar any information they have out of their minds before you get it out of their mouths, that way."

Major Llewellyn stood massaging one hamhock fist, smearing blood over the knuckle he'd cut on the edge of McKay's tooth. "You were part of this little setup, Russki. Why don't *you* tell us the details?"

The trim head shook again. McKay fuzzily regretted not being able to break it open, back in the living room of the apartment that had briefly been his. At that moment it hadn't mattered one damned bit what kind of kung-fooey master the Russian was, if McKay caught him he was going to be prime USDA hamburger and no two ways about it.

Unfortunately, one of Llewellyn's goons had kicked him in the nuts when he went for Vesensky, and even if you're Billy McKay that takes the wind out of your sails, and then Llewellyn, grinning like a big bearded jack-o'-lantern, had pulled his head up and back by the ear and rammed his fist into it, and all the lights had gone out.

They were back on now, but they kind of flickered, and McKay still wasn't too sure anybody was home. He glanced at Casey Wilson, tied in a chair facing him with his sharp chin sunk to an olive drab undershirt covered with brown mottled bloodstains. He wasn't looking too good, either.

At least Tom and Sam had gotten away somehow. Or maybe not. Maybe they were both dead. He thought he'd heard their captors saying something about that, but maybe it was a dream. He couldn't tell. His thoughts kept sliding away like mercury from a fingertip. Couldn't pin 'em down. . . .

Concussion? he wondered muzzily. He knew getting hit on the head wasn't like the movies, where you just neatly went out and came back some scriptwriter-convenient interval later rubbing the back of your neck and going *Where am I?* It was heavy-duty shit. You might wake up with half your marbles. You might not wake up at all. Your cranium might be filling right this second with blood, pressure building until your brain just imploded. . . .

Which would be better than having to live much longer with the flat certainty of failure. McKay was cheering up a little when Vesensky spoke.

"I only know part of them," he said smoothly, in that plastic-laminated Midlantic accent of his. "I know what was discussed between the president and my former master Chairman Maximov. But I didn't take part in the planning session with the Motor City Madman . . ."

Lying shit, McKay thought. *Lying renegade shit.* It was some consolation that he'd turned his coat for Maximov, too. Good to think of Chairman Max getting hosed by his best boy.

". . . and I still don't know the details of the Canadian connection. And that's what Colonel Morrigan is most interested in—not how long it takes you to tenderize the prisoners' brains with those fists of yours."

Llewellyn growled something. McKay didn't catch it. Sound was pulsing in and out of focus like a movie when they fiddled with the length of the lens.

Canadian connection? Canada? What the fuck, over? Was this fucking faggot Russian spy giving the weenie to his new bosses, too?

He raised his head, prying open puffed blood-glued lips, trying to talk, trying to blow Vesensky's little game for him. He owed the cocksucker that much.

But the words wouldn't come. They were bubbling like boiling lava inside him, but somehow he couldn't make them come out.

"However," Vesensky said, moving around behind McKay and putting his hands on his shoulders, "I think you'll find that the drugs have taken effect now, so if you'll just refrain from battering our prisoners into unconsciousness, perhaps we'll learn what we need to know."

Drugs, McKay thought. *Fucked again.* Torture you could stand. But drugs . . . sooner or later they'd hit on a combo that would peel you right open.

And wouldn't Vesensky be the one to know it?

From behind McKay the Soviet began to speak. His voice was low, almost soothing. And now McKay found his mouth worked fine, and the answers were coming out of him, slowly but surely. He wondered at what he was saying—*hey! That ain't right!*—but it wasn't worth it, nothing was worth it, and he subsided gradually into a roaring grayness shot with red where his own words played like a tape recorder in a dream.

"I told them everything," Merith Tobias said.

McKay moaned and shook his head. It felt as if it might come off.

"What time is it?" he asked.

"A little after ten. At night."

He shifted. He was lying on a sofa in what seemed to be be an efficiency apartment. His wrists were secured behind him—nylon passive restraints, by the feel. He wasn't going to be cleverly working free and taking Morrigan's new squeeze hostage any time soon.

With a grunt he sat up. His head and gut contrarotated.

"Is it still today?" he asked, squeezing his eyes shut and opening them again. It didn't help.

It was a pretty obscure question, but she read him. "Yes. William's deadline isn't until day after tomorrow at dawn."

"William, huh?" He looked around, trying to spot monitoring devices. He didn't see anything. They were there; just no reason they should be obvious enough for him to spot them. Especially in his current state.

"So does my man William know what kind of loyalty you got? Pretty elastic." He fastened a bloodshot glare to her face. Care made it haggard. It still was as beautiful as any face he'd ever seen. "You just couldn't even wait to sell us out."

"B-but I didn't." Her eyes filled with tears. Well, she was an actress, after all. Hadn't even been that bad, though the critics, of course, saw nothing but a pretty face and body and automatically assumed *no talent*.

"Bullshit."

"It's true. I heard you'd been discovered, arrested. You know how word gets around. And I—I knew Major Llewellyn had it in for you."

"*That's* why you sold us out?" There was an itching ache at the back of his head that told him somebody'd hit him there with something hard. He longed to rub it, and wondered if this conversation would make any more sense if he hadn't been sapped and doped to the follicles.

She held her hands up in front of her as if offering him a washcloth. She looked just like Captain Kirk overemoting in the final scene of a *Star Trek* episode. Third season.

"I didn't sell you out. I . . . I couldn't stand the thought of them hurting you. I knew Llewellyn would torture you, knew he was just looking for an excuse, after the way you showed him up yesterday. Especially after you came back from the tower, and Bill was bragging about what terrific new soldiers you were, how men like you could rise fast. Llewellyn's a crazy man, he's jealous."

Tears and words were pouring out of her now. "Hey, hey. Calm down, calm down now. It's okay. Everything'll be fine."

It was a lie; things *weren't* okay. And things didn't look to be fine ever again, not for the Guardians, not for America—not for the whole damned entire *world*, now that Vesensky had jumped ship. But for some reason his urge to hurt her was all gone, evaporated. What he mostly felt now was embarrassed. The way he'd always figured he'd be if he could see people crying at his own funeral. Come to think of it . . .

"Now, just let me get this straight," he said. "You didn't want them to hurt us? I thought you were on Morrigan's side now."

She looked past him. Her fingers were knotted in front of her right cheek. "I'm his woman. I have to be. That's the way I am. But you're my friends. You and Casey and Sam and Tom. Even Ivan."

"Huh." McKay lay back down. It didn't ease the dizziness much. "What about Tom and Sam? I didn't see 'em when they were working us over."

The speckled amber eyes flicked around the room. She was figuring bugs, too; well, he knew she was no dummy. "I heard they, they got away. It was supposed to be hushed up. But I heard Llewellyn bellowing about it to some of his men."

Well, that was something. Maybe Tom could organize a guerrilla war when Morrigan got made emperor of the fucking world. If he could find guerrillas dumb enough to go up against a man who could exterminate all human life in a given area easy as snapping his fingers.

"I'm sorry. So sorry."

"Yeah. Well. Don't suppose you could get us out of here?"
Wordlessly she shook her head. "Didn't think so. What happens
now?"

Her eyes eluded his. "Bill has ordered you to be executed.
There's nothing I could do."

He sighed, gazed up at the ceiling. It wasn't revolving anymore.

"Thanks," he said, and the word stuck in his throat. "I mean,
you didn't give anything away. Not really."

She stared at him. "But I told Bill everything. *Everything*."
Something on her face said she was lying—and wanted him to
know it. Well, fuck that; his brain hurt too much for subtext.

"Don't mean jack. It was Vesensky who turned us over. He
already told the fuckers everything. You're off the hook,
sweetheart."

He closed his eyes and listened to her sob. After a while he
heard her stand up, move softly to the door. A man's voice spoke
to her as the door closed—guard out there: no surprise. There was
the sound of big locks being locked from outside. Apparently, the
efficiency had seen use as a holding cell before.

It wasn't until an unspecified time after she'd left that he snapped
awake to the realization that she'd said nothing at all about Nguyen.
*So maybe she held just a little something back from her main man
Bill.*

*—Not that it'll do the doc a bit of good. 'Cause that fucking
fairy Vesensky blew her anyway.*

But what was a little futility among friends?

Sam Sloan swallowed a curse as a solid chunk blanketed by the
amorphous urban-decay crud twisted under his right foot. *I fetch
up lame*, he told himself wryly, *Tom's going to have to just shoot
me.*

A few meters ahead Tom turned back to see what was wrong.
Had it been Billy McKay, he would have stamped and blas-
phemed—"We need to be *quiet*, goddammit!"—at the disturbance
and delay. But vaguely, in the darkness, Sam could tell Tom was
just checking on him.

The very *dark* darkness. A lid of clouds hung low over the
tormented skyline of the city, sealing it off from the stars; the
only light at all was the orange backscatter from bonfires dotted
among the ruins, which qualified more as special effects than
useable illumination.

"I'm okay," he subvocalized. For some reason Morrigan's

people hadn't ever gotten around to relieving them of their personal effects, which was an odd oversight of basic intelligence gathering and made Sam think Morrigan was getting overconfident, which wasn't real surprising in a megalomaniac who was in the process of successfully blackmailing the entire human race. Even with everything crashing down around their ears he and Tom had had time to scoop their communicators off the dresser in the quarters they shared. *"I'm fine. Everything's great. Let's go."*

Tom stared at him, then turned and began moving ahead, seeming to flow like fog over the treacherous rubble. Ahead, beyond his right shoulder, Sam could make out glows of firelight like a dozen tiny one-eyed rats peering from the dark Marina Towers across the river. Sam scrunched after him.

Half a block, down an alley; what was underfoot here didn't crunch so much as squish. Tom still made no more than a shadow, while Sam glumly wondered if he should just go ahead and whistle a tune to keep his spirits up; he was making enough noise for a marching band, or so it seemed. *Didn't I learn* anything *in Guardians training?*

A hand on his forearm stopped him, and he just managed to restrain an impulse to jump right out of his Detroit cammies.

"Bridge up ahead," Tom subvocalized. *"Careful."*

Sam peered nervously around a stone wall that glistened unpleasantly in the billowing light of a pair of oil-drum fires to either side of the bridge entrance. He could make out at least three wild-haired figures in the crazy glow, one of them carrying a very modern Franchi SPAS-14 riot gun on a sling made out of a length of nylon rope. Pretty bold, these Street People.

But just his brief exposure to Citadel scuttlebutt, mainly that afternoon when they were checking his proficiency on their uncomfortably sophisticated commo gear—the Guardians had listed qualifications for their *personas* that matched their own fairly closely; Sloan had been going under the name Marino, since he might conceivably pass for Italian with a brush—had made it clear that the Street People *owned* the night, even here within a few blocks of Morrigan's stronghold. He wished fervently and futilely that they'd had a chance to grab longarms on the way out. But those they'd had to check in the basement armory near the complex's gym, and the warning they'd got made it clear they had time for nothing but fast movement. The Beretta under his arm felt like a plastic toy.

Of course, that wasn't bothering Tom. Tom would be fine if

you dropped him stark naked into a pit full of hungry tigers. To Sam's mind Tom was invincible. Which wasn't much help, because Sam knew *he* wasn't.

A breeze off the lake probed down the alley, bringing a smell of dirty water and general decomposition that stuck in the back of Sloan's throat. *"How're we going to get across?"* he asked, eyeing the sentries. They had a casual arrogance about them and were probably cannibals.

"Tom shrugged. *"I go talk to the man,"* he said. *"Sit tight and watch my back."*

He slipped around the corner and instantly blended into the night. Sam stared after him with his heart hammering in his throat. He was all Guardian, no less hard-core in his way than Billy McKay, but he'd had a tough day. The world was probably just about to end, most of their team had been captured, and here were just the two of them in the middle of the home turf of a lot of urban savages he'd been hearing lurid torture tales about all day. He was entitled to some nerves.

To his credit he didn't scream when a gigantic spidery hand clamped itself on his shoulder. He just turned his head and looked up and up and *up* at a black figure looming above him, tall and skinny as a telephone pole. And calmly thought, *That's it for me*.

"What are you doing here?" a conversational voice asked from up among the reddened clouds.

CHAPTER
TWENTY-THREE

The hands guiding Suzette Nguyen along the tiled corridor were not ungentle. That made it more hateful, somehow, along with the familiar smells, the lab smells of disinfectants and acids and Bunsen-burner char that had meant shelter and security for most of her life.

Now they, like old friends, were about to turn against her.

And that was all wrong, as bad as the rest of what was about to happen, because *people* betrayed you, not the certitudes of science, not the appurtenances of the cloistered life she'd devoted herself to. Why else had she always walled herself off from human contact, than to avoid that inevitable people thing, betrayal?

"In here, girlie." Her two escorts, one black, one white, had the sort of half-friendly gruffness of seasoned floor nurses, and the same sort of build: compact and square. It was the white one who spoke, with the saggy sad water-blue eyes and lank short hair. She had an accent that made it hard for Nguyen to comprehend her. As a matter of fact, she was one of prewar Chicago's large population of ethnic hillbillies, but Nguyen didn't know anything about that.

She stood there staring at the door. The white terry robe suddenly seemed to be scratching her all over her body. She thought vaguely that she never expected the clinic to be so large, since it was just an adjunct to the apartment complex and all. But the builders of the place, like lots of builders in the last few years before the end of the world, had sunk its roots deep into the soggy, sandy soil, as if knowing it would have to weather storms.

The door. A chunky black arm reached out and opened it. She stared at it. Just a door, metal, painted orange, which hadn't even acquired the networks of dents and scratches doors in places like this practically came equipped with. She stared at the knob, focusing on it, as if by that she could shut out the rest of the world, the rest of time.

Those competent, neutral hands urged her forward. If she were a trained killer, like the vulgar American bandits she'd been thrown in with—or like the sleek and sinister Vesensky, who'd ordered her to submit to violation for the Greater Good—she could have done something about it. She was small and quick and kept herself fit; she could have dealt with these ungainly Occidentals. But she had always studied the arts of healing, never violence. She wasn't a vicious animal or soulless killing machine.

But Sam's not an animal, or a machine, she thought, and wondered why her thoughts reached out to the tall American like a drowner for a chunk of driftwood. Perhaps because he had been gentle, and kind, without ever seeming to be seeking for strings by which he could manipulate her—

The door closed behind her. It was buff-colored on this side. Or as far as she could tell; the light in here was a dim, diffuse purple that was almost more disorienting than pitch blackness would have been.

"Come in," she heard Cromartie gurgle, with mucus gurgling at the back of his throat. "I've been waiting for you."

She could say no, now. They would kill her; probably they would torture her first. But she could endure what they did, and die undefiled.

How petite-bourgeoise *and selfish you are!* she reproached herself with sudden vehemence. *All your life you've prated about serving humanity. Now you must sacrifice to save thousands of lives, millions, perhaps, and all you can think about is your childish squeamishness.*

Because Vesensky was right. This was her duty. Still, she hated him; hated him more than what awaited her down the short corridor, in the larger chamber from which the weird purple light seemed to pulse. . . .

Whatever it had been before, the room had been transformed into some kind of bizarre harem fantasy. Ten meters on a side, it was seemingly carpeted in fat, tasseled silk cushions. There were pornographic magazines and whips and rocket-shaped dildos scattered carelessly around, and by one wall stood a contrivance of seats and tubular metal frames that seemed to suggest a playground or an exercise machine, at whose purpose she didn't want to speculate. The walls were covered with tentlike swatches of silk, interspersed with photographs that appeared to be laser-printed blowups from sex magazines and with crudely executed paintings on black velvet in which men and women with exaggerated sexual characteristics did things to each other that startled even someone who'd interned briefly in a free clinic in Amsterdam.

In the midst of all this the focal point of the faint light weeping down through cyan and magenta gels, sat an enormous circular bed. In the middle of the purple expanse of its coverlet lay Magnus Cromartie, naked and exalted as one of the grosser Roman emperors at an orgy.

She swallowed. He was ugly even for a white man. But there was her duty.

He was staring at her with eyes like jellied eggs. She let the terry robe whisper to the floor. Beneath it she wore a men's magazine fantasy of a sexy woman's underclothes: electric blue bra and panties, blue garter belt, blue stockings, even blue high-heeled shoes. He stared at her and slowly ran a lump of tongue around his lips.

She forced herself to smile, and bending slightly slipped the panties down the curves of her thighs.

Later, Nguyen lay on her stomach, which was slowly lurching in harmony with the surface of the waterbed. *I never thought I'd be grateful to a man for being quick.*

Cromartie lay propped beside her on a fat pillow, swigging some kind of horrible homemade wine Morrigan's goons had extorted as tribute from some squatters' nest or another. She was also grateful for the smell of her own sweat; it crowded the smell of him from her nostrils, at least a bit. She wished he could have rolled over and gone to sleep after finishing his brief flurry of fumbling. But apparently he was still too excited by the acquisition of his new sex toy to sleep.

It had been on her mind to lie there like a slab of meat fresh from the icebox. She had not. First, the gossip she'd heard from the other women in the lab harem indicated he had ways of making you either enthusiastic or very, very sorry. Also, it occurred to her that the better she made it for him, the sooner he'd be done.

He dropped a hand to her upturned buttocks, absently began caressing her. Her flesh shrank from his touch, and she felt the irrational conviction he'd leave *smudges*.

Oh, well. The only way to do this was the best she could. Having learned from her exposure to the Guardians—especially McKay, who was as subtle about matters sexual as a stallion who smells a mare in heat—that American men thought nothing in the world was quite so sexy as a girl with a French accent, she raised her head and looked at Cromartie through the square-cut bangs that had fallen across her eyes.

"So tell me," she purred, trying her best to sound fifteen.

"They say you are a doctor, *non?*"

With a heave of effort, Billy McKay peeled the slab of callus from the underside of his right big toe. It took a half-centimeter wide swatch of live skin with it, leaving raw pinkness from which a dozen pinpricks of blood oozed.

"Ow! Fuck. Fuck, fuck, fuck, *fuck.*"

He squeezed his foot with both hands and bounced up and down on the sofa bed in his skivvies and T-shirt. How could he've been such a jerkoff? This was gonna gripe him for *hours*. Major wounds, you could bear the pain, he knew from hard experience; it was a badge of honor, at least that was something you could tell yourself. Little persistent penny-ante pains like this were what made you nuts.

He gave up and lay back down with his fingers laced behind his close-cropped head. They'd taken the restraints off him when he asked if they were gonna take his peter out for him when he needed to take a pee. Now he almost wished he hadn't, if the boredom was going to make him pick at himself.

He tried for an outlet in violent exercise, but there's only so many push-ups and crunchies you can do when you're penned in a little room without even an outside view. Especially when inside of twenty-four hours the world is either going to end or a mad dictator will be placed in charge of it all, and incidentally you're going to be executed. That kind of thing tends to give you a lot of nervous enery.

Maybe I'll just kick through that cardboard door, he told himself, and take as many of the pukes outside to Hell with me as I can.

But not just yet. Billy McKay wasn't the kind to just give up, even now.

He sighed and started to count the million tiny plaster stalactites poking down from the ceiling.

The room was full of guns, but his hands were immobilized behind his back again.

"Some days it don't fuckin' pay to get out of bed," Billy McKay said under his breath.

William Morrigan, dba Marcus Aurelius, would-be emperor of America, the world, and no doubt the goddamn solar system, looked up from the futuristic Franchi prototype shotgun he was examining. It was stubby and black and kind of raked-back looking: a bullpup design with the fat magazine behind the pistol grip, fully

automatic with a silencer built in. It looked like what Buck Rogers
might pick up if he got tired of messing with lasers and wanted
to kick some *serious ass*.

"I beg your pardon?" Morrigan asked mildly.

"I said you could kiss my ass."

That got him a rifle butt in the kidneys. His knees ached for
the feel of the vomit-colored carpet underfoot, and red lines of
electricity crackled from the soles of his feet to the center of his
brain, but he managed to keep upright. He just swayed a bit and
looked back over his shoulder at the nametag BARNES.

"Son, I'm gonna shove that FN up your ass, by and by. Bet
to it."

Barnes glared at him with his cut-up fish-eyed Willem DaFoe
face. Major Llewellyn laughed a deep-down laugh.

"Lieutenant McKay," Morrigan said, laying the fancy shotgun
almost reverently on a foam sheet spread on a wooden table, "I
have to admire your spirit: I really wish I could ask you and your
friend here to join us. But—" He shrugged. "You committed a
serious offense, infiltrating here to disrupt my plans. It would be
a serious injustice to permit you to live, don't you agree?"

"It would be a mistake, man," Casey said casually. "I'll buy
that."

"You already got one turncoat working for you, Morrigan. You
don't need more," McKay said, jerking his chin at Ivan Vesensky,
who stood discreetly behind Morrigan's left elbow, hovering at
roughly the same orbit as burly red Llewellyn.

Morrigan smiled thinly. "Colonel Vesensky and I are colleagues. We both well understand the exigencies of the trade of
intelligence. The colonel is clear-sighted enough to desire to serve
the strongest possible master, and since I am in fact and soon to
be acknowledged the most powerful man in the world, he's made
a proper choice."

"Yeah. He likes to suck the biggest dick around. Like Merith
Tobias."

Morrigan's face turned to an ice sculpture, like something you'd
see at a ritzy Jewish wedding, if you knew any Jews peculiar
enough to want an ice sculpture of a pinched asshole. "Don't ever
mention that name again," Morrigan said, strangling on the words.

He spun away. "The woman loves me. Worships me! And I
worship her, do you understand?"

"If the bullshit in here gets any deeper, we're all gonna drown
and save the world that way," McKay observed.

This time the kidney shot dropped him to his knees. He turned red and bobbed his head and cursed the pain and his captors.

Casey started to laugh.

Morrigan stared at him as if he thought he'd gone mad. "What on earth do you find funny?"

"You man. Your goons are, like, afraid to go outside the wire at night in groups of less than ten. And you think you can take over the world?" He was laughing so hard he was having trouble keeping his long legs beneath him, to say nothing of speaking clearly. "What a trip! You must've dropped some heavy acid in the sixties, man."

Morrigan went white. A couple of spare guards moved in on the former fighter jock, as if they were going to dent his kidneys, too, but Morrigan called them off with a shake of his head.

"The disorder you speak of is a temporary condition. It will end as soon as I have power."

"Dream on!"

"And don't interrupt me," Morrigan said without breaking stride, "or I'll have your fingers broken, one by one. It occurs to me, Lieutenant Wilson, that you may anticipate some kind of rescue attempt by your two comrades who remain fugitives. It will give me some pleasure to lay those expectations to rest."

He turned, held up a long, thin finger. "First, they are liable to have found the night as hostile as my men. The Street People have long since abdicated any semblance of humanity. They're merely predators now, two-legged predators. Your friends, who are still men, are to them simply prey.

"Second, in the unlikely event they should be able to enlist support, this compound is prepared to defend itself indefinitely against any number of starving rubble rats. You've seen the defenses, and as professionals, you know it's true."

He was striding back and forth. Now he stopped and turned to them. "But suppose, for amusement, that my defenses *were* penetrated. I would simply come—*here.*"

He gestured around at the racks of guns that lined all the walls, with fluorescent lights jittering on the glass faces of their cases. "As you may have observed as you were brought here, we stand within a special underground chamber with reinforced cement walls and steel vault-style doors. The designers intended it as a fallout shelter. Fallout turned out to be the least of the former inhabitants' worries, but it will serve me admirably as a final redoubt. Inside this compound I and my *corps d'elite* can hold out for months. But we won't need to. For from within it I can disperse nerve gas from canisters secreted throughout the rest of the Citadel. And, at the same time, I would send the orders to release the virus and sterilize the North American continent of human life.''

He smiled. ''And in a matter of days I and my loyal few would emerge, masters of all we surveyed, to build a new dream of American greatness.''

Having struggled to his feet during the speech, McKay looked at the guards standing watchfully near. ''What about you? What if you get caught outside when it all goes down?''

Barnes's eyes glittered. ''We're M.A.'s personal bodyguards. We go down with him.''

''Junior,'' McKay said, ''I'll make sure that's true. This I swear.''

Llewellyn rumbled a laugh up from his incipient gut. ''Big talk. *Big talk.*''

Ignoring him, McKay turned to Morrigan. ''Well, what the hell did you bring us here for? To show us your toys?''

Morrigan picked up a gleaming WWII-vintage Schmeisser machine pistol. ''Hugo Schmeisser had nothing to do with the design of these, did you know? I wanted to share my collection with you; I'm quite proud of it. And I thought it only polite to inform you in person that your fate had been decided, and what it would be.''

''Glad you didn't ask us to the trial, man,'' Casey said. ''I never could stand courtroom dramas.''

'' 'Trial'? '' Morrigan smiled. ''No trial was needed. I knew the facts of your crimes, and weighed them, and came to a just decision. In the new America we will have less of trials and more of justice.''

''I'll fucking bet,'' McKay said.

''Bet your life, McKay,'' Llewellyn said, ''hur, hur.''

''I won't keep you in suspense any longer,'' Morrigan said. ''You gentlemen may be pleased to know that you're about to become bigger celebrities than you ever were before. As you're aware, the upstart President MacGregor is due to offer his capitulation to my New Order at seven hundred hours tomorrow morning. Now, he might entertain notions of resistance, or possible double dealing—in fact, thanks to your compatriot Colonel Vesensky, I'm fully aware that he does.''

McKay glanced at Casey under his shaggy brows. Casey, who

was nowhere near the flake he seemed to be, returned the tiniest of shrugs. Was it possible Vesensky had some kind of under-table deal with MacGregor that he'd blown to Morrigan?

No fuckin' way, McKay decided. *Jeff's a liberal wimp, but he ain't that kind of fool.*

"However," Morrigan went on, "I plan a demonstration that may encourage his good faith. Because at 0700 hours tomorrow, I plan to have you both executed by means of my virus and broadcast the proceedings nationwide via satellite. In fact, I may just broadcast it worldwide. That could be very instructive, don't you think?"

He paused for effect, smiled to the eyeteeth. "*Good Morning America* was never like this, eh?"

McKay shook his head with a grin that Morrigan took for admiration. Until the ex-marine said, "M.A., you are one major asshole. You know that, don't you?"

This time Llewellyn hit him. He turned and spat in a blue eye. Llewellyn glowered through snot, cocked his fist to smash McKay's face.

McKay pulled his head back on his neck, gave it a prissy little shake. "Uh-uh. You want me to look nice on the TV tomorrow, and makeup don't cover bruises."

Llewellyn looked at Morrigan, who shook his head. Growling— literally growling, like a polar bear who's just had an overadventurous tot plucked out of his pen—Llewellyn lowered his fist.

"Take them back to their rooms," Morrigan said. "I'm sure they'd like to spend the last few hours alone with their thoughts."

"How about a final harem outcall for the condemned?" McKay asked.

Morrigan shook his head. "I'm afraid not. You might get notions about hostages, and I'd hate to waste a perfectly good girl. They tend not to last long anyway."

"Speaking of sex, you know he's queer, don't you?" McKay asked, nodding at Vesensky as the guards took his elbows to haul him away. "What do you think about having a faggot working for you? How does that set with your traditional goddamn virtues?"

Morrigan shrugged. "In our new society—*my* new society— homosexuality will not be permitted. But exceptions can be made, for those whose services earns them that privilege—as the colonel has already, by exposing your perfidy and the connection with the holdouts in Canada, who will be dealt with as soon as the usurper MacGregor is brought to heel—"

"Canada?" McKay asked. "What fucking Canada?"

Llewellyn slapped his face. "Shut up while M.A. is talking."

"Yes, I know all about the Canadian army awaiting the intelligence you intended to gather before it moves against me—a futile gesture even had you succeeded, for reasons I've explained. But still, a valuable datum which has helped earn Colonel Vesensky an honored place in the New Order."

He shook his head. "Besides, after a year of Magnus Cromartie, I find myself learning to take a broader view of human sexuality."

CHAPTER
TWENTY-FOUR ————————

Magnus Cromartie was ugly even for a white man.

Of course, Suzette Nguyen reflected, sitting astride his naked bloat of body in tonight's red garter belt and stockings, the additional puffiness in his face didn't help, nor the way his protruding eyes goggled at the cheap Madras prints hung from the ceiling, nor the way his cratered asteroid of a tongue stuck out between his lips. But the blueness—greenish black, really, in this light—to his lips and face and the fingers clawed deep into the rumpled satin sheets, *that* was a marked improvement.

He had closed his eyes at the moment of climax. She'd observed that the night before, along with a good many data that were even more interesting, if not so immediately pertinent. So tonight when he gobbled his ecstasy and buried his hands in the sheet as if afraid he were about to float up to the silk ceiling, she'd been ready. When his eyes closed was when she knotted the matching red brassiere around his all but nonexistent throat, so tightly it almost vanished.

He'd flailed for his life even more energetically than he had for sex, and even less successfully. He'd come a second time, then, as he went. She'd forgotten that would happen. Now she could feel his little sad dick diminish within her.

She felt nothing. Not triumphant, not vindicated, not purified— but likewise not soiled nor sorry nor sad. Not anything at all. What she felt was as if a chromed steel cylinder had been implanted at the center of·her, encapsulating mind and heart alike.

A cheap little Spartus clock TV glowed the time at her from amid a jumble of pillows, foolish luxuriance gone tawdry and sad. She swung her leg off the body, grimacing slightly as he slipped from her.

She had much to do, and little time to do it.

The technician on watch in Morrigan's command center glanced up from the brightly colored pages of an unusual kind of coffee table book, printed in Denmark, that had come over with the Effsee occupation force a year before. His skinny pale delayed-adolescent hands were already in motion, trying to stuff it back under the console out of sight, when he realized that the intruder wasn't M.A. himself on one of his midnight tours of inspection.

"Uh, hi," he said.

Ivan Vesensky nodded back. He wore a navy turtleneck and blue jeans and deck shoes, and his narrow face had a distracted look on it. The tech took advantage of his apparent preoccupation to poke the book away out of sight in a cubbyhole along with yellowed old log sheets and some paper clips.

He brushed hair the color and general consistency of straw back from his forehead and watched the newcomer, expectant and curious. He and the other communications technicians had been introduced to this one earlier today; he was supposed to be some kind of hotshot who would be advising M.A. on his own signals intelligence, as well as how to make his communications more secure.

The tech had been startled that a newbie was given such free rein right off the bat, especially since the rumor mill said all kinds of wild things about him—that he was a renegade KGB agent, that he'd come in with that team of spies Morrigan had caught the day before, the ones who came dressed as Detroit soldiers and knocked that bastard Llewellyn's dick in the dirt for him. But M.A. had his own way of doing things.

It didn't occur to the tech to question the Soviet's right to be here. The center was aboveground, right over one of the high-rise's three restaurants, not down in the mysterious underground bolt-hole, though M.A. had more gear down there, which he let no one but a handpicked few touch. Security was the concern of the two sentries posted outside the room's armored door twenty-four hours a day. If they let him past, he had to be okay.

Vesensky frowned at the console. In fact, he'd been able to impress Morrigan by telling him a few things he didn't know about it. By great good fortune, he'd bought a TeleVideo satellite communications driver system virtually identical to the one that lay at the heart of the Citadel's setup a few years ago and shipped it to the USSR via cutouts in Israel and Czechoslovakia—and then he'd told his bosses a few extravagant but eminently plausible lies about the cloak-and-dagger dodges required to get it past the U.S.'s barriers on technology export, with the result that he still had five hundred ounces of gold stashed away in a Swiss bank from that job.

"I couldn't sleep," he said. "The Guardians' Canadian allies had truly frightful communications security. I'm worried that we've haven't picked up more traffic from them.''

The tech nodded. His eyes were blue and empty. "But I have an idea. If you'd like to bring up the freek-scan menu on that screen *there*—''

He pointed past the tech's right shoulder with his right hand. The kid's eyes followed, and he obediently reached for the keyboard.

Vesensky's other hand, which had been scratching the back of his neck in a bleary, sleepy way, flashed down and punched the needle-slim blade of a commando knife through the side of the tech's neck. As the boy's eyes widened in shock his right hand caught the back of the swivel chair and spun him around, so that when the dagger slashed out through the front of his throat the torrent of blood wouldn't splash the delicate communications gear. It wouldn't do to have it malfunction just yet.

A scream drowned in veinous blood. Vesensky held the tech by a thin shoulder until his struggles subsided. Only in the movies did you simply fold up and quietly expire from a single knife wound, even one as comprehensive as the one Vesensky had given his victim. The two fools on watch in the hall he'd momentarily incapacitated with two quick blows before slitting their throats. No need to expend such effort in here.

He let the body, the whole front of it drenched in blood, slump sideways in its chair. He brought up the controls for the master transmitter, locked on a satellite that had survived the war, punched in coordinates. The signal was going to travel quite a few thousand kilometers in order to wind up a few blocks away; amusing.

The message he keyed in was clear, in German: *"Der Adler ist gelandet."* An outside observer might have thought he was harkening back to the line that the first moon landing mission *hadn't* fluffed, translating it for obscure reasons, but he'd have been wrong. It had in fact been chosen in honor of Yevgeny Maximov, Chairman of the Federated States of Europe, from one of his favorites of the spy novels he adored.

Vesensky waited for the numerical sequence replay, broke the link, and broadcast a quick short-range pulse. On the roof a relay clicked and a timer began its countdown to self-destruction with idiot complacency.

Vesensky popped the console's scratched off-white plastic cover and made a few unauthorized hardware alterations with the Sykes-Fairbairn dagger. Then he went out to drag the two dead guards inside the command center. Finally he pulled the pin from a thermite grenade and left it lying in the middle of the expensive hive of electronic equipment.

Then he left. Not running. He had much to accomplish, but he was a man who had learned never to rush himself.

The process of making the Citadel a suitable headquarters from which to rule the Whole Nine Yards was a continuing one, and had been since William Morrigan ran across Magnus Cromartie and conceived his grand plan. The lab hadn't originally been *in* the Citadel, of course, but rioters had wrecked the original even before the Effsees hit town. Once the connection was made, Cromartie and those willing to follow him in pursuit of Morrigan's New Order had moved crosstown into the Loop. Dr. Wendell Carter and the other holdouts had mostly moved to graves of varying degrees of shallowness.

But important as they were, the lab boys were Johnnies-come-lately. Increasing the security of the compound was M.A.'s main priority, and preparing his plush bolthole beneath the high-rise tended to be his second. The lab never went begging, but except when Cromartie threw one of his legendary tantrums it was never at the top of the list. The techs were civilians, after all.

As a result, no security system more elaborate than the electronic locks (tougher for those persistent inner-city junkies to pick) extant when Morrigan took possession had been installed. Then again, they and the round-the-clock guards were deemed sufficient by the Man. Morrigan didn't encourage undue curiosity in his followers, and one or two colorful examples convinced everyone that if they were going to risk the penalties for breaking regs, it would be for something with more entertainment value than the biolab. Who the hell wanted to get close to Crazy Magnus and his bugs anyway?

The guard sitting with his feet up on a desk in the anteroom of the main laboratory looked up from his book and his eyebrows practically shot off the top of his face as the door opened.

"Hi," said the incredibly beautiful Oriental woman who stood there, naked except for a red garter belt, stockings, and shoes. She pulled the card out of the slot, slipped it under her waistband, and shut the door. "Doctor Cromartie thought it would be nice to send you a little treat."

As a general rule Cromartie seemed to think Security could all kiss his smelly ass, but he was also a noted nutbag. Besides, who the hell would argue with a naked woman?

The paperback slithered to the floor. Nervously licking his lips, the guard started to his feet. "Oh, no," the woman said, in an accent that made his balls tingle. "Just sit there. I will take care of you."

One thing you could say about working for M.A. You got well provided for. The guard sat himself back down, about ready to bust from eagerness.

"Moment," she said. He almost went off in his pants when she glided past, trailing her fingertips along his arm. The nails were blood-red, to match her getup.

He glanced back. "No peek," she giggled. "I have the surprise."

He grinned a slack grin, shrugged. Hell, he'd play along. Why not? She looked like she knew some pretty *interesting* games.

He was humming unconsciously to himself and crossing and recrossing his arms when she stepped close behind him and drove a ballpoint pen into the hole of his right ear. A hefty black marble pen holder snatched up from the desk pounded the pen into his brain with a single quick blow.

The guard exploded from the chair like a spear from a gun. He clutched at the side of his head, eyes rolling back, jaw clenched so hard the strings stood out on his neck and his teeth creaked. He made a funny thin keening sound and collapsed kicking to the thin carpet.

Grunting with effort, Suzette Nguyen dragged the body out of sight behind the desk. Then she picked up the guard's Uzi from the desk, worked the bolt, and moved to the inner door. There was a second lock here—those junkies could be *awfully* persistent. She put an ear to the door, listened, heard nothing, slid Cromartie's card into the slot, turned the knob and stepped quickly inside.

The room was crowded with cluttered benches interspersed with chunks of equipment: centrifuges, a gas chromatograph, a gene sequencer. Monolithic freezers stood by one wall, humming to themselves, like bleached slabs from *2001*. Remarkably well equipped for such an ad hoc operation, she thought. *But one would hardly think it sufficient to tailor a major viral variant.*

She smiled and sat down at a Compaq terminal. The vinyl chair seemed to grip her naked rump like a clammy hand, but she barely noticed. She frowned, hoping she had correctly memorized the access codes this morning when she'd wheeled Cromartie into showing his new sex kitten the place he did his important and mysterious Science, and began to type.

Billy McKay looked up from the sofa bed to see Ivan Vesensky standing in the door to his one-room efficiency cell. The Soviet was dressed all in tight-fitting black.

McKay made an animal sound clear at the center of him. A happy sound, but not a pleasant one. "Forget to bring your bodyguards, you cocksucking traitor? Well, I'll—"

Casey Wilson stepped past Vesensky into the room. "Everything's cool, Billy," he said. "Put this on." And he tossed what looked like a deflated black man onto the rug at McKay's bare feet.

CHAPTER
TWENTY-FIVE ──────────

"*Good* shit," Denny said, in a wisp of condensation and smoke that glowed greenish in the light of the partial moon coming up out of the lake.

Justin sucked the joint and nodded his head in enthusiastic agreement.

It was the middle of the night and cold in the 105-mm recoilless emplacement out in front of the high-rise, and neither man was in the mood to say nope, to dope. M.A. would have skinned them alive if he caught them, of course. But they weren't too worried about being on the receiving end of one of his infamous spot inspections.

"I mean, shit," Justin said, sounding like Donald Duck breathing helium. The dope didn't affect his vocal cords all that much, but he was kind of a weed, always had to overdo it. "Shit, if *you* had Merith Tobias to keep you warm at night, would you run around in the cold looking at a bunch of guys?"

"Maybe I would," Denny said, studying the ember end of the joint, which he was holding down below the sandbag rampart out of the way of prying eyes," if I was as big a faggot as you." Denny was a more strapping kind of lad, with black brushcut hair and an army mustache and a well-packed ballplayer look. He'd been airborne and never let anybody forget it.

"Hey, man," Justin said, aggrieved, "hey, now." He didn't sound as if he wanted to make something of it. He was stoned, and anyway he never wanted to make anything of it, not with somebody built like Denny. That was why Denny picked on him. "I ain't no fag."

"Just a wimp," Denny said absently, and lifted the joint for a hit.

His dark eyes widened, then, because spiraling at them, at *him,* right out of the night, spewing a huge trail of sparks like a dragon with Montezuma's revenge, came a LAW, making that hateful waspy antitank rocket buzz.

"Shit," he said, and dropped right to the pavement.

Justin blinked around. "What the fuck?" He was really pretty useless.

He abruptly realized that this weed was *nowhere near* good enough to give you light-show hallucinations, and then he stood there with his nub of chin hanging down and his Adam's apple kind of bouncing around his chicken neck, waiting to be vaporized.

Instead, the LAW did a barrel roll and slammed into a concrete planter. It if had been aimed true the volcano spray of sparks and incandescent gas would still've shaved the top half off him notwithstanding the sandbags, but instead it blew a big section of ground-floor window into what used to be the offices of a travel agency, sending huge jewelry sheets of busted glass and flaming chunks of the plywood that had been fitted over it flying all over everywhere.

"*Righteous,*" he said in awe.

"What? What?" Denny demanded from the deck, where he lay with his hands behind his head as if he were surrendering.

"It's okay, man," Justin assured him. "Missed."

That made stoned sense to Denny, who started to get up. There was a flash above their heads, and they both looked up to the sound of the sky cracking open to see the main dish of the fancy antenna array up on the roof go spinning into the night like a giant Frisbee.

They were so entranced by that that they never noticed the second LAW until it hit their nest and knocked the recoilless into a U-shape and blew the two of them into a bunch of steaming, sticky little globs of stuff. They didn't notice it then, either.

"You mean I can't kill the puke?" McKay demanded in an outraged whisper.

The three were running down the hall with the hoods of their wetsuits bobbing at the backs of their necks like outsized condoms and Uzis in their hands.

In the lead Vesensky never looked back. "It's *okay,* Billy," Casey hissed. "He's still on our side."

"I don't trust the fucker."

"Billy, he *let us go.*" He sounded exasperated, which McKay had never known he could. It occurred to McKay just how cagey Vesensky had been to set Casey loose first.

A corridor crossed theirs up ahead; Vesensky stopped, pushed a three-second look around the corner, drew back. "Looks clear."

"If he's a good guy, why'd he blow us up in the first goddamn place?" McKay said.

The Soviet grinned. "It broke the logjam, did it not? We were getting, as you would say, nowhere fast."

He started around the corner.

"And Canada," McKay persisted. "What was that Canada shit?"

"I had to tell them something."

"You told them plenty, dude."

"But Morrigan was not about to buy that we'd come marching in here with no plan except to wing it. He'd never accept that we were that stupid."

"Oh," McKay said.

From outside came the crash of explosions, shouts, the sudden snarl of an M60.

McKay scowled. "What the fuck, over?"

Vesensky checked his watch. "Our friends. Right on time."

"Our *friends?* What the hell is going on here? Are you nuts? Jesus, all Morrigan has to do is put the word out over the airwaves and what's left of the nation is History 101."

The building vibrated briefly as if a tic had run through it. "Not anymore. The antenna just blew down. The Citadel is cut off."

"It did, huh? What blew it down? Wind?"

"The explosive charges I set an hour ago," Vesensky explained cooly. He checked the cross passage again. "Now, come *on.* Nguyen can't hold on forever by herself."

Fingers outstretched, pink tongue tip protruding between full lips, Nguyen scanned the racks of beakers and carboys. Much of what was here was more appropriate to a high school chemistry lab than a recombinant-DNA research facility, even a small and jury-rigged one. She wasn't surprised. The files she'd skimmed made it clear Cromartie hadn't really been much more of a scientist than he was a lover. The real work had been done by Dr. Carter, who was evidently brilliant and just as evidently dead.

But the late Dr. Cromartie could still claim credit for Marcus Aurelius's secret weapon. *That* he didn't have to share with his former boss. Such delicious irony—

"Hey, you little bitch! What do you think you're doing?"

She spun. It was one of Cromartie's half-witted bottle washers he glorified with the name of lab technicians, his lab coat buttoned lopsided and doing Christ alone knew what coming here in the middle of the night. Single-minded dedication to the work had not been a big feature of Cromartie's shop.

She made no attempt to run. She had a job to do, and it had to be done here. If she died trying, so be it.

He was advancing on her, huge and menacing, smiling with a face that reminded her of a rubber fright mask. "Magnus's new bimbo, aren't you? Getting in where you don't belong." He laughed. "I think I'm gonna enjoy this. He may just let me take care of you, since I caught you. I think maybe I'll make you sit with your sweet little bare ass on an iron plate, and start heating it up *real* slowly—"

"I warn you," she said, "do not interfere with me."

He laughed, his face rumpling into a pantomime of incredulity. "Interfere with you? Sweetheart, I'm going to fuck you, front, back, and sideways, and then I'm gonna get a guard in here and stash you somewhere." He reached for her.

She spun and splashed a vial full of clear liquid into his face.

A sharp smell and a horrible shriek filled the air. He clapped hands to his face and reeled away as the nitric acid went to work on him, knocking equipment over left and right.

She watched him a moment, then followed, looking for something to finish him off with. The lab was heavily soundproofed, but she couldn't take the chance of his screaming attracting any more attention.

"Hey," Billy McKay said, "there's a dead guy under this desk. Jesus God, he's got a *pen* in his ear. Casey, get a load of this."

Standing watch at the door of the lab's anteroom, Casey said, "No," very firmly.

"You really oughtta. I mean, I seen some scaly shit in my time, but a guy killed with a pen? Come *on*."

Vesensky tried the knob on the inner door. It opened. White smoke rolled over him like a human wave attack. He staggered back, coughing.

Casey looked around. "Uh-oh."

"Shit," McKay said. He raced to the door, bellowing into the smoke, "Suzette! Doc Nguyen! Are you all right?"

"I'm perfectly well, Lieutenant." The muffled words emerged like a wraith from the dense, chemical-stinking smoke. A moment later so did she, wearing this red garter belt and a respirator mask and not one damned thing else.

"Now, that's something you don't see every day," McKay remarked approvingly. He noted her breasts were a nice cone shape. The nipples were chocolate brown.

Vesensky never batted an eye. "What happened in there?" he asked, waving a hand at the smoke.

"A technician discovered me. He gave trouble. He knocked over some racks, spilled chemicals. A fire started. Now, will some of you oh-so-strong men give me a hand?"

She turned around—*nice ass for an Oriental girl*—and tugged in a dolly with three canisters on it. They resembled big fire extinguishers, or maybe freon cans. They were black with broad yellow bands top and bottom.

"What the fuck, over?" he asked, picking one up.

"Cromartie's magic virus," Nguyen said, dragging in two more canisters.

"Bull jive. This is your basic VX nerve agent. Deadly as shit, but there's no virus about it. Case, give her a hand."

"It is what I try to tell you before, what I did suspect in Cleveland." She was dragging in more of the heavy nerve gas containers as she spoke. "There is no virus."

Casey and McKay stopped dead and stared at each other. "No virus?" Casey said. "Then what has Morrigan got stashed all over the country?"

"Jack shit," McKay suggested.

"He has this nerve gas. Cromartie knew where it was, how you say? Stockpiled. He made the deal with Morrigan. They pretend to have some horrible artificial virus, use it to frighten everyone to do what they say." Her English was eroding like the earth under a busted main.

"But why?" Casey asked. "Nerve gas is, like, pretty heavy all by itself."

"Yes. But people are more afraid of disease, you see? And a virus can spread, can reproduce itself. Mere gas cannot."

"That sonofabitchin' M.A.," McKay said, not without admiration. "He hosed everybody and his dog Jake. Damn. Say, what are we doing with this crap?"

"We'll use it to neutralize the defenders," Vesensky said. "That's why the wetsuits; they use them for NBC protection. I have respirator hoods, and—".

"Well, well," a familiar voice said. Heads turned to see Major Llewellyn standing in the door, covering them with an Uzi. "What do we got here? An orgy?"

CHAPTER
TWENTY-SIX

The machinegun on the roof of the mini-mall half of the Citadel went off with a spasm of orange flame. Samuel Roberts Sloan, formerly of the United States Navy, hugged rubble and thought about how the movies had betrayed him.

In movies when people shot at you, it was like hail pattering down. The bullets kicked up little spurts of dust around the hero's feet as he dodged from cover to cover, went between his legs, that sort of thing.

Sloan had been shot at before, of course. But mostly with 5.56-mm rounds, NATO standard, small-caliber high-velocity stuff. It had a nasty crack to it when it went by, and the little needlelike slugs could mess you up amply if they connected. But it wasn't truly impressive.

This was. This was full-sized 7.62, that made the earth shake for meters around where it hit and made you fear God. It was like having John Henry the Steel Drivin' Man come looking for you with his sledge. John Henry on *speed*.

Sam had taken position behind a big mound of rubble nuggeted with cinderblocks and blocks of stone that seemed to him to offer what they called Cover and Concealment in abundance. It showed what he knew. In fact, the mound did offer good cover and concealment. It was just that the M60's bullets weren't easily discouraged. Sam remembered a book of reminiscences about the Vietnam War he'd read years back, how somebody mentioned that in the average block you would not see too many *buildings* it was safe to hide from an M60 behind.

That made sense to him now, it surely did.

"Hail Mary, full of grace—" The quiet, high-pitched words emerged from Francis, the black kid who'd put the arm on him in that alley near the bridge last night, whose body was laid like a stretch of blacktop highway next to his. Francis was sixteen years old and seven feet tall, and if the world hadn't blown up he would probably be explaining to all the basketball scouts in North America right now that he couldn't consider accepting their offers

181

because he'd be entering a Catholic seminary as soon as he graduated from high school. He was a gentle, soft-spoken youth who had grown up amid sheltered upper-middle-class surroundings. Now he was a Street Person like the rest. He seemed to feel some responsibility toward Sloan, having captured him last night, however briefly, and had attached himself to him.

"Boy, those M60s," Francis said, and admiration hummed in his piping voice. "They sure can crank 'em out."

Sloan turned his head to look at him.

The onslaught stopped. Sloan peered around a fallen cornice, hoping the gunner had burned the barrel out. Unfortunately, these murderous bastards got lots of live-firing practice. They had some seasoning and the sense of security an apparently impregnable position can give you. Burning through a barrel was a panic reaction, and the Citadel defenders had no reason to panic.

Grimly, Sloan hoped that'd be changing real soon.

Unfortunately, right now their confidence looked justified, even though half a dozen hardpoints had been neutralized by the barrage of rockets scarfed from the Effsees that had opened the evening's—early morning's—entertainment.

Unfortunately, the apparent success of the rocket attack had inspired the Marquette Park Marauders with wild overconfidence. They had come whooping and screaming out of the rubble and into the killzone, waving Molotov slings in blazing circle, filled with a special field-expedient napalm that was heavy on dissolved Styrofoam soft drink cups looted from Wrigley Field, which went by the pleasant name Necklace in a Drum, after Winnie Mandela's favorite form of political expression.

The problem was while some of the weapons pits had gone spectacularly to Hell, not *all* of them had. Sloan had seen beehive rounds at work during the fight with the *Cristeros* in Texas, and he had to admit it was even less pleasant to be anywhere near on the receiving end of a few of them than M60 fire. Marauders, RIP: *Rest in Pieces*.

"Anything?" Francis asked, peeking around his own personal chunk of masonry at the machinegun nest, four hundred meters away, that had singled the two of them out for its undivided attention. He pushed his glasses up his nose. They had a piece of tape wrapped around the bridge, holding them together.

Sloan shook his head. Tommy Rogers assured him that the woman handling their communications from the former toy depart-

ment of Marshall Field's was a veritable wizard, despite the
magenta hair and the human fingerbone hung from one ear.

Normally, Tom's word was gospel to Sloan on military matters,
but it wasn't in him to trust *anyone* who called herself a Cyberpunk.

Francis pursed his lips as their friend the machinegun got lonely
and started reaching out for them again. "Hoo. I certainly hope
they hurry."

Sam barely heard him. He'd never had any conception how
loud a 7.62-mm machinegun could be four hundred meters away.
When it was pointed right at you it sounded darn near as loud as
McKay's did twenty meters off. Or maybe that was just his imagination.

A bullet hit the jutting edge of the cornice and whined right
over his head, leaving his face feeling as if it had been bee-stung
from the shower of cement chips and realizing he was one lucky
dog to have both his eyes.

"Jesus, can't they find somebody else to shoot at?"

As soon as he said it he felt guilty about it, wishing death and
disaster on his comrades. It was unworthy, even in the heat of
battle. Besides, they at least had a modicum of protection. . . .

"What do you think I been praying for?" Francis said.

His head crackled, and a surly female voice said, "—Sloan.
Have you gone to sleep at the switch, jackboot?"

He fumbled between his vest of 40-mm grenades and his chest
for the communicator in its special pocket, hit the transmit switch.
The M203 launcher slung under his Galil—he'd never realized
how sentimental he could be about an implement of death and
destruction until he was reunited with it this morning—would have
settled the hash of those pesky gunners once and for all. They
were within range, but once the defenders spotted a forty mike-
mike launcher *everything* they had would be hunting for him, even
their own 40-mm automatics, which were right now raking the
rubble beyond the killzone littered with mostly motionless Marauders. And he had a job far more important than distributing little
inch and a half cans of heavenly joy.

Which maybe, *maybe,* he was going to get to start doing.

"Sloan here," he said, not bothering to subvocalize. "Go ahead,
Jade."

"You're on, Sloan. Keep your ass down so your brains don't
get shot out."

Mother Teresa? Sloan thought. *Forget her. They should saint*

Tommy *for dealing with people like this on a constant basis without killing them.*

"I love you, too," he said.

"Of course you do," said a rich, black, male voice, "and well you should, because this is Grand Admiral for Life Achemba of the Detroit Navy, on board the good ship *Jesse Ventura,* ready to kick ass, take names, and teach your women the meaning of satisfaction."

"Achemba? Thank God."

"God, thank Achemba, you mean. Coordinates?"

Sloan didn't have to check his map; the numbers were hardwired in his brain. He recited them quickly. Achemba chanted them back, then said, "It's on the way."

Sloan waited through an enternity ticked off in the hammerfalls of 7.62-mm bullets. Then in a lull between bursts he heard it, the sweetest sound in an old navy man's life: the rising whistling whine of an incoming naval barrage.

Not that it was really a barrage. It was a single round, in fact. And it was *naval* only by virtue of having been fired from the reinforced deck of one of a pair of field-expedient Detroiter gunboats anchored off Jackson Park. It came in fact from a plain old 105-mm howitzer, a landlubber gun. But *still* . . .

It missed. By a mile. It flared off somewhere in the killzone beyond the compound.

"Amateurs," Sloan moaned. "Goddamn *amateurs!*"

"We are still pretty new to this," Achemba agreed. "Now, you can call us off the corrections, or you can abuse us some more. In which case we take the *Jesse* and the *Gorgeous George* and sail back to Muskegon and a hero's welcome. You choose, white devil."

Sam goggled. He'd never been called a white devil before. The icy professional kicked in then, the expert Forward Gunnery Observer plying his craft, and he called out the corrections.

The next round fell short, splashing a lot of prostrate Marauders, including a wounded few who were beginning to suspect they might just pull through. Sloan swallowed a curse; *that* was a panic reaction, and a Guardian didn't panic, even with an evil black machinegun probing for him with copper-jacketed fingers that were getting ever closer. He may have been as fine a gunnery officer as Annapolis ever stamped out, but these really *were* amateurs, and for amateurs they were doing a hell of a job.

"All right," he said. "You've bracketed them." He recited

more careful adjustments, then settled back for another endless wait in the noisy night.

And Francis said, "I think I'm hit. Oops. Mom's gonna be pissed."

"Oh, Jesus," Sloan said. *The boy's killed. And I'm responsible!* "Jesus."

Francis's face was gray. He rolled onto his side and started to feel at himself. Sloan wriggled over to offer what help he could.

Then it hit him: "Your *mom?* Your mother is alive?"

"Sure. She's living in Chicago Heights with my twin baby sisters. My dad's dead, but I've got an uncle who looks after them."

"What are you doing here?"

The kid shrugged. "Volunteered to fight the Effsees last year. Stayed on to help give the Butcher a bad time. You know how it is. Gets kind of exciting."

Sloan grimaced. He was about to deliver a sort of Say No to War homily on how excitement could turn ugly unexpectedly when Francis grinned and held up something between spidery fingers. "Look at this!"

Sam squinted through the weird neurotic light of a parachute flare fired from the high-rise. Francis held up an object that looked like a horse capsule, pointy on one end, flattened on the other, and copper colored: a 7.62 bullet, slightly used.

"Spent itself burrowing through the rubble. I'm only bruised. Boy, am I gonna say some Hail Marys *tonight.*"

Burning people ran screaming from an erstwhile office building where a burst of WP rounds from a Mk19 had found them. A couple of rockets snaked their lazy lurid way across the sky and dug holes in the pavement beside the high-rise. The M60 kept probing ever closer to Francis and Sam.

Then the *Jesse*'s third round landed. Their personal bullet storm stopped abruptly.

Sloan looked at Francis. Both grinned and shot each other thumbs-up. *Selfish of me to solve my personal problem first,* he thought, *but, you know, I don't really give a fuck.*

"Achemba? Good shooting. Now, we've got a recoilless emplacement—"

The anteroom filled up with Llewellyn's troopies, grinning unpleasantly over Uzis held at hip level. Their grins seemed mainly to be leveled at Nguyen.

"Officers got first dibs on booty, boys," said a man with newly minted lieutenant's bars and HOSPERS stenciled on his chest. "Ain't that true, Major?"

"You got that right, Lieutenant." Llewellyn smiled and lit a cigar. "Boys, you secure these swinging dicks while Hospers and I take this female captive aside for some in-depth interrogation."

Face practically cut in two by his grin, Hospers started for Nguyen. Two things happened simultaneously.

A trooper sniffed and stared quizzically at the door to the lab proper, which had swung shut. "Major, I think I smell smoke," he said.

And Nguyen stooped and picked up a black and yellow canister, holding it before her bare breasts.

"Fools. *Pigs*. You cannot shoot in here. Don't you know, this is nerve gas! If it breaks open, we all die!"

CHAPTER
TWENTY-SEVEN

Hospers froze in midstep, reaching for her. "She's bluffing," Llewellyn said, but McKay saw beads of sweat springing up around the fringes of his beard and hair.

"No, she ain't, sir," said a soldier whose face had been tan a moment before. "I was with a Chemical Warfare unit in Bad Hersfeld. Them's the real thing."

"Well, for Christ's sake," Llewellyn snarled, "take 'em *anyway*. We outnumber them."

Somebody switched the projector of Hospers's life back on again, and he resumed motion toward Nguyen. She threw the heavy canister at him as if it were a plastic toy. It caught him full in the face. Teeth snapped. He flew over backward, shouting blood.

With a mutual bellow of "This puke's ass is *mine*," McKay and Llewellyn charged each other like sumo wrestlers. Two soldiers grabbed Casey's arms. A third launched himself at Ivan Vesensky in a flying tackle.

Vesensky jumped straight up into the air, tucking his legs below him, hauling his P7 from the sexy black shoulder holster he wore over his wetsuit. The soldier rolled right beneath him, crashing into the legs of the desk, as he fired twice in midair, like Ozzie Smith turning a double play.

The two soldiers hanging onto Casey screamed and fell away, one clutching his shoulder, the other his gut. Their comrades froze again, staring at the Soviet in mixed horror and admiration as he touched down light as Bojangles, covering them, a wild light and a shock of blond hair in his eyes. It was the finest display of combat pistolcraft anyone in the room was ever likely to see—even if they survived tonight.

The soldier he'd dodged suddenly spun from the floor, holding the canister Nguyen had thrown at Hospers two-handed by the valve. It struck Vesensky on the left forearm.

Bones snapped with a sound like another gunshot.

The pistol clattered away. Vesensky staggered, then using the

187

momentum the blow had lent him spun all the way around, shooting out his right heel in a reverse kick. The troopie took it in the throat. His trachea collapsed, and he fell, face blackening as he strangled.

All the figures in the petrified tableau lurched into action again. A soldier made a grab for Casey, only to collect a foot flailing *up* and *around* and *back* in a reverse wheel kick in the face and sit down hard with the clatter of his slung Uzi. Two troopies converged on Nguyen, who knowing full well her lack of size and strength wasn't going to do much good in hand-to-hand combat, scurried behind the desk in search of weapons.

McKay and Llewellyn collided like a pair of water buffalo banging the bosses of their horns. Grappled head to head, straining all his strength against all of Llewellyn's, his nostrils full of the reek of the major's booze-laden breath, McKay knew at once that the other man had the advantage of weight. *But it's beer muscle,* McKay thought. *I can take him.*

About then Llewellyn uttered a triumphant bellow and pitched McKay back. McKay groaned as the edge of the desk slammed like an axe against his lower spine.

"Gonna break you *in two!*" Llewellyn roared, and threw himself on him.

Casey was a wild man.

He had three modes. One was the ultramellow California kid he showed the world most of the time. One was the Yeager Clone fighter jock, ultimately cool, ultimately in control, that came on him when he drove or flew in combat, or nestled himself behind the high-tech scope of his sniper's rifle.

Then there was the *other* other Casey Wilson. The one that flunked out of Aggressor training—the air force equivalent of the navy's Miramar Top Gun program—on the first go-round for being too aggressive. The one that just lost it in an explosion of fury you'd never associate with a laid-back pretty boy in yellow Zeiss shooting glasses and rock conert tour caps. It was a Casey Wilson that seldom got let out into the light of day.

Hand to hand combat opened the cage for that Casey. The others had hated unarmed combat instruction, because Casey couldn't control it, even in sparring. He could only go all out.

So now he was slashing through the Citadel troopies with a fighter jock's leopard strength and reflexes matched to a total lack of concern for anything but inflicting bodily harm on his enemies.

A tornado of whirling arms and legs, breaking bones, gouging eyes, impossible to defend against for its sheer unpredictable fury. He wasn't taking many opponents down to stay, but he was single-handedly occupying the attention of half a dozen men.

Vesensky was cool. He had three of them all to himself, trying to circle him in the confines of the room while avoiding catching Casey's foot in an ear. He faced them with his good right hand extended, his broken left arm held close to his black-rubber clad chest. He was smiling.

The man to his left darted forward, trying for a flank. Vesensky danced a step toward him, jabbed two fingers at his eyes. He shied, threw up an arm to block.

Vesensky kicked him in the balls.

Alert, the other two were closing. As the first doubled over clutching himself, the Soviet crowhopped back two steps and fired a straight rear kick into his midsection, doing him little hurt but sending him flying backward.

The third grabbed Vesensky by his left wrist. He twisted. Broken ends of bone grated audibly against each other. He smiled.

Through a patina of sweat Ivan Vesensky smiled back. "You . . . like that?" he gritted.

He grabbed the man's wrist with his right hand, torqued clockwise with his hips, yanking the soldier's arm straight. He pushed his right foot left, crossing between their bodies, and suddenly snapped it up and around, letting himself fall backward off-balance, further extending his opponent's arm and locking the elbow.

His thigh hit the elbow with all Vesensky's wiry strength and popped the joint clean.

"Gotcha now, sweetheart," the soldier grunted, grabbing Suzette Nguyen by one slim ankle and dragging her bodily out from the under the desk. He leered at the perfect moon-pale cheeks of her ass and the wedge of coarse dark hair between.

Then her upper body slid out. Her right hand flashed out. It held the fancy Rambo combat knife the dead sentry had worn in a hip sheath.

The soldier let go of her ankle and fell back howling, clapping his hands over the spurting ruin of his eyes.

Okay, so he's stronger than I thought, McKay told himself, as

Major Llewellyn bent him backward over the desk.

He bashed his forehead down with all the strength of his bull's neck on Llewellyn's lumpy yam nose. Blood fountained.

Llewellyn laughed. His powerful arms were wrapped around McKay's rib cage, pinning his arm. His thighs pinned McKay's against the desk. He was just bending forward at the waist, forcing McKay inexorably backward millimeter by millimeter.

In a matter of moments McKay's spine would split against the adze of the desk-edge. He hammered his head into Llewellyn's face, puking curses. And the bearded major just grinned at him, teeth shocking white through a scarlet wash of blood.

The two men Vesensky had kicked hit him simultaneously from both sides. Vesensky backfisted the face of the one he'd nailed in the balls, breaking his nose. Then he whipped his arm down in a hammer fist—balls *again*—and finished with an elbow in the solar plexus. The man fell down again, whimpering, and tried to crawl away.

The other one got his hands on Vesensky's throat and started to choke him.

Past his shoulder the KGB renegade caught Billy McKay's eye. And winked.

Then he extended his right forefinger, drove it savagely into the hate-twisted face. The soldier howled. Vesensky clenched his fist, yanked it back with a heave of effort that sent pain rocketing up his broken arm. There was an instant's resistance, then a moist popping sound.

The soldier dropped, convulsing like a snake in a campfire. Vesensky turned.

The man whose arm he'd broken was aiming an Uzi at his gut, one-handed.

That fucking faggot is getting fresh *with me?* McKay wondered in outrage. *He* winked *at me. He*—
Oh.

And he smiled into the terrible dripping mask of Llewellyn's face. "Tryina . . . *fuck* me, are you? We got somethin' we do to . . . people—like—you."

His right hand pivoted, grabbed a handful of Llewellyn's crotch, and *squeezed*.

The major screamed like a woman. The crushing bear hug went slack.

McKay's arms exploded upward, blasting Llewellyn's arms away from him.

"Gonna break *me*, are you?" he roared. He drove his right fist into Llewellyn's face with every gram of mass he had.

"I got him!" Lieutenant Hospers yelled. And even if the words came out of his ruined mouth "Aya'im," like some kind of weird Arab curse, the fact that he'd managed to catch Casey Wilson in a half nelson from behind was unmistakable to his three buddies who were still on their feet. Bruised, bloody, and vengeful, they started to close in for the kill.

Then Suzette Nguyen, holding her knife with both hands, rammed it with surgical precision into Lieutenant Hospers's kidneys. He screamed and let go of Casey.

Major Llewellyn came flying across the anteroom and knocked Hospers, Casey, and two troopies in one big heap.

Face expressionless, Ivan Vesensky extended his right fist toward the man holding the Uzi on him, palm up. The man frowned, trigger finger forestalled by sheer confusion. Vesensky opened his hand.

An eyeball stared up at the man with the Uzi.

The gunman lost it. He screamed louder than Hospers with the knife in his back. Vesensky swept the gun from his hand with a kick. He flipped the eyeball into the squirming heap of Casey and foes, where a little confusion would do the most good. Then with a brain-shattering *kiai* shout he drove his right fist into the trooper's sternum and stopped his heart cold.

McKay was all over Llewellyn, his fists smashing into him like pile drivers. He ignored everyone—Hospers still shrieking as if he were afire, Casey pulling the knife from him, the prostrate troopies trying mainly to get the hell *out of there*, naked Nguyen dancing around the perimeter looking for something else to bash people with.

The major was fighting back, sledging his own fists into McKay's sides. He might as well have been the Cerebral Palsy Poster child.

"Beat the shit out of me when my hands are tied, huh?" McKay grunted, breaking Llewellyn's jaw.

"Gonna watch me die, were you?" he said, breaking the major's left cheekbone.

"Gonna break me *in two,* were you?" he screamed, breaking Llewellyn's other cheekbone, along with the second knuckle of his left fist.

Nguyen hove into McKay's sweat and blood-blurred view, holding a VX can. Llewellyn jackknifed, lifting McKay's bulk clear of the carpet in a last desperate spasm of escape.

McKay rode him like a bronc. At the top of the arc he plucked the heavy canister from Nguyen's hands.

"Thanks, kid," he said, and smashed the butt end of the canister down into Llewellyn's face.

What seemed an hour of methodical pounding later McKay snapped out of it to Casey tugging on his arm and going, "That's enough, Billy. That's enough, man. He's *dead.*"

McKay stopped. He looked at the canister in his hands, which was now as much brownish-red as it was black or yellow. Then he looked down at the floor.

Lasagna city.

He set the canister down carefully, suddenly very aware he was holding a lot more deaths than Llewellyn's. "Gotta move," he said, picking himself up, feeling as if every bone he had was broken or at least cracked.

He looked around. If the room had been a drive-in movie, Joe Bob Briggs would have given it at least four stars: Spam in an Office.

Nguyen was binding Vesensky's left arm, using his Sykes-Fairbairn in its sheath as a splint. Casey was holding down on the outer door with an Uzi. Smoke was just pouring out from under the lab door, thick and white and reeking of Christ alone knew what toxic chemicals. Nobody had been paying much attention to it; other things to think about.

Finished with her first aid, Nguyen skinned the wetsuit Casey had carried with him over her garter belt. She'd brought respirator hoods, gloves, and elastic-sealed feeties out of the lab with the VX cans. They put them on.

"Let's go," McKay said through his mask.

Case held up a hand. "Somebody out there, I think."

McKay shrugged. "No good guys here. You take right, I take left. Rock'n'roll, yes?"

"You got it, man."

At a nodded signal Nguyen hauled the door inward. McKay wheeled out one way, Casey the other, firing full auto from the hip. Camouflaged soldiers screamed and went down to the strobo-scopic flicker of muzzle flashes.

A moment, then silence came crashing down like a hotel mez-zanine. McKay nodded. "Let's do it. Case, you better go get the harem broads out. I hate to waste good gash, and when this nerve gas goes—"

Casey's eyes shifted nervously behind his goggles. "Billy, I don't think we'd better," he said.

CHAPTER
TWENTY-EIGHT ―――――――――

"Say what?"

The building shook. *One-oh-five,* McKay thought. *Our friends from Detroit musta showed up on schedule.*

"We can't control this stuff," Casey said earnestly. "We don't know if we can keep it inside the building. If it gets loose, what's it going to do to our friends out there?"

"How the hell do I know? I thought that was Ivan's big plan." He looked at Nguyen. "How about it, Doc? Will this stuff stay inside the building if we set it off? Or do we wipe out our buddies?"

She shrugged. "All that matters is stopping that madman Morrigan," she said fiercely.

"Uh-*huh.*" This complicated things.

"I was improvising," said Vesensky, who'd stepped out to help cover with an Uzi in his right hand. "I didn't have time to get all the details straight. If you're willing to listen, though, I may have a solution to our problem."

McKay rubbed his chin through the hood. "You've come through for us so far, bud. Though I gotta say some of them details you did get to weren't much fuckin' fun."

Vesensky nodded at a body crumpled against the wall, ten meters down the corridor. "That one's faking. We could send him out to tell his comrades what we can do if we have to."

McKay made a mouth, nodded, sauntered over to the "corpse" Vesensky had pointed out. He swooped, grabbed the man by the hair, and pulled him up to his feet. The building shook to another two-stroke salvo.

"Wakey-wakey, asshole. *Say,* I know you; you're the dickmuncher who kept poking me with his gun. Remember what I promised to do to you?"

Miserably the man nodded. "Now, I'm a man who keeps his promises. But I'll break that one, *if* you're a good boy and do just what we tell you."

He slammed him facefirst into the wall, stooped to pick up the

194

fallen FN-FAL. It was a very long rifle. He turned Barnes around,
held it up under his nose.

"Fuck with us, though, and you're gonna be walkin' around
with this muzzle brake sticking out of your *mouth*. Do you hear
me, buzzard puke?"

Miserably, the man nodded.

The Citadel had been fortified with an eye to keeping ill-armed
ragged-ass gangs of Street People in their place. Nobody had
suggested to its personnel that they'd have to defend it against
naval gunfire. Even two-bit naval gunfire.

Under Sam Sloan's expert direction the Detroit gunboats wiped
out Morrigan's heavy weapons nests inside twenty minutes. Then
they went to work on any centers of resistance Tom's guerrillas
or the Detroiter infantry company that had landed in Gary the
night before the Guardians arrived in Chicago could spot.

The message Barnes came running out waving a white bedsheet
to spread was no more than a handy excuse to do what the would-be
heroes of the New Order desperately wanted to do anyway.
Whofuck can fight against nerve gas? *Come* on.

Honor satisfied, the defenders began to lay down their arms.

And as the scroungy, cheering attackers began to stream through
holes blown through the wire, a voice crackled from the pole-
mounted loudspeakers that were still functional:

"Nice try, McKay. But you lose."

They stood in a bunch before the vault door of Morrigan's last
redoubt: the Guardians, Vesensky, Nguyen, a couple of blood-
smeared Street People bosses, Captain Wu of the Detroiter infantry.
Nguyen, her hood off and eyes red, clung to Sloan as if she'd
been born his Siamese twin. He had an arm draped absently around
her shoulders.

There was a TV screen inset in the wall next to the steel door.
Smiling out at them was William Morrigan, looking haggard but
triumphant in a dark green robe with his rose and fist device picked
out in silver thread on the breast. He drank brandy from a snifter
the size of his head. Merith Tobias sat behind him on a bed with
what looked like one of his white shirts on.

"Gentlemen—ladies." One of the Street People leaders was a
black woman who called herself Ice. "I can see you, you understand; if you'll look closely, you'll observe a video pickup below
the screen."

"Yeah, we got that," McKay said. "Now, why don't you just pack it in? You've lost, Morrigan. Might as well face it."

Morrigan laughed. "Ah, but I haven't. It was a clever plan, I grant that. Colonel Vesensky is to be congratulated on his ingenuity. His apparent defection had me quite taken in."

Vesensky tried to look modest.

"But he isn't superhuman. He destroyed my broadcast array. Unfortunately, I have backup landlines run out of my inner sanctum he didn't know about."

They looked at each other as horror unfolded within them like diseased roses.

"You know by now that I had no virus. Oh, Magnus had a strain he was working on, which he repeatedly promised me would be ready soon. But what I used in Cleveland was nerve gas."

He sipped again. "And what my agents will release in a number of population centers at my command is also nerve gas. Not as comprehensive as the chimerical virus would've been. But it will suffice to thin the remaining population of America considerably. My retribution is terrible, gentlemen; you should have considered that before you opposed me."

"You're going to murder thousands of innocent survivors?" Sloan demanded.

"Didn't I just say so? Though I daresay the figures will likely run into the millions."

"But *why?* McKay's right. You've lost."

"Commander Sloan, you disappoint me. You should know that, as soon as you've all watched me transmit the signal to release the gas, I will also open the remotely controlled nerve gas canisters hidden within the Citadel. Those of you who don't happen to be wearing protective clothing will not be able to move quickly enough to escape."

"But what good will that do?" Sam persisted, trying for a tone of reason and ignoring the fact his death was one of the ones Morrigan was so blithely discussing. "There are hundreds of men and women outside any possible dispersal radius of the gas, who'll be waiting for you when you open this crypt of yours. And you'll have Billy McKay and Ivan Vesensky waiting for you.

"Why don't you just surrender? You could go into exile. You have our word as Guardians you would not be harmed."

He didn't look at the others. But one by one they nodded.

Morrigan laughed. "You know, I believe you're so naive as to honor that agreement—though I'm not so sure about your slippery friend Vesensky. But I'm afraid I'll have to decline.''

He backed up a couple of paces and sat on the bed. ''First, I won't be deprived of my vengeance. The nation has stubbornly resisted the imposition of due authority. Like any spoiled brat, it's overdue for the rod. I don't propose to spare it.''

Merith Tobias slipped from the bed and moved beyond the camera's glass eye. Morrigan paid no attention. ''Also, I can hold out for months in here, as I mentioned before.''

''You gotta come out sometime,'' McKay said. ''And I'll be waiting. And my buddy Ivan and me, we know some tricks, you know. I bet we could keep you alive every bit as long as you can hold out in there. But not having near so much fun.''

''Ah, yes.'' He hoisted the snifter in salute. ''But it won't be an unpleasant captivity, alone with my books and writings and the most beautiful woman in the world. And the satisfaction of having made so many pay for the wrong that was done to me.

''And then, when we reach the end of our supplies, I can emulate the Romans of old and take my own life. I can yet cheat you at the end—if I have to.''

He grinned. ''But I doubt I will—''

McKay blinked. A pair of small feminine hands had appeared in the side of the picture, behind his right ear. They held a very large snub-nosed revolver. He could see the fingers trembling as they tried to exert the force necessary to work the double action.

''It's funny,'' William Morrigan said as the hammer crept inexorably back, ''how things tend to fall your way when you have right on your side.''

The hammer fell.

His head exploded.

Several minutes later the vault door hissed open. Merith Tobias stepped out, holding the .357 magnum slackly in one hand. She fell against the thick cement doorway and stared at them with unseeing eyes.

''We all have limits,'' she said. ''I guess I just found mine.'' And she collapsed like a marionette with the strings snipped.

EPILOGUE ————————————————————

"I'm staying," she said in French, turning away from the window. Miraculously it had survived the most recent battle.

Colonel Ivan Vesensky sipped his scarfed Perrier and regarded her with blue-green eyes that betrayed no emotion. "So you've found love?" He spoke French, too. Perfectly, of course.

"Sam?" Nguyen laughed, bitterly, shook her head. "No. He is my friend . . . for now. He knows better than to ask for more than I'm ready to give."

"But your country did."

She looked at him in the darkness. The light of bonfires outside gilded the curves of her cheek and turned strands of her hair to fire wire. "But the FSE did. I have no country."

Outside the victory celebration continued into the night. The victorious mob had received the personal telecast thanks of President Jeffrey MacGregor that morning, but what they were mostly celebrating was the death of the evil wizard whose keep they had taken at long last.

"Will you try to stop me?" she asked, her eyes on his.

He scratched at the inflated cast on his left arm. "You're brave. You're also a fool. Which is an almost certain concomitant of bravery."

"You're brave. The Guardians are brave. Are you all fools?"

He smiled. "The Guardians are brave. And they are fools, though magnificent ones. Myself? Perhaps I am, too."

He looked away. "Or it may be that I am not brave, but merely have nothing I mind losing. No, I won't try to force you. And I won't kill you. The Federated States have other biochemists."

"Then I'll be going." She rose and started for the door.

"One moment."

She stopped, fear winging up like a startled bird in her chest. He hadn't asked her the question she most dreaded yet. Now she knew beyond doubt he would.

"That fire in the lab. All Cromartie's records and specimens

198

were destroyed, though it was more smoke than substance. It wasn't an accident, was it?''

His voice was low and infinitely sinister. She looked at him with rabbit eyes and said nothing.

''If you lie to me,'' he said, ''do not expect me to keep my faith with you.''

''I set the fire,'' she said. ''The fool Cromartie was closer in his virus than he realized. I could have completed the work in weeks. Any competent researcher could have, especially if she had the resources of the Federated States of Europe backing her.''

''And you took it upon yourself to destroy what might have been a very powerful tool for the FSE?''

''Not a tool!'' she flared at him. ''A weapon. Nothing else. The death of humanity, perhaps. I would not hand that over to the likes of you. Nor Chairman Maximov. Nor anybody.''

She crossed her arms defiantly. ''Kill me now, if you wish.''

He just sat on the edge of the bureau and looked at her. ''Chairman Maximov is a wise man, and a very powerful man. I think that you perceive he is not a good man, and by your lights you are correct. But he is a very good man by mine, in that he is an appreciative master, and you have no idea how rare a commodity that can be. And he will be the most powerful man in the world.

''Yet he can be the most powerful man in the world without having the power to destroy it. And though I am loyal to him, and shall in time give up my life for him, I see no need that he should possess such power. Accidents happen, if nothing else.''

He stood. ''Should you attempt to use our little talk here as leverage to blackmail me, I will kill you. Now, shall we go down to join the party?''

He offered her his broken arm.

After a moment she took it.

''You're really going out there?'' McKay asked, staring out at the silent ruin of the city. A few crows circled in the gray morning sky. ''Alone?''

Merith Tobias nodded and brushed hair the color of honey from her face. ''We go through life alone, McKay. Anything else is just pretend. And I'm through with pretending.'' She smiled. ''For now, at least.''

The others hung discreetly back by the gate through the Citadel wire. They were alone with the wind and the city and the crows.

"So that's what it was with me, huh?" he rasped. "Just pretend."

"No, Billy. Not with you. But not with the Madman, either. Or even with Morrigan." She shook her head. "My pretense was that I needed to live like that, as an appendage of a man. That's why I'm going."

She reached forward and touched his cheek. "I don't blame you, Billy. I don't blame anyone, because I did what I chose to do. But now I'm choosing differently, and I hope you don't blame me."

He wanted her. He ached from wanting her, and his tongue ached from the need to cry, *No! Stay with me! I want you!*

But what he said was, "Naw." And he meant it.

"Then it's good-bye, as we say in the movies."

He grabbed her arms. She didn't flinch away. "They'll kill you. The ruins are full of crazy nesters who'd be more than happy to rape you, then cut you up and cook you in a pot."

"Then that's what they'll do. If they can catch me. If I can't make it on my own, I won't make it at all. Either way is fine with me."

And she grabbed him behind the neck and drew his head to hers, and her tongue was moist fire in his mouth. He crushed her against him with all his strength, ignoring the butt of her .357 gouging his ribs from its shoulder holster.

She broke away. Her eyes were awash with tears. He let her go and stepped back.

"See you around," he said.

"Yes," she whispered. "I think you will."

And she turned and walked down the rubble-strewn street, with her Jansport pack—tawny, to match her hair—bobbing between her shoulders, and her rump working inside her khaki pants like every schoolboy's dream.

AMBUSH AT OSIRAK

A novel by
HERBERT CROWDER

Israeli forces are prepared to launch a devastating air
strike on the Iraqi nuclear production facility at Osirak.
Iraqi forces are fully aware of the oncoming attack. And
the Soviets have supplied them with the ultimate super-
weapon—the perfect means to wage nuclear war...

J JOVE